THE
BRIGHTEST
STAR

THE
BRIGHTEST
STAR

A NOVEL

GAIL TSUKIYAMA

HarperVia

An Imprint of HarperCollinsPublishers

HarperCollins books may be purchased for educational, business, or sales promotional use. For information, please email the Special Markets Department at SPsales@harpercollins.com.

FIRST HARPERCOLLINS PAPERBACK PUBLISHED IN 2024

Designed by Yvonne Chan
Fan pattern on pp. iii, 3, 119, and 219 © Daniela Iga/Shutterstock
Frame on pp. 1, 15, 121, 221, 259, 307, and 331 © Tartila/Shutterstock

Library of Congress Cataloging-in-Publication Data is available upon request.

ISBN 978-0-06-321376-0

24 25 26 27 28 LBC 5 4 3 2 1

CONTENTS

For my family,
past and present

I have nothing more; I've given my all. What they'll never understand was how alike we all are, not the butterflies or dragons they made me out to be.

—Anna May Wong

PROLOGUE
SANTA MONICA, CALIFORNIA

1961

In my dreams I hear their voices, those young boys who were already cruel when they chased me through the schoolyard yelling, *Chink, Chink, Chinabug.* It's no wonder that so many of them have grown up to be the kind of men they are. Their voices may have deepened, their hair thinned or turned gray, their bellies softened and grown larger, but their hearts and minds remain as hard as stone, impenetrable. They are still those small-minded boys who tormented me. To them, I'll always be foreign—a porcelain China doll, or a fire-breathing dragon lady, neither of which belongs in their world. I had such high hopes for them. I thought they might know better as grown-ups and realize that there are more ways than one to view the world. Even so, I tried to make a difference. And I can't help but find some peace in knowing that I did. Hollywood certainly never saw anyone like me. I am Anna May Wong, a *real* Chinese-American girl who acted, sang, and danced into the hearts of movie fans around the world. I was once young and tenacious, always reaching for the brightest star. And for one brief moment in time, it glowed brilliant and beautiful in the palm of my hand.

PART ONE

Outside of our home, we were thoroughly American in dress, action, speech, and thought. Right and left we were smashing the traditions of our forebears.

—Anna May Wong

June. Already hot and dry. A different kind of heat from that of my childhood when I stood in the back room of my father's laundry with my older sister, Lulu, washing and ironing, my damp hair pressed against my forehead. That moist, muggy heat had risen from the steaming vats of hot water, simmering like *ma ma*'s boiling soups. The dripping clothes that hung from the racks left the floor wet and slippery. The air then had felt so thick, I could hold it in my hands, but this is a dry heat, the wily kind that sneaks up and attacks you from behind.

Walking from the taxicab to the entrance of the train station has me sweaty under the collar, my silk blouse sticky against my back. I look up at the palm trees lining the walkway, just another Hollywood illusion of a paradise that is anything but. Still, Hollywood hasn't completely forgotten me. Four months ago, I was awarded a star on the newly inaugurated Hollywood Walk of Fame, the first Chinese-American actress to receive the honor. My name, **ANNA MAY WONG**, gleams in shiny gold letters encased in a star on the 1700 block of Vine Street for the world to see. Nevertheless, it's easy to see the irony of it too. I've been stepped on so often during my career, why not be immortalized on a sidewalk.

I can hear Lulu scolding me yet again. "It's a great honor," she'd say, shaking her head. "You should be thankful."

Lulu, the oldest, has always watched over all the siblings, becoming our surrogate mother after *ma ma* died. She followed all the rules I broke when we were young. If she was here walking with me now, I would tell her that I do appreciate the recognition, while adding I also worked like hell and suffered through years of prejudice and discrimination for that star. And then I'd be off on a rant, reminding her once again that the *real* Hollywood isn't the magic that fans see on the big screen. It isn't what I dreamed about as a young girl, bursting with so much hope and ambition. I was naive to all the prejudice and politics that ran rampant behind the scenes, along with the Hays Code, and all the rules and regulations made by those close-minded, cigar-smoking, whiskey-drinking studio heads, who wouldn't know a *real* Chinese if they saw one. It's the other side of the coin, which isn't always as bright and shiny as my star embedded in the sidewalk. No one gets away untarnished.

I can hear Lulu sigh. Without hearing a word, I know what she'd be thinking. It's hard to be completely disillusioned by a life that has put me up on the big screen, brought me fame, a small fortune, and a legion of fans from around the world, even if it all came with stipulations.

"I am thankful," I whisper to myself, pulling open the glass door.

I'm even more thankful stepping into the beautifully cool, cavernous train station with its tall, majestic, brass-adorned windows, art deco chandeliers, polished marble floors, and hand-painted mission tiles, all providing an immediate respite from the heat.

WAITING AT TRACK 5 is my train for Sacramento, where I'm scheduled to switch trains and continue to Chicago's Union Station for my first interview during the three-hour layover. From Chicago, the last leg of the trip takes me to New York's Penn Station, where my dearest friends, photographer and writer Carl Van Vechten and his wife, actress Fania Marinoff, will be waiting for me five days from now. I'm excited to see them, to be in New York and back on the road again on my first big press tour in years for a highly anticipated Hollywood movie, *Portrait in Black,* starring Lana Turner and Anthony Quinn. I had a small part, procured through Tony, whom I've known since we made *Daughter of Shanghai* together in 1937. I was the big star back then, when he was young and up and coming. How the tables have turned. Tony's reached leading man status now, and while I can't be considered up and coming at the age of fifty-five, I've made something of a comeback in the past year: a flurry of television appearances, the star on the Hollywood Walk of Fame, and this small role in Ross Hunter's *Portrait in Black.* (If there's one thing I've learned, it's how to make a small role expand on the screen.) And, the best is yet to come; I have another movie, a musical, with Ross on the horizon, playing Auntie Liang, one of the leads in his next big project, *Flower Drum Song.* Rarer still, it has a largely *Oriental* cast. Singing and dancing, right up my alley, if not four decades too late.

The day has finally arrived, and I'm happy to be working again.

I used to think that making a "comeback" meant taking one last, labored breath before you were "going and gone." Now, I'm not so sure. I feel as if I've been resuscitated from a long and restless sleep. Maybe that's why I've been given this publicity tour, getting my name back out there and prepping for the next movie. Ross, or someone else at the studio, must have decided my story isn't quite over yet.

I hand my suitcase to a porter with a smile and a generous tip. I've booked a private compartment on the train for the overnight trip that's scheduled to arrive in Sacramento early tomorrow morning. For a moment, I stand clutching my handbag, feeling lost on the hot, oily-aired platform, alone among crowds of people hurrying about their lives at a dizzying pace. My younger brother Richard offered to come with me, but I declined. He needs to stay and promote his Oriental novel decor shop, as christened by the local papers. I don't need a babysitter, not this time.

A young man rushes past me, his bag bumping against my leg. Without a word of apology, he hurries on. There was a time I would have been instantly recognized, surrounded, and gushed over by men and women, young and old, asking for my autograph. You couldn't miss me: my smiling face and dark round eyes framed by my short hair and my trademark Chinese "virgin-child" bangs—worn only by unmarried girls in China—had been displayed on posters, billboards, and movie magazines all over the world during the twenties and thirties. By the mid-forties and fifties, my career had dried up, shadowed by my chronic health problems and the dark moods that threatened to overtake me. Years have slipped by, erasing that eager young girl who once graced all those movie magazine covers.

I feel all but invisible as I walk toward my train car. I'm dying for a cigarette, just one to hold between my fingers, press between my lips. I know I'm reaching for the old security blanket again. Dr. Bloom, my doctor for the past nine years, has warned me off both cigarettes and alcohol. At least I'm making an effort with the cigarettes, though it's the latter that's done most of the damage. I saw him just a few days ago for a checkup before the trip, and I can still hear his stern, disapproving voice.

"This is serious, Anna May; Laennec's cirrhosis of the liver is not to be taken lightly. It's not going away. Do you want to have another relapse?" he asked, as if I were a child.

He's too serious for someone just barely forty, with his full head of dark, curly hair that springs every which way. He always appears a bit disheveled, as if caught in a windstorm. Some things can't be tamed into place, no matter how hard you try. It's one of the reasons I've stayed with Dr. Bloom, his unruly hair. The other is that he doesn't pull any punches; he tells me like it is. I, on the other hand, am meticulous to a fault. Appearance is everything, right down to my trademark long and tapered fingernails. I was often said to have the most beautiful hands in Hollywood, even as I was unraveling on the inside.

I politely answered, "No, I do not want to have another relapse."

It's the truth; I don't. When I suffered an internal hemorrhage seven years ago, I ended up in the hospital and felt as if I was being squeezed dry by the terrible stomach pains. Nausea and fatigue, along with a lack of appetite, kept me hooked up to clear bags of fluids and bedridden for weeks. In the past few years, I've had to convalesce more times than I'd care to admit.

My response drew a quick smile and nod from Dr. Bloom.

"Good then," he said, as if my scarred liver will somehow make a miraculous recovery if I play by the rules—something I've never been very good at. "It's up to you to keep it in check. I can't do it for you." He has told me this more than once.

Nothing new there, it has always been up to me. But I won't let my illness disrupt the happiness I feel at this moment. I'm back on my feet and buoyed by this trip.

ONCE ON THE TRAIN, I settle into my small, efficient cabin, my luggage stowed away, and I sit by the window to watch the last-minute passengers hurrying toward their cars. I could have flown to New York, it's what the studio had originally planned, but I wanted to take my time and leave a week earlier than scheduled. Although I've taken trains for much of my life, I've actually seen little of the places I passed through, always rushing from one location to another, scripts in hand to memorize my lines, working to keep my movie career afloat.

So I specifically planned this longer train route, taking me north from Los Angeles to Sacramento, and eastward along the route of the first transcontinental railroad through the Sierras, Nevada, Utah, and then on through Colorado, Nebraska, and Iowa to Chicago. Now that I've been given this opportunity, I want to see the America that I was always made to feel I didn't belong in. I want to ride along the same tracks that were first laid down by Chinese laborers who were brought over to do the most treacherous, most unforgiving work. Many came from my ancestral province of Taishan, yet were never accepted as citizens by the country they helped to build.

The Chinese Exclusion Act of 1882 suspended Chinese immigration and declared Chinese immigrants ineligible for citizenship. Ten years later, the Geary Act of 1892 upheld the law for ten more years and declared that every Chinese, including Chinese Americans, had to carry identity papers to prove they were American citizens allowed to be traveling in and out of the United States. I flush with anger to think I carried those papers with me until 1943, when the law was finally repealed. Now I want to see the blazing sunsets as well as the mountains and tunnels where the Chinese laborers worked and died so far from home. This time, I want to pay more attention.

I'm also considering a new project: writing my autobiography. Once I was thrown into semiretirement, I found myself with more time on my hands, coupled with new money worries. I waited for the next audition call for a new movie or play, which never came. Instead, I sold my beloved property on San Vicente Boulevard, moved to a smaller house, and spent those years finally slowing down, using my free time to read, to garden, and to cook more elaborate Chinese dinners for old Hollywood friends I invited over: Edith Head; Tony Quinn and his wife, Katherine DeMille; the Victors; Laskys; and Knopfs. My brother Richard is never far away and neither is a game of poker at my place, or *mah-jongg,* and a few laughs and drinks down at The Dragon's Den in Chinatown with childhood friends. It isn't Hollywood's bright lights, but I've been happy enough.

In between, there have been trips to New York to see Carl and Fania, Kitty Clements, Hazel Stockton, and other old and dear New York friends, including Bennett Cerf, who's the big-time publisher at Random House. Over the years, he has sent me books that I've read eagerly, and since my semiretirement, he has been nudging me to write my autobiography.

"Who would want to read about my life?" I asked.

He smiled, cradling his pipe in the palm of his hand, and said, "You should ask yourself, who wouldn't?"

I've never forgotten the way he looked at me that day in his office, tall and bespectacled, always dressed in a perfectly tailored suit, his eyebrows raised as if to say, Don't play coy with me, you know your life has been anything but ordinary.

"Write about the allure of Hollywood, and your experience of *Orientalism,* which unfortunately hasn't gone away," he added. "Think of it as your chance to tell future generations what it's like to live in that kind of racist, small-minded world."

"But I never even finished high school," I said.

"You're one of the smartest people I know," Bennett said, putting his pipe down and choosing a stack of books from his shelves. "I don't know anyone else in the movie business who sang and spoke in three different languages for the same film."

It was true, I did learn to speak German and French well enough back in the day. "I'll think about it."

"You should," he said. "Do you think I'd ask this of just anyone? I have a reputation to keep!"

I laughed, and shook my head. "I'll try not to ruin your reputation," I told him, reaching for the books he passed to me.

THE TRUTH—ALTHOUGH I'VE NEVER told anyone, not even Lulu or Richard—is that I've already written down my story in three composition notebooks I bought at a local drugstore. What else was I going to do during my forced retirement? I smile to think they're the same kind of notebooks I used in high school, black-and-white hardboard covers with lined pages and stitched binding. Unfortunately, my story includes others, and there are family and friends to consider. I can't imagine what Lulu will say of me parading our family secrets in public. Haven't I caused enough uproar to last a lifetime? But Bennett has planted the seed on purpose, knowing I can't ignore a challenge. I've written articles over the years for Hollywood and European film magazines, and volumes of letters and postcards, birthday and Christmas cards to family and friends around the world. I've also written down these significant events in my life so they wouldn't be lost in the fog of old age. I've brought the notebooks along on this trip. They're in my bag on the seat next to me now. The thought of resurrecting my past terrifies me, as if I'm taking two steps back, just so I can move one step forward.

But as Bennett tells me, I have the power to change the discrepancies, tell my real story as I've lived it, "if you have the strength," he adds.

I have the strength, but I'm not sure I have the courage.

And yet, I've convinced myself it's time to face my fears. This train trip will give me the peace and quiet to read through the notebooks, to determine if I have a story worth telling. If so, maybe Bennett will get his book after all. And if not, no one will be the wiser.

"ALL ABOARD!" A VOICE cries out from the platform.

A horn blasts twice.

I sit back as the train trembles to a start before moving slowly out of the station, gradually picking up speed. Only when we're at the outskirts of the city do I finally look away from the window, pick up the first notebook, and turn to the opening page.

We are defined by our history, my father always told us. If so, I'll always be that little girl who was tormented at school. It remains one of my clearest memories, the first of many times I would be bullied into realizing what I'd have to do all my life: fight to prove that I was as American as everyone else.

BITS OF LIFE
1913-1928

CHINABUG
California Street Elementary School—1913

"Where you going, Chink?"

I walked faster, glancing back to see the small group of boys following close behind, their voices nasal and nasty.

"Chink, Chink, Chinabug!" they taunted. "Go back where you belong!"

Where was I supposed to go back to? I was born here in Los Angeles eight years ago, just like them. My parents were born in California too. My father, Wong Sam Sing, started the Sam Kee Laundry a few blocks from Chinatown, where I was born on Flower Street. My grandparents came over during the Gold Rush back in 1855 and never left. We were Americans, no matter how they tried to exclude us.

"I belong *here!*" I yelled back at them.

But they wouldn't leave me alone. "Go back to China, Chinabug!"

My older sister, Lew Ying, called Lulu, was usually waiting for me outside after school, but this afternoon she was nowhere in sight. We used to go to school in Chinatown before my father moved the Sam Kee Laundry to North Figueroa Street, a neighborhood on the outskirts of Chinatown where people of all different nationalities lived, so we could attend a public elementary school and adapt to others outside of the Chinese community.

"This is America! Study hard and get good grades. Education will take you far," my father repeated to me and Lulu so often I'd stopped listening. The move had been hard for both of us. We were the only Chinese family on the block, and it felt very far away from my friends at our old school in Chinatown. Lulu, who was in fifth grade, also suffered through the name-calling, the pushing and bullying, but she was three years older, her body solid and strong compared to my thinner, more fragile build, which made me the easier target. We both tried to tough it out, saying nothing to our mother or father about the constant harassment. They were busy enough with our younger brothers and sister, and there was also the laundry to run.

Only when I was at school did I wish I were back working at the laundry, even with the piles of clothes we had to iron and fold and the steamy heat that flattened my hair. The reddish singe mark on the back of my hand was a constant reminder of the burn I suffered the past weekend while ironing. I couldn't wait until the ugly mark faded and my skin was smooth and spotless again. *Ma ma* said I was too vain, that working hands were a sign of character. I have a lot of character, I told her, though I wasn't sure what it meant. I knew I could never be like my sister, Lulu. She was a natural at washing clothes and pushing that heavy iron back and forth, while I always preferred to work up at the front counter, or to deliver the parcels of clean laundry to the houses and apartments throughout the neighborhood. I learned early on that if I said all the right things, *"Your dress is so pretty,"* or *"Something smells so good in there,"* batted my eyelashes innocently, and smiled, I'd receive a bigger tip.

But every morning, there was still school. My stomach began to hurt as soon as I stepped onto the schoolyard, anxiously waiting for what was going to happen next. There were only a handful of Chinese kids at the school, and I was the only one in my class. I was afraid my teacher wouldn't like me if I complained about the boys and their bullying. What I'd learned growing up was that Chinese shouldn't complain, shouldn't draw attention to themselves, so I remained silent in the chalk-dust air of the crowded classroom. I endured the boy who sat behind me pulling on my pigtails or jabbing me in the back with a sharp pin, just hard enough to poke me but not draw blood. I didn't make a sound. When the teacher wasn't watching, I quickly turned around and swatted at him, but he leaned back just out of reach. Each morning my mother looked at me questioningly, mumbling, "Too hot," in English, but I only shook my head when, even on a warm fall day I wore two layers of sweaters and on top of them, my thick, wool coat as protection against those pinpricks.

AFTER SCHOOL, WHEN I saw the boys headed in my direction, I didn't wait for Lulu. I ran across the schoolyard where I liked to play tag or kickball at recess and had just made it to the gate and out to the sidewalk when a hard tug on one of my pigtails jerked my head back. "Where you going, Chinabug?" one of the boys asked, shoving me hard against the fence.

My cheek stung as it scraped against the rough wood. It hurt, but I refused to cry in front of them. Instead, I clenched both my hands into fists, turned around, and swung hard, hitting the boy who pushed me into the fence in the stomach. He folded over, red faced with surprise. Just as I stepped back, ready to swing again, I heard Lulu calling my name. I looked up to see my sister running across the yard toward me, closing the distance, swinging her book bag in the air.

The boys scattered like ants in all different directions.

Lulu, breathing hard, dropped her book bag and gripped me by the shoulders, her dark piercing eyes scrutinizing the scrape on my cheek. "Are you okay?" she asked, and then pulled me closer to her.

I nodded, and breathed in the scent of mothballs and Tiger Balm on my *ma ma*'s old blouse that Lulu was wearing. Every time my sister outgrew a blouse, another appeared from our mother's old wooden chest. Other orphaned clothing also appeared from the laundry my parents owned, shirts and pants abandoned by customers like forgotten pets. My *ma ma* was a magician; she cut them down to size and sewed them to fit her three daughters and two sons. I pressed closer to the comforting scent and finally began to cry, more out of anger and relief than fear. I wanted to tell Lulu how furious I was, how awful those boys had been to me the past two months, but I couldn't find the words through my tears.

"I know," Lulu said, rubbing my back. "They don't know anything. It'll be okay, Liu-Tsong, it'll be okay," she added, using my Chinese name, which meant Willow Frost, to comfort me just as *ma ma* would. "Tonight we're going to tell *baba* how terrible it is at this school."

I pulled away from Lulu and nodded, wiping my tears with my sleeve. Lulu rarely used my Chinese name except when we were at home where *ma ma* almost always spoke to us in the Taishanese dialect of her ancestors from Southern China. Out in public, among our new German, Irish, and Mexican neighbors, we kids always used our English names—Lulu, Anna, James, Frank, and Mary—given to each of us by our parents at birth so that we'd always know that we were Chinese *Americans*. I looked at Lulu and put on a brave face, once again reminded that this was just as much home for us as it was for those boys.

THE SILVER SCREEN
Nickelodeon Movie Theater—1914

Names scrolled up the flickering screen in fancy black letters followed by the last of the movie credits before the screen blinked and faded into white, the silent movie over, the spell broken. I hated every time a movie ended. It felt like a candle had been suddenly blown out, leaving me alone in the dark. The electric piano music continued to play as the lights slowly rose, illuminating the shabby, sticky-floored, bare-walled theater below. There was a stale, greasy smell in the air. Mesmerized by the movie, I stayed seated on the hard wooden chair up in the first row of the balcony where the Chinese sat, and watched all the Caucasian people downstairs walking out, as the few people around me stood and began to leave. *Tess of the Storm Country* was one of the best movies I'd ever seen, Mary Pickford at her greatest. I was in love with Mary Pickford. Her expressive eyes said so much more than words on the screen ever could.

To be at the nickelodeon again, I had skipped my afternoon class at the Chinese language school. When *baba* and *ma ma* transferred Lulu and me away from that awful public elementary school to the Presbyterian Chinese Mission School in Chinatown, we'd left those bullying boys far behind, and we were much happier to be back among other Chinese kids. I'd also taken a real shine to sports and games, and liked to play baseball and kickball during recess. But we were taught Anglo-Christian values at the school in English, which *baba* wasn't happy about, so he insisted we attend Chinese school after our regular school day ended, and also on Saturdays. He wanted us to read and speak Cantonese, the language of our ancestors.

"China has a history that's thousands of years old. It doesn't just go away," my father repeated, adding, "You mustn't forget: who we are is a reflection of where we come from."

How could we forget that we were Chinese? I wanted to ask him, but knew to keep quiet. At nine years old, I was already a pebble in my father's shoe, always irritating him. All I had to do was look in the mirror to see my black hair, the slant of my eyes, and wide cheekbones. I also knew I was just as much American as anyone else, even if my face told a different story. I was both Chinese and American, different and the same.

What I began to realize was the face I saw in the mirror wasn't a face I saw on the big screen. So why didn't I ever see any Chinese actresses in the movies? It was one more reason I wanted to be an actress. One day, movie audiences would know how alike we all were by seeing me, and knowing what a real Chinese-American girl looked like on the big screen. I'd show them all. But first, I needed to study the actors and actresses in as many movies as I could. Every chance I had, I'd forge a note to excuse myself from Chinese school, then sneak off to one of the many nickelodeons several blocks away from Chinatown. For the five cents I saved every week from my tips delivering laundry, I could see the opening newsreels and several short movies, or if I was lucky, a full-length movie starring Mary Pickford or Lillian Gish.

I lived for my trips to the nickelodeons. I memorized every expression and movement of the actors and actresses. In the dark and musty air of the theater, there was no longer any school or laundry to swallow me up, only the adventurous and glamorous lives I watched up on the screen. Everyone and everything else faded away. Later, I would recreate the same looks and gestures in front of the mirror in the crowded bedroom I shared with Lulu and my four-year-old sister, Mary, in the house we lived in behind our father's laundry.

I finally stood when the piano music came to an abrupt end. The thought that one day audiences would come to see me up on that big screen filled me with happiness. I didn't want to leave until I glanced at the clock on the smoke-tinged wall. I was already late meeting Lulu, who knew I'd snuck off to the movies again.

I STEPPED OUT INTO the blinding sunlight and back into the real world. Since we'd changed schools, Lulu and I had seen so much more of the surrounding neighborhoods while taking the bus, or walking back and forth to our school in Chinatown from North Figueroa Street. Two-story buildings with shops downstairs and apartments upstairs lined many of the streets. The shops were run by German, Irish, and Mexican families, their children playing stickball in the streets while wonderful spicy smells wafted through the air. I couldn't get enough of all the new sights and the voices and music that blared loudly and happily from the opened windows.

I hurried the five blocks from the nickelodeon back to the Chinese language school. The sidewalks became increasingly crowded, and noisy, as I drew closer to Chinatown, where the unpaved streets turned into muddy cesspools during the rains, lined with two-story brick-and-adobe buildings, crowded tenements and gambling houses, narrow dark alleyways, and peddlers selling their wares on every corner. I was happy to be back in the thick of it, walking through boisterous crowds gathered around the outside stalls, bargaining for fruits and vegetables. I peeked into the herb and Chinese mercantile store my parents shopped at, and slowed down in front of a chop suey restaurant with red and gold lanterns hanging in front. The aroma of roast pork and salted fish coming from the doorway reminded me of how hungry I was.

I heard a voice and glanced up quickly to see a tall man with dark eyes and a high forehead in the crowd who looked so much like *baba* from the distance, my mouth went dry from fear. I lowered my gaze and quickly turned around, waiting for him to walk pass. *Ma ma* had been the first to discover my lies. A few months after we returned to school in Chinatown, she ran into my Chinese school teacher at the market, and he had expressed his concerns about my constant "headaches." She gave me a warning but had kept quiet, protecting my secret so I wouldn't be punished. It didn't last for long. The first time *baba* found out I had skipped Chinese school was when a customer from the laundry told my father he'd seen me at the nickelodeon. I'd never seen him so angry. He yelled so loud I had to cover my ears. Lately, it seemed the air between us was so thick with struggle at home I felt like I was suffocating. Couldn't *baba* understand that movies provided me with a different kind of language to express myself?

It all seemed so simple to me. I didn't need either American or Chinese school to become an actress. I was learning so much more from the newsreels that were shown at the beginning of the movies. They covered everything from the latest Paris fashions to the Siege of Tsingtao in China to the awful assassination of Archduke Franz Ferdinand of Austria. I was convinced that sitting in a classroom every day was a waste of my time.

I swallowed, imagining *baba*'s fury if he knew what I was thinking. From the moment that all of his children were old enough to understand, he had drilled into us that a good education was the key to success. It meant everything to him.

Sighing, I turned around slowly, and was greatly relieved to see that the man walking down the street wasn't my father after all.

LULU WAITED FOR ME a block away from the Chinese language school whenever I skipped class and went to the movies. She'd given up trying to talk me out of it, and stood at the corner looking hot and annoyed. "You're late again," she snapped.

"I'm sorry," I said, but she simply shook her head, turned away, and began walking down the street. "I'm sorry," I said again, louder.

Just past the Wah Ming Herb store, Lulu suddenly stopped. "What's happening over there?" she asked.

A large crowd had gathered in front of a blocked alleyway. I instantly perked up, hoping it was a film crew shooting a new movie. In the past year, the movie industry had moved from the East Coast to Los Angeles, and suddenly the movies I loved watching were no longer just at the nickelodeons, they were being filmed right down the block from us on any given day of the week. According to the newsreels, "the mysterious and exotic *Oriental* world has captured the imaginations of American audiences." Did that mean more and more movies were going to be made with Chinese themes, even while Chinese were *still* forbidden to immigrate to the United States?

Although I didn't quite understand it all, I was thrilled to be living in a location where movies were now being made. I read in a movie magazine that the brick-and-wood buildings in Chinatown could easily pass for a Chinese setting, and it seemed like every few weeks a new film was being shot in an alleyway, in front of a storefront, or inside a restaurant. *Ma ma* always told us that it was a "good omen" when something lucky happened. Hollywood was suddenly right in front of me, and I was more determined than ever to take advantage of my good fortune.

"Come on, we have to go home," Lulu said, pulling at my arm.

I stood my ground. "You go home first, I'm coming," I told her, smiling innocently. "I just want to watch for a little while longer."

But Lulu didn't budge. "*Baba* won't be happy if you come home late again. You know what happened the last time you stopped to watch," she reminded me.

How could I forget? I returned home late to find *baba* sitting in his chair waiting for me, the bamboo switch lying across his lap. "How many times do I have to tell you to stop this foolishness!" he said, his voice angry. "The only thing you should be concentrating on is your studies."

My father stood, and I followed him obediently into my parents' bedroom. That night *ma ma* and all of my siblings were nowhere in sight. I kept quiet as I'd been taught, swallowing down the stinging pain as the bamboo switch whipped against my legs and backside. The swollen red welts on the back of my thighs made it difficult to sit on the hard wooden chairs at school for days.

Still, I was willing to accept my punishment again.

"How will he know?" I asked, holding my breath as I waited for my sister's response.

Lulu stared at me before looking away. "He'll find out sooner or later . . . but not from me," she finally said.

"It'll be later, then," I said, and smiled. I quickly hugged her. "Go home," I urged. "I don't want you to get in trouble."

Lulu hesitated and turned back to me. Her face was flushed. "They'll never let you act in their movies," she said, forcefully. "They look at us like objects. We'll always be different from them."

For a moment I didn't know what she meant. I was tongue tied amid my scattered thoughts. "They'll let me," I finally answered, defiantly. "They will, you'll see."

Lulu shook her head. "They see us differently," she repeated.

For just a moment, I hesitated. How did Lulu know so much about the movies? I realized then that just because she was the good daughter, she wasn't unaware. I turned to her and said, "Please, you have to trust me."

Lulu watched me as the crowd pushed us forward. "I won't say anything," she said, "but promise me you'll be careful and come home soon. Promise."

"I promise," I said.

My heart raced. Did my sister disapprove of the movies as much as my parents, or was she just worried I'd get in trouble again? I wanted to reassure her, but she nodded and turned away, quickly disappearing back into the mob of onlookers. For now, all that mattered was that Lulu would keep my secret.

I inched my way to the front of the crowd, squeezing in just behind a rope barrier to see Hollywood moviemaking right in front of my eyes. The glaring, bright lights with blinders were as tall as trees, and on a wooden platform, a large black camera was perched on a tripod. Next to it, a man wearing a suit and straw hat sat in a chair, holding a big cone-shaped megaphone. He shouted his directions for the actors to move onto the set, which was made to look like the front of a Chinese restaurant. The crew buzzed around making sure everything was in place while the actors entered to take their spots. Suddenly, the director, the camera, and the platform slowly began to rise high above the ground, looking down on the actors.

I watched, entranced. It was all I'd ever dreamed about.

The lights dimmed, the crowd hushed, someone clapped a board, and when the director yelled, "ACTION!" everyone on the set came to life.

From the distance, I couldn't tell who the stars of the movie were, but when I saw a Chinese actress enter the scene, I was so surprised, I felt dizzy. It was the first time I'd seen someone who looked like me acting in a real movie. I couldn't hear what she and the Caucasian actor were saying, but from her expressions and movements—the real language in a silent movie—she seemed to be pleading with him, wrapping her arms possessively around his neck, only to have him push her roughly to the ground.

The director lifted the megaphone, asking for more fight from the actress. She stood, nodded, and they replayed the same scene several more times.

"And that's a wrap!" the director yelled through the megaphone, and the wooden platform he was on slowly descended to the ground.

I STOOD THERE, STUNNED.

Even after the crowd dispersed and the crew began dismantling the set, I remained there alone, waiting and hoping for a closer glimpse of the Chinese actress who had stopped to talk to the director. When I spotted her walking toward me, I took a deep breath and stood tall. I was only nine, but I already knew that I wanted to be an actress more than anything else in the world. I hoped she might help me.

But as the Chinese actress approached, something wasn't right. She looked strange. She wore a *cheongsam*, a typical Chinese high-collared tight-fitting dress with a slit down the side, but the corners of her eyes were pulled upwards unnaturally, and she was wearing a coarse, black wig. Her eyebrows were too dark, her lips too red, and her skin appeared a ghostly white with pink blush on her cheeks. I glanced down at the skin on my arms, which was so much darker than hers from playing kickball outdoors during recess. Up close, the actress looked scary and unreal, reminding me of the *Frankenstein* story, a book Lulu had borrowed from the library about a monster that had been all stitched together.

Only then did I realize she really wasn't Chinese. I remembered reading in a movie magazine about Caucasian actors and actresses appearing as Chinese or Japanese in movies. I'd stood at the magazine rack at Scolari's drugstore, wondering why Hollywood wouldn't want to use real Chinese or Japanese actors and actresses in films.

"Hey there, sweetie," the actress said, as she walked by.

I turned away, heart beating in my ears, pretending I didn't hear her as I watched her walk past.

I was confused and didn't know what to think. I pulled at my collar, feeling hot and sweaty. I looked back at the set as it was dismantled, the exterior of the restaurant pulled apart section by section and packed into wooden crates. It was then I understood that the magic I saw on the big screen wasn't just created by good acting, but by lies and trickery too.

YET NOTHING WOULD STOP me from becoming a Hollywood star. Whenever movies were being filmed in Chinatown, I'd steal onto the sets either before or after Chinese school, asking questions and getting to know the actors and film crews. It wasn't long before they nicknamed me CCC for curious Chinese child, letting me stay on set, and laughing when I begged to be in the movie.

"I know I can act," I said, angry when they didn't take me seriously.

"You're a cute kid," one crew member said. "What's the rush to be a grown-up?"

I wanted to be in the movies. I didn't like to be known as CCC. But it didn't matter how they remembered me as long as they did.

NORTH FIGUEROA STREET
The Wong Household—1916–1919

I considered my reflection in the mirror. At eleven, I'd grown taller and lost most of my baby fat, my features thinner, my large dark eyes more expressive and all seeing. I definitely appeared older than my age. Last year, I was thrilled when I was given a job modeling fur coats for a furrier whose laundry I delivered. The newspaper photo of me modeling a mink coat even impressed my father, but more importantly, I looked at it as my first professional job.

After two years of watching and studying silent movies, I knew that a good actress could convey what was emotionally important through her eyes and by physical movement—the tilt of her head, the sway of her body, the use of hand gestures to express what she needed the audience to believe. By paying close attention, I could already tell a good actress from a bad one just by the way she moved and reacted. I practiced every evening after dinner, accentuating and exaggerating my movements in the mirror to show what the absence of my voice could still communicate.

I brushed my hair and pursed my lips, every transition reflected in the mirror. The short movie I'd seen that afternoon with Norma Talmadge was inspiring. I mimicked the expression on her face, the look of surprise when she found out her husband had been killed.

I smiled knowingly into the mirror, distracted, reflecting upon the first of many important decisions I needed to make about my acting career, choosing my stage name. I couldn't go by my Chinese name, Tsong, which didn't translate easily to an American name, and though I'd been named Anna by my doctor at birth, all of us Wong girls had simple four-letter names. I was searching for something more expressive than just plain old Anna Wong. I wrote down several names that I thought would not only sound good but also look good as my signature. I'd just written down *Lily Sing Wong* when I heard my little sister, Mary, running up the stairs and down the hall, bursting into the room and throwing herself onto her bed.

"I knew I'd find you here," Mary said, jumping up from her bed. "Why are you always sitting in front of the mirror making funny faces at yourself?"

I turned and stuck my tongue out at her playfully. At six years old, she had the sweetest nature of all the Wong kids. "Come here," I said.

Mary came closer and stood by my side.

"I'm studying to be an actress," I told her. "I'm looking in the mirror so I can see how I should look and react to different situations, just like they do in the movies."

Mary looked a little confused.

I smiled. "If you were afraid, how would you look?" I asked. "Look into the mirror and show me."

Mary stared into the mirror, her eyes suddenly wide with fright, her mouth opened wide in a silent scream. It was exaggerated, but she was on the right track.

"Was that good?" she asked.

I nodded. "Very good," I said, and squeezed her tight. I stared at the two of us in the mirror.

"What else?" she asked.

"Give me a happy look?"

Mary smiled big, her eyes clear and bright.

"Perfect! Now, tell me," I asked, gesturing toward the mirror. "Who do you see?"

Mary laughed, and said, "I see you and me, silly. Anna and Mary."

I laughed with her. "No," I said, "you're seeing the next big Hollywood movie star to grace the silver screen!"

Mary squirmed out of my arms, and yelled, "Yes, I see Anna, the next big movie star!"

I was happy to see that someone in my family believed in me, even if she was too young to know what she was really cheering about. Watching my sister prance around the room, I made my first big career decision, choosing the name I hoped to see one day on every screen and marquee across the country. Close to the two of us, but all my own. I whispered it once, twice before it rolled off my tongue. "And from now on," I said aloud, "I'll be known as *Anna May Wong*."

LATER THAT NIGHT I couldn't sleep. I heard voices and sneaked downstairs to overhear *baba* talking to *ma ma* in our small kitchen that smelled like an herb shop. Glass jars lined the open shelves with what looked like orange berries, twigs, and flat slivers of wood that *ma ma* used in her soups to keep us healthy. I moved quietly, and stood to the side of the partially opened dining room door, holding my breath and listening. My father was sitting at the old wood table we'd brought from our first house, his legs crossed, smoking a cigarette. My mother poured him more oolong tea before sitting down across from him. The lingering smells of the peanut oil used to cook dinner, mixed with the cigarette smoke and the mustiness of the tea and herbs, was always home for me.

I flinched when I heard my name.

"If Anna keeps pursuing this movie foolishness, she will be seen as nothing more than a prostitute," he said. "And then what respectable Chinese man will want to marry her?"

"She's young, let her get it out of her system," my mother said, trying to reassure my father.

It wasn't often that I heard my mother voice her opinion. She usually remained silent, letting my father rant on about his children while she quietly protected us. Lulu favored my mother in looks and temperament. She was shorter, solidly built, and reserved, while I had inherited my father's height, stubbornness, and persistence.

Had he even heard her? He shook his head. "She'll only learn responsibility when she marries and has a family of her own."

"Let her be," my mother said quietly.

Baba frowned and banged his teacup down on the table. "She has always had a mind of her own, even when she was a young child. She's becoming uncontrollable!"

I pressed my body against the wall. *Was it so wrong to yearn for something more?* I wanted to ask him. Nothing would ever change. At home, I would always be Anna or Liu-Tsong, the second daughter of Wong Sam Sing, who had hoped I would be his first American-born son after the big disappointment of having his first American-born child, Lulu, be a daughter. Instead, I was just another girl, double the frustration for him. I remember seeing a family photo where my mother had dressed me in the traditional Chinese outfit of a baby boy prince with an ornate, gold embroidered cap and plush silk robes, just to make my father happy. As a young man, *baba* had gone back to his ancestral village where he already had a first-born Chinese son with his number-one wife. Still, he wanted an American-born son more than anything else. Two years after my birth, his dream finally came true when my brother James was born.

It didn't take long for my father to see that I had what *ma ma* called a "spirited nature," along with the stubborn determination that better suited a son. From the time I was a small child, I was always breaking the rules, always curious and unafraid to wander away from the family when we went to the park, or asking too many questions and speaking up when I should have remained quiet. There always seemed to be a tug of war between us. I pulled one way, *baba* pulled the other. I was much more trouble than my father ever antic-ipated, already bringing shame to him and to our family by skipping school and going to the nickelodeons. He also didn't like me lingering around movie sets and coming home late. I was everything a proper Chinese girl shouldn't be—stubborn, independent, with a mind of my own.

Was that so bad?

And yet, my heart raced at the sound of his anger. Again and again, my mother remained silent, even when she didn't always agree with everything my father said. For the past two years, our count-less arguments, which often led me to tears, hadn't changed either of our minds. If anything, they made me more determined to be in the movies. I knew that *baba* believed in tradition, he wanted me to receive a good education and settle down into a favorable marriage. Preserving our Chinese history and traditions was what my parents had instilled in their children every day of our lives. Lulu, Mary, and I were to marry husbands who were good providers and raise families of our own. My brothers were to find good professions, marry obedient wives, and carry on our family name. *Baba* ran our lives like his laundry business—wash, dry, iron, and fold into neat, tidy bundles. There was nothing more important than family. Through it all, I never once heard the word love mentioned.

Not like in the movies.

"She's spirited," my mother repeated quietly.

Baba made that throaty sound he always did when he was displeased. "Her spirit must be broken then," he said, "before she's too old to listen."

"I'm not so sure," *ma ma* said. "Liu-Tsong has a mind of her own. Sometimes it's better to let the water flow rather than try to stop it with cupped hands. The water will simply seep through your fingers and you'll have nothing."

I smiled to hear my mother voice her thoughts. I peeked at them as my father drew from his cigarette in thought. But then he shook his head. "No, I'm her father, and she will listen," he finally said to my mother.

I stepped away from the dining room doorway when I heard footsteps. I was relieved to see it was my fourteen-year-old sister, Lulu, who had walked into our small, cluttered living room to see me listening there. If it had been one of my brothers, I would have been revealed by them just to get me in trouble. I put my finger over my lips so Lulu would stay quiet, though she didn't need reminding.

Lulu nodded her head with sympathy. "Let's go back to bed," she whispered, taking my hand and leading me upstairs.

Despite all my father's objections, I was more determined than ever to become an actress.

The following year, at the age of twelve, I worked as a counter girl and model for Ville de Paris department store. If I couldn't be an actress right away, I could be amid the latest fashions and furs, which I already had an eye for.

BY 1919, AUDIENCES STILL couldn't seem to get enough of Chinese-themed movies like *The Forbidden City*, starring Norma Talmadge, and *Broken Blossoms*, a new film by D. W. Griffith and starring Lillian Gish—and studios were more than willing to produce them all over Chinatown. I wondered if it was because we really were an unknown entity, mysterious and exotic, adding flavor to otherwise bland stories. Not long after my fourteenth birthday, I got an idea one day after school. I stood outside the Baptist Church in Chinatown waiting for Reverend James Tong, who was a go-between for Hollywood producers hiring Chinese extras for the movies. On a film set, I'd heard about Reverend Tong and the shortage of Chinese extras due to the influenza epidemic, and I knew this would be my opportunity. We rarely attended church since the laundry was open seven days a week, but I knew my father had met the reverend through the local Wong and Tong family associations. As soon as the reverend, who was short and portly with thinning hair, stepped out of the church, I introduced myself.

"Reverend Tong?"

"Yes," he said, buttoning the jacket of his dark suit.

"My name is Anna May Wong. I'm the daughter of Wong Sam Sing from the Sam Kee Laundry."

"Ah yes, I know who your father is," he said. "What can I do for you, young lady?"

"I need your help," I said. "I love everything about moving pictures, from Mary Pickford to Crane Wilbur. I've saved my laundry delivery money for years just to see the latest movies. I've been hanging around film sets since I was nine years old, hoping to become an actress. Please, can you help me get a role?" I asked, finally stopping to take a breath.

Reverend Tong stepped back and sized me up. "And what does your father think about all of this?" he asked.

"He's not very happy with me," I answered, telling the truth.

The reverend smiled. "Then he won't be very happy with me helping you," he said.

"He doesn't have to know," I said, "at least not right away. I promise, I can act."

I was taking a chance, but I also suspected the studios were paying the reverend for recruiting Chinese actors and actresses for bit parts.

Reverend Tong cleared his throat and looked at me for the longest time. I was beginning to feel uncomfortable, ready to give up, when he finally said, "You're tall and thin. Your face is also round and pleasant, and your eyes are big enough. You won't go unnoticed," he added. "Let me see what I can do. But don't get your hopes up. Even if you do get a bit part, you'll most likely be lost among hundreds of others in a crowd scene."

I nodded happily.

I knew I would be a star.

MY FIRST ACTING ROLE was in the 1919 movie *The Red Lantern*, starring the "Queen of the Silent Screen," Alla Nazimova, who was not only a sophisticated Russian actress and producer, but also a teacher and mentor. Unlike other actors or actresses, Alla was also very sensitive to ethnic portrayals on screen and had written an article for *Motion Picture Story Magazine* about racial sensitivity. It must have been the reason she'd taken a liking to me, amused by my curiosity and my relentless desire to be in the movies. She let me stay on the set when she was filming her scenes and invited me to her trailer when she wasn't.

I was one of three hundred extras hired to carry a lantern for a crowd scene. At last, I was able to watch a movie being made up close. Everything was so much more time consuming and technical, from setting up a scene to getting the right lighting. Alla Nazimova played two sisters, one of them Eurasian. By then, yellowface had become so common it no longer surprised me, even if it disturbed me to see actors and actresses made up to look so ridiculous. But I was confused as to why they weren't using real Chinese or Japanese in movies, and it was the first time I knew a real actress well enough to broach the subject.

"It's that foolish law," Alla told me.

"What law?" I asked.

"The one telling people who they can marry and who they can't marry, who they can kiss or can't kiss," she said. "Only in America are people so provincial."

She didn't explain more and I didn't dare ask, not wanting to be a nuisance, but it made me curious to find out more on my own. After years of daydreaming about it, I was suddenly making headway in the movie business with the help of a famous friend.

WHEN BABA FOUND OUT I'd been working in a movie, he was livid, even if I was nothing more than an extra among hundreds of others. *Ma ma* was busy with my new baby sister, Marietta, and was constantly reminding him to lower his voice and not wake the baby. I heard his restrained anger as he forbade me being on the set without someone watching over me. Otherwise, I had to be kept apart from the rest of the actors and locked away in a separate room until it was time for my scene. My father thought I'd surely give it up, but he had no idea that it was Alla Nazimova who was watching over me *and* helping me along with my acting career. Fortunately, he also didn't know she was a famous actress. The only life he envisioned for me was marriage and motherhood, a life filled with stifling rules and restrictions. He couldn't understand that I felt more alive on a movie set than I did in my real life.

When *The Red Lantern* played in theaters, I could hardly find myself in the crowd scene. At first, I was disheartened to see I was only a small blip on the screen, but when the camera lingered on a close-up of my face for just a second longer, it was enough. I was the only extra that stood out. Afterward, directors began to pay a little more attention to me when they needed an *Oriental* on screen. My career in the movies had finally taken a small step forward. I refused to be an "object," as Lulu had said Hollywood thought of us. I refused to simply be background decoration and used my facial expressions and height to stand out, even as an extra. I was determined that, one day, Anna May Wong would be a name they'd all remember.

BABA'S DISAPPROVAL OF MY acting career only grew over the following months. Then, the sudden death of my baby sister in her sleep left us all reeling. For months I'd been run ragged working at the laundry, going to school, and whenever I could, looking for bit parts in movies against my father's wishes. We were stuck in an on-going war, but I was too old at fourteen for the bamboo switch now, having grown to over five feet six inches tall. I also appeared older and more grown up. *Baba* began to use words as his weapon instead. And in many ways they hurt much more.

"You need to settle down and find a good husband before no one will have you," he said. "The way you flaunt yourself in front of everyone is degrading. Can't you see, Anna, you'll be worthless in the eyes of any good, respectable family?"

His words stung more than I cared to admit. I hated myself for falling into his trap, but there was a part of me that was always afraid he was right.

It didn't help to see how *Orientals* were constantly being por-trayed in the movies. The more time I spent on film sets, or watched movies in the theaters, the more I understood what my father was saying. It *was* degrading to see how we were being depicted. The *Oriental* women characters were constantly depicted as villains or prostitutes who always died in a tragic ending. Or we played the weak, fragile damsels in distress who needed to be saved, only to be discarded. Most often, we were merely the maid who bowed and poured tea for her mistress, suffering in silence, yet lending credibility to the scene. There was some satisfaction in knowing that even the Caucasian actors and actresses who wore yellowface didn't always fare well by the end of a movie.

They were just as likely doomed from the start.

For the first time since I'd dreamed of becoming an actress, I felt a wall in front of me that felt too high to climb. I was suddenly aware of the real possibility that there wouldn't be a "happily ever after" for me in the movies. And then what would I do? According to *baba,* if I didn't marry in the years ahead, I wouldn't be able to find happiness in my real life either. This much I already knew. I would rather have a few stolen moments of happiness as an actress than be forced into an arranged and unhappy marriage. I wondered if *ma ma* ever felt the same.

The continuing arguments at home wore me down. I wasn't sleeping well and had a constant sore throat. I was tired and scared and confused about my future. Since *The Red Lantern,* I had picked up some small parts playing extras in movies that were filmed around Chinatown, but as the weeks and months passed, I was no further along in my career. Alla Nazimova, who had helped to guide me, was away filming another movie in London. It felt as if time and my career had stalled.

AS MUCH AS I hated going to school, the one thing high school did was nurture my love of sports and competition. Since elementary school, I had enjoyed playing baseball and kickball. At home, it irked my father to find me sprawled on the floor shooting marbles with my brothers. In high school, I discovered I was good at tennis, which gave me back some control over my life. Hitting tennis balls back and forth was a welcome relief from all the tension I felt at home. I was told I had a natural backhand, and before I knew it, I was winning tournaments and moving up to the next levels under the watchful eye of the tennis coach. I couldn't help but wonder, Would it make *baba* happier if I gave up acting to be a famous tennis player instead?

At fourteen, I was away at camp playing tennis and preparing for the next round of tournaments when I started to feel cold, even under the hot sun. The chills were followed by a strange tingling feeling that ran through me, right before I felt all my strength drain from my body. I collapsed on the court and had to be brought home. I faintly remember the car ride back, lying motionless in the back seat and opening my eyes just long enough to see the tree branches waving their goodbyes, already knowing that yet another thing I loved was coming to an abrupt end.

When I opened my eyes next, I was home.

I heard my coach's voice. "Anna has been working really hard on the court. Maybe she just needs to rest for a few days."

"Too much sun," *ma ma* lamented, as I was carried up to my room and put to bed.

Lulu held my hand and gave it a squeeze. It was always our

unspoken way of saying, *I'm here and everything is going to be okay*, which we'd done since we were girls, bullied in elementary school.

My words felt trapped in my throat. "What . . . what . . ."

"Don't try to talk, just rest," Lulu whispered.

I wanted to know what was happening to me. One minute I was hitting a tennis ball, and the next, I was lying on the court unable to get up. I'd been feeling tired, but it was only natural since I'd been training for hours every day. I felt weak and powerless, my arms and legs disconnected from my body and brain. I was reminded of the puppet shows we used to watch when *ma ma* took us to the park when we were young. It was one of my favorite family outings. I couldn't take my eyes off the puppet, and I always felt sorry for it, slumped over after the show ended, no longer controlled by the puppeteer pulling the strings. Lying in bed, I felt like that limp and listless puppet.

The next morning, the first spasms hit me just after I managed to get out of bed. My arms and left leg began trembling, then jerking frenziedly, wild and unrestrained. I thought I was going crazy. I was that puppet again, only now, the strings attached to my arms and legs were being pulled in all different directions without my control.

NORTH FIGUEROA STREET
St. Vitus's Dance—1919–1920

What's happening?

I can't . . .

stop

moving.

I can't . . .
Stop!
I thought to myself,
Just stop!
Please . . .

My arms and left leg kept twitching, my face and tongue moved in crazy spasms. I couldn't call out. My body wasn't listening to my brain. Stop, just stop! The increasing tremors in my limbs kept coming and wouldn't stop, couldn't stop. My heart raced. What was happening to me? I had lost all control of my body.

"MA MA, MA MA, something's wrong with Anna," I heard Mary downstairs yelling for my mother. "She's dancing funny."

Lately, nine-year-old Mary followed me around whenever I was home, watching and listening to everything I did and said. She must have crept up to the bedroom and seen me moving and twitching out of control.

Normally, no one in my family would think twice of my dancing. I was always practicing different facial expressions and repeating dialogue from movies in front of the mirror. I often sang aloud, or danced around and around the room like Alla Nazimova or Mary Pickford. Only this time, it wasn't of my own free will. Mary must have been scared by the anxious and frightened look on my face, by the way my hands and arms moved crazily through the air without restraint.

Ma ma hurried upstairs to see the terrified look on my face. "I can't . . . ," I mumbled. "I can't . . ." I couldn't stop jerking long enough to get the words out.

"*Gweil*," my mother said aloud, seeing me. *Gweil* meant ghost. She quickly sent Mary to get my father from the laundry.

Was I possessed?

There was a ruckus downstairs as the front door slammed, my father rushing up the stairs. "What is it?" he asked, irritated and breathing heavily. He wiped his still wet hands on his pants.

Mary stayed by the doorway.

"Something's wrong with Liu-Tsong, she can't stop moving," my mother answered.

My parents helped me back to bed as I twitched and jerked. Even *baba* was perplexed and worried enough to summon an American doctor.

I couldn't stop wondering if this was my punishment for disobeying *baba* all these years, for not being an obedient Chinese daughter. Now, not only would I never become a famous actress, but *baba* would never be able to marry me off.

I was damaged goods.

I WAS DIAGNOSED WITH having St. Vitus's dance, which sounded like a holiday, but the dance in the title was too ironic for words. My arms and left leg continued to jerk, but I was far from dancing. The older, heavyset doctor, who smelled like black licorice, said it appeared to be neurological and caused by a bacterial infection that most likely started with the bad sore throat I'd had weeks before.

"It afflicts a handful of young people Anna's age," the doctor said. "It will most likely calm down in the next two months with plenty of rest. Then, it should gradually stop on its own a few months after that."

Two months might as well have been a lifetime to me. Every contact I'd made in the movie business would have moved on or forgotten me by then. What was I supposed to do? My movie career was over before it had begun.

I couldn't even cry, I was twitching so much.

Only when I was lying down did the twitching relax, merely to start up again just when I thought it was over. I wondered if my limbs stopped moving when I was asleep, wishing I could just sleep the next two months away. As I lay in bed the following day, the twitching had moved to my fingers on my left hand, leaving me to play an imaginary piano in the air. My leg also continued to twitch, but what I hated most was when my tongue slipped in and out of my mouth. I felt and looked as if I had gone insane.

I imagined *ma ma* telling Lulu that the spasms were a result of my own vanity. She was never happy to find me spending so much time in front of the mirror when there was work to be done at the laundry and at home.

"The mirror will still be there after the books are balanced and the laundry is folded and wrapped for your brothers to deliver," *Ma ma* had said to me just last week.

As always, her voice remained calm and neutral, which was more disturbing than *baba*'s yelling, but I knew it was a scolding neverthe-less. I had hurried to the laundry.

I should have told her what I was really trying to do when I stared into the mirror, but I was afraid she wouldn't understand. I would have said, "I'm sorry, *ma ma*, but when I look in the mirror, it's not to see me, but to see the 'me' I hope to be."

Ma ma and Lulu did stay by my bedside in the evenings, keeping Mary and my brothers away. My mother stroked my cheek while I continued to twitch, and all I could think of was how sorry I was to be such a burden.

When Lulu finally turned out the lights each night, all I could do was quietly cry.

IT WAS *BABA* WHO finally took control of my situation, asking Dr. Hong, our Chinatown herbalist doctor to come to the house. The thin doctor with the high forehead checked my tongue, lymph nodes, and fingernails before trying a series of remedies that were unsuccessful. I remembered visiting his cramped shop, which had barrels and wooden crates filled with different dried herbs, plants, fruits, and horrible-looking things soaking in large murky jars. He had me drinking herbal teas and soups, and then began using a gold coin to scrape against my arms and legs every few days until he drew blood. It was so painful, part of me would rather have remained a freak for the rest of my life than continued his tortuous treatment, but *baba* believed the Chinese doctor knew best and I wasn't about to complain.

Baba had called a truce to our battling long enough to take care of me, something I would never forget. According to the American doctor, St. Vitus's dance would eventually run its course and hopefully come to an end in a few months. Dr. Hong thought differently. By scraping my skin, he was driving the toxins out of my body and ending my affliction faster. Ten days later, when I finished drinking the last of the bitter-tasting teas that left my pee dirt colored, I woke up, still weak and very tired, but the tremors and twitching that had taken over my body were gone. I lay motionless, heart beating, and kept waiting for the spasms to return. When they didn't after what felt like an eternity, I slowly sat up, daring to hope I'd regained control of my body.

THE FOLLOWING EVENING, I found *baba* closing up the laundry, sorting through the last of the clothes that had been washed and needed to be ironed while they were damp. He was heating up the iron when he heard me come in. I was never so happy to be back in the wet heat of the laundry and able to work again.

Baba smiled when he saw me. He had grown slightly older looking in the past few years but he was still a tall, good-looking man.

"You've found your calm again," he said.

I nodded. "Thank you, *baba,* Dr. Hong's teas and the coin treatment worked."

My father pulled a damp shirt from the rack of clothes. "Thousands of years of history don't lie," he said, not unkindly. "Our long culture and your family will help you through anything. Remember that, Anna."

"Yes, *baba.*"

At that moment, all I wanted to do was give him the respect that he deserved. Even after all our heated arguments, he'd shown me that beyond everything, I was still his daughter.

"And now you can return to your studies," he added, glancing at me to see what my reaction would be.

"Yes, *baba*," I said again.

He smiled.

I checked to see if the iron was hot enough before I took the damp shirt from his hands. I wasn't ready for our truce to end yet. I wanted to hold on to this small piece of harmony between us for as long as possible.

FAMILY AND EDUCATION
First Steps—1920

The peaceful pause between *baba* and me didn't last for long. Once I had regained my strength, I stepped right back into the movie world, which angered my father all over again. The battles between us resumed and intensified. I took whatever bit parts I could get, staying on sets to get to know the directors and crew, talking to the actors and actresses who would give me the time of day. I kept telling myself that, one day, they would be seeking me out. I was fifteen, and it took all my courage to keep pushing, especially when I saw nothing but obstacles in the way. Being Chinese already limited the number of movie roles I could play, but I was also a woman in a business run by men. I had to learn to sidestep the predators who leered and grabbed at me as if I were a steak on a plate. And most difficult of all, I had to continue fighting against the angry will of my father. I balanced it all against my everyday life working at my family's laundry before school and on weekends, and I cringed to think I still had more than two long years to go until I finished high school.

MY BIG BREAK FINALLY arrived at the end of 1920. After two years of playing bit parts, I secured a role in the movie *Dinty*, directed by Marshall Neilan, which was set to film in San Francisco Chinatown. *San Francisco!* I was excited by the added adventure of travel. I'd never been farther than North Figueroa Street. My heart also leapt to learn I wasn't playing one of a hundred extras that usually filled a crowd scene, or one of the many servants in a household; I was being cast in a small role as the main servant. I was ecstatic. For the first time, I would be in a scene all by myself and it left my heart racing.

While *baba* wasn't at all happy with the idea of my traveling by train with the cast to San Francisco, I was being paid as a real cast member and he knew there was no stopping me. Instead, my father arranged for me to be looked after by a Chinatown friend who worked on the crew, but it was easy to skirt his vision between my few scenes. My first taste of freedom was exhilarating.

San Francisco Chinatown was so much larger and grander than Los Angeles Chinatown. I walked down real sidewalks, and crossed paved streets that were lined with dragon-entwined iron lampposts, past brick and stone pagoda–topped buildings like nothing I'd ever seen before. There were endless restaurants and bazaars selling Oriental-style artifacts, along with churches and nightclubs and two Chinese theaters. I was especially happy to see the theaters playing Chinese operas, much like the ones *baba* had taken us to see when the opera troupe traveled to Los Angeles. Here, the theaters were open every day from two o'clock in the afternoon to midnight, so I could sneak away and attend any time I wasn't working. I loved the retelling of the Chinese myths and stories, the costumes and makeup, the pageantry of the performances. During a free afternoon, I hurried over to the theater with another young actress, Rhonda Yee, and we sat up in the balcony of the enormous theater and watched both the opera and the Caucasian tourists seated below us. Among the crowd was a particularly raucous group of young men who began to talk and laugh louder just as the second act began.

"I don't understand a word you're saying!" one of the men yelled toward the stage. The others with him laughed.

"Why are they even here?" Rhonda whispered, incensed.

"Why don't you leave then?" I yelled loudly down at him.

He looked up and I wanted to sit back and out of sight, but instead, I stayed hovering over the railing, the blood rising to my face in anger.

At first, I was happy to see so many Caucasians, delighted that other people were interested in the Chinese theater. But as I scrutinized the faces of the troublemakers below, I saw an uglier truth. They weren't there to see the beauty of Chinese culture; they were there to make fun of the differences. They were watching the actors on stage as if they were animals in a zoo. I felt sick to my stomach.

The young man glared at me. "Yellow bitch!" he yelled, rising, but was pulled back down into his seat by his friends.

Instead, I was the one who stood. "I need to get some air," I said. Rhonda looked at me and followed.

WHEN I ARRIVED HOME from San Francisco with the largest paycheck I'd ever made, my parents were more accepting of my career. My role in the movie, though small, allowed me to leave a lasting impression. This was my chance to make sure the camera captured me as I walked in and out of a scene, pouring tea or relaying a message to the daughter of the prominent judge I worked for in the movie. The film did reasonably well. More importantly, I also caught the eye of film directors who began to regularly cast me in small roles in other movies.

MY BOUT WITH St. Vitus's dance had kept me out of school for over a month. Soon after my recovery, I left for San Francisco to film *Dinty*. By the time I returned to Los Angeles and was back in high school, I was restless and distracted. After two months away, I felt completely out of place. I'd also fallen behind in my studies, and the classroom walls seemed to be closing in on me. I loved learning and knew I could easily catch up if I wanted to, but I hated the slow pace and repetition, the young kids sitting in front of and behind me without a thought beyond lunch. My experience making movies had given me a freedom I'd never felt before, both on and off the set. Learning to act and traveling to new places offered so much more than I could ever learn in a classroom. Each day dragged on, feeling heavier and heavier until I just couldn't stand it anymore.

When I returned home from school one afternoon, I couldn't stop crying and I didn't know why. All I wanted to do was sleep. I stayed in bed the next morning, and no coercing could get me up for the next two days. I was afraid the malaise I felt would become a lingering ghost, returning to haunt me throughout my life if things didn't change. I knew I had to do something, and so I came to a quick decision. The third morning, I dressed, went downstairs to the kitchen, and refused to return to school, upsetting both of my parents.

It hurt to know that I was such a big disappointment, a failure in their eyes. According to my father, education and family were always the keys to success. A good daughter obeyed her parents and did what she was told. *Baba* raised his voice and his hand, adamant that I finish high school.

"You have no idea how difficult the world is without an education and family," he said to me, coldly.

His eyes were dark with anger. His words stung. Did giving up one mean I had to give up both?

"I've always wanted to be an actress," I told him, holding my ground. "I'm making movies now. There's no use wasting any more time sitting in a classroom."

"You'll learn what wasted time is," my father said, furious. He walked out of the kitchen, his words lingering heavy in the air.

I couldn't go back. High school was a life I had already left behind. I'd had a taste of Hollywood magic and I was finally on my way to becoming an actress. I refused to let it all go after I'd worked so hard to make inroads.

For weeks after I'd left school, my father remained frighteningly silent, watching me come and go, waiting for me to fall.

Instead, my movie career began to soar.

CENTRAL VALLEY
1960

The train slows to a stop at the Fresno station. I put down the notebook and turn my attention to the growing commotion outside the window. The thump of the train doors opening is followed by the dull thuds of footsteps down the corridor. I watch as passengers disembark, while others wait to board. Moments later, someone bangs into the compartment next to mine, stowing luggage under the seat so forcefully our adjoining wall shakes. I hear voices, laughter, someone clearing their throat. I'm left hoping they'll settle in quietly for the remainder of the trip.

I get up to stretch my legs, walking the four steps to the door and back several times. This train trip is my calm before the storm. When I arrive in New York, there will be a whirlwind of friends, dinner parties, and a slew of nonstop interviews and events. I didn't think this opportunity would come my way again; now it leaves me feeling anxious.

My last big interview was nine years ago, in 1951, when I was given my own television show after years of having little work. It was about a woman detective, called *The Gallery of Madame Liu-Tsong*, in which they used my real Chinese name. At the time, television was a new form of entertainment and just finding its way, and it was quite a breakthrough moment for me. I thought I was finally on the road to a comeback then. Unfortunately, the show didn't last and the years have been quiet since then.

My life turned another corner when Ross Hunter and Universal Studios approached me about this press tour for *A Portrait in Black*. "Just give them what they want, a retrospective of your career," the studio publicist told me when he dropped off my itinerary. "You're the first Chinese-American woman to become an international movie star, from silent films to the talkies. You've been in the movie business for over forty years. Talk it up," he urged. "Tell them what it was really like for you. The time is right now, people will understand how hard it was for you in Hollywood back then."

Back then, I think to myself. What about now? What I should be asking is, Why hasn't Hollywood changed after so many years? What of the anti-miscegenation laws that kept me from so many leading lady roles that should have been mine? Why is it so difficult for a Chinese to play a Chinese role, while all those Caucasian actors and actresses in yellowface are playing Oriental characters on the screen? Didn't the role of the Japanese neighbor in the upcoming movie *Breakfast at Tiffany's* just go to Mickey Rooney? The offenses seem endless.

But I know I'm going to have to play nice once again, tell them how lucky I've been in my career, even if it has nothing to do with *luck*, but all the hard work and the willingness to accept disparaging roles that were less than flattering. What choice did I have? I've perfected the dragon lady, the prostitute, the opium dealer, and so many death scenes, I finally had to leave the United States. Nevertheless, I believe that seeing a *real* Chinese on the screen was better than never seeing one at all.

OUTSIDE THE WINDOW, the fields flash by heavy with bounty. The late afternoon light changes as we move through the Central Valley, where farms and fields blanket the countryside and the sky feels so much more expansive than in the city. The wide-open space is not only brighter but also lonelier. The train suddenly slows, and it seems as if we're traveling through the middle of a field. I fumble in my bag for the Leica camera Carl gave me years ago, but by the time

I pull it out, the train has picked up speed again and sweeps past any decent shot of the farmhouses and barns, leaving only the flat fields.

Farther along, farmworkers gather their belongings, wiping sweat and dust from their faces as they walk slowly back toward the dirt road. It's the end of another long day of back-breaking work. I imagine it's the best part of their day, going home to their families. It's the reason why they're in the hot sun working for low wages, all for their families, so that their children can find a better life in America, just as my father wanted for us.

MY FATHER, WONG SAM SING, found his American dream. He was a self-made man who owned property back in his village in China and started his own laundry business in Los Angeles, one of the few businesses Chinese men were allowed to own in the early 1900s. Even during our angriest disagreements, I tried to remember how hard it was for him: the long hours of washing other people's dirty clothes in the big vats of boiling water, the drying, ironing, and folding all day, every day. But he built a successful business and found his niche. He was respected by his peers, and raised his seven American-born children straddling the same racial lines. I can still hear him telling us over and over, "We are Americans, but we are Chinese too."

For the most part, he never looked for anything beyond raising a large family to help him with the family business. Even reading my old notebooks, I did not find a window into his thoughts. Had he ever secretly wanted more? He returned to his village in China in 1934, several years after my mother died and he had retired. In China, he was a prosperous and respected elder in his village.

His eldest son, my half-brother Dounan, was educated at Waseda University in Japan and had a growing family of his own. At least Dounan had fulfilled *baba*'s dreams. My father was proud of the life he built in Los Angeles. Wong Sam Sing looked to us, his American-born children, to carry on the American dream he'd already begun here. I know I had taken that dream in a direction he never fully understood, or accepted.

Still, it was my life, my *American dream.*

HOLLYWOOD
A New Life — 1921

I was sixteen when Hollywood finally cracked open its door wide enough for me to slip through. A steady stream of contacts and growing friendships with other actors and actresses introduced me to Hollywood social life. My first grown-up party was at actor Sessue Hayakawa's mansion after I'd appeared with him in a movie called *The First Born.* He was the only major Japanese star to make it big in Hollywood, and the only other *Oriental* actor working in silent movies who looked like me. We were the token two. I'd read in movie magazines that he was born and raised in Japan, but even after years of seeing him in silent movies, I was surprised to hear his heavy Japanese accent when we met. Already a famous actor in Japan, Sessue was in his early thirties when he came to the United States to find fame in Cecil B. DeMille's *The Cheat.* In 1915, Sessue bucked the trend—a Japanese actor who crossed over to leading man territory; he was as popular and adored as John Barrymore and

Douglas Fairbanks, commanding similar salaries. He played a host of other exotic nationalities beyond Chinese and Japanese characters, and had a huge following of female fans from all over the world who were mesmerized by his dark, brooding good looks. The thought of "forbidden" love with him, as all the magazines wrote, drove up the fantasy and made him a big Hollywood star.

Over the years, I closely followed all of his films and studied his career. His many movies almost always dealt with interracial love, ultimately followed by disaster and tragedy. He usually played the villainous romantic character who challenged the Caucasian leading man for the affections of the Caucasian leading lady in a film, though he was destined to never get the girl. This was the common theme in movies whenever a character wasn't Caucasian, and it was a standard I was determined to change.

SESSUE AND HIS WIFE, actress Tsuru Aoki, were also known for the lavish parties they threw for the Hollywood elite—their cocktail parties, luncheons, and sit-down dinners for hundreds were the talk of the town, often featured in the movie magazines. He drove a gold-plated Pierce-Arrow, and they lived in the famous "Castle" in Hollywood, a mansion that was the replica of a Scottish castle, complete with turrets, leaded windows, and large tapestries.

When our movie, *The First Born*, wrapped up, Sessue approached me with an invitation to a cocktail party that he was hosting at his house to celebrate the completion of the film.

"You must come," Sessue said. "There will be many people at the party that you might benefit by meeting. It's very important to know the right people in this business, and you mustn't let them forget you." And then he added with a smile, "One of those people is my wife, Tsuru. She's very eager to meet you."

I blushed. "Thank you," I said. I couldn't believe the famous Sessue Hayakawa was talking to me as if he were my older brother and confidant.

He laughed. "You will do just fine, don't worry."

Sessue had given me my first priceless lesson in surviving as a Hollywood actress: it was important to be invited to and attend as many Hollywood parties as possible to meet all the right people.

"WHAT WILL YOU WEAR to the party?" Lulu asked.

In the back room of the laundry at closing, she was folding the last of the day's wash that had been dried and pressed, wrapping each garment meticulously in a sheet of brown, waxy paper. The bundles sat like gifts on the long wooden table waiting for the next day's delivery. My brothers, James and Frank, did most of the deliveries now, while I handled the accounts. Although I didn't like sitting in a classroom, I read constantly and was quick with numbers. I recorded the day's income, closed the ledger, and locked it in the top drawer of *baba*'s desk.

"I'm hoping to borrow something from *ma ma*," I answered.

It was my first big Hollywood party, and I was well aware that whatever I wore would have to make a big impact on everyone there. Even as a young girl, I was mindful of what people were wearing. I watched how fashion played such a big part in what the actresses wore in movie magazines, and sat mesmerized when the latest fashions were shown in the newsreels. In Paris, Coco Chanel was the reigning queen; her free-flowing styles were the current rage. Hollywood stars were trendsetters and everything they were seen in was for a reason.

Lulu paused in thought. She never spent much time thinking about fashion the way I did, and was usually the last one to care how people dressed, but even Lulu realized I couldn't go to a big Hollywood party wearing my schoolgirl clothes.

"You could borrow *ma ma*'s embroidered jacket," she said.

I paused before I answered, "Yes, you're right, that's a wonderful suggestion!" I looked over at Lulu as if it was all her idea. I had already sneaked the jacket out of *ma ma*'s wooden chest days before to air it out. I knew *ma ma* would definitely allow me to wear the jacket with Lulu on my side.

Lulu smiled happily. I stood and gave her a quick hug. She was everything I wasn't: steady, practical, and obedient.

I didn't have much money, but I knew I could create a unique outfit with a few pieces from my mother's trunk. A simple black *cheongsam* topped with her brightly embroidered turquoise silk jacket would be stylish enough for me to stand out in a sea of Coco Chanel designs. It was all I could hope for.

SESSUE HAYAKAWA'S "CASTLE" WAS large and imposing, the grounds clearly taking up half the block of the large corner lot on Argyle and Franklin Streets. I pulled *ma ma*'s jacket tightly across my chest as I walked up the stone steps and through the large wooden front doors into another world. I nervously stopped just inside the high-ceilinged entryway. Large tapestries and paintings hung from the walls, behind pedestals of Chinese and Japanese vases and antiques. As beautifully dressed people greeted one another, moving around me in expensive dark suits, a flurry of furs, and glittering dresses, I felt completely out of place. When someone in a white jacket offered to take my coat, I pulled it tighter, smiled, and shook my head.

"Anna May!" a voice called out.

I turned around to see a smiling Oriental woman walking toward me.

"I'm Sessue's wife, Tsuru," she said, introducing herself.

"Yes, I know," I said, and smiled. "I'm so happy to meet you."

She smiled kindly, gave me a quick hug, and then hooked her arm in mine as if we were old friends meeting at a train station. Tsuru had a round face and kind eyes. She was shorter and a bit heavier than I was, but seemed immediately protective of me, for which I was grateful. A well-established actress in her own right, both in Japan and in Hollywood, she was often photographed with Sessue in the movie magazines. Friendly and unassuming, Tsuru wore a simple black cocktail dress and a long, shiny strand of pearls.

"Come then, let us find Sessue," she said.

Tsuru led me through the enormous, high-ceilinged living room with dark wooden beams, a huge stone fireplace I could have stepped into, and a bank of tall windows that opened up to a huge terrace. We slowly moved into the thick of the boisterous crowd. Al Jolson was singing and playing the grand piano on a raised platform in the back corner. Along the way, Tsuru stopped a server and handed me a drink from the tray.

"Okay?" she asked.

"Yes," I answered, not knowing exactly what kind of drink was in the beautiful, wide-mouthed glass. I liked the way it looked, the green olive lying in the clear liquid. I tried not to spill any of it as we continued, but just holding the glass in my hand made me feel like I belonged in this liquor-laced, smoke-filled room, among the famous and sophisticated.

Tsuru followed my wide-eyed gaze and leaned closer. "They're mostly here for Sessue, but also for the liquor. Since the Prohibition, everyone knows he serves the best liquor, and in unlimited quantities." She smiled, and added, "Sessue was very smart. He bought hundreds of cases just before liquor was banned. It's always good to plan ahead, don't you think, especially with life changing so quickly?"

I nodded, not quite sure what I should say. My own life had changed in the blink of an eye. I stopped and stood, transfixed, watching Clara Bow chatting with John Gilbert, Fay Wray talking to John Barrymore, followed by loud laughter from the corner of the room. Even without his white makeup and bowler hat, I knew it was Charlie Chaplin by his smooth, quick movements as he pantomimed drinking and falling down drunk for a small group of onlookers.

We walked through a large, beveled glass doorway and out to the large terrace surrounded by a stone wall with turrets. The breeze felt good.

"Here she is," Sessue said, greeting me kindly.

"It's some party," I responded, happy to see a familiar face. "Thank you for inviting me."

He smiled. "The first of many," he said, and then lowered his voice. "After all, this is where most Hollywood movie business is done."

Tsuru smiled, and squeezed my arm. "I'll leave you in good hands, then," she said, and wandered off to talk to other guests.

I looked around the crowded terrace, filled with so many of the movie stars that had colored my imagination and desires for most of my childhood. I kept wondering when I was going to wake up from this glorious dream.

When I turned back, Sessue had been joined by the director Marshall Neilan, a tall, thin man, roughly the same age as him. "Do you know Mickey Neilan?" Sessue asked.

"Yes, we've met," Neilan quickly answered. "Anna May had a small part in my movie, *Dinty*. My friends call me Mickey," he added with a smile.

I'd also read all about him in the movie magazines. Neilan was currently building quite a reputation for himself as a director, as well as quite a partyer and ladies' man, although he was married. I didn't see his wife anywhere nearby.

"It's nice to see you again," I said, shaking his hand. I was surprised he knew who I was. I hadn't spent a lot of time on the set, slipping away whenever I could during the filming in San Francisco to walk around Chinatown and attend performances of the Chinese operas at the theaters there.

I quickly swallowed from the drink I held and coughed, spilling some of the drink. The burn of the alcohol sent a warm flush to my face.

"Careful there," Mickey said, laughing. "Sessue's martinis are deadly."

"She'll soon get used to them," Sessue said.

Mickey handed me his handkerchief and leaned closer. "Sip slowly next time," he said, and laughed.

My mouth went dry and my tongue felt numb, but I liked the sound of his laugh and the way his gaze was focused on just me, even with so many famous and beautiful women at the party.

I glanced away when the warmth rose to my face again.

HOLLYWOOD
Growing Up—1921–1922

Sessue had been right. After the party, Mickey Neilan gave me my first screen-billing role in a drama called *Bits of Life*, set again in San Francisco Chinatown, and starring Lon Chaney in yellowface. In the movie, I played his wife and the mother of a baby girl so successfully that audiences and movie magazines began to take notice. I also liked Lon, who was generous and worked hard, taking nothing for granted. Playing my first adult role at sixteen brought me some international publicity as well. I was thrilled to be featured in a major British magazine, *Picture Show*, which showcased me on the front cover. Being in demand for supporting roles in major movies with famous stars had surprised and impressed my family, as did my making $150 every week, while I continued to do my bookkeeping duties at the laundry.

MICKEY NEILAN BEGAN SPENDING more and more time with me. He was a major Hollywood film director and I was a fledgling.

I could hardly believe my new life. As happy as it made me seeing him, I knew my parents would never approve of me going out with someone who wasn't Chinese and was almost twice my age.

"Hey, beautiful!" he said, when he saw me approach.

"Hi, Mickey," I said, a flush rising to my cheeks.

He leaned over and pushed the passenger-side door open for me, a cigarette dangling between his lips. I usually met Mickey on a side street, a few blocks from the laundry and away from prying eyes when he picked me up in his big, shiny convertible. We would drive down the coast and away from the city to walk on the beach. I loved the feel of the sand beneath my bare feet and the roar of the waves rolling in and out. We stopped at small, charming restaurants that overlooked the ocean, while Mickey talked about the movies he wanted to make with me as his leading lady, and gave me gifts of bracelets and gold necklaces. I was on my way to becoming a movie star, a dream come true. A few months later, we no longer stopped at restaurants, but at out-of-the-way seaside motels where he told me to wait in the car while he secured us a room. As I waited for Mickey the first time, I was both scared and excited. He was risking it all for me; I was not only Chinese but only sixteen, legally underage. He was breaking the law and could be accused of rape and sent to prison. All I knew was that we no longer cared. We loved each other.

THE FIRST TIME MICKEY undressed me and laid me on the big bed, I felt as if I was watching everything from a distance, like a camera shot being filmed from above. I was startled by the weight of his warm, pale body as he lay on top of me and began kissing and touching me, whispering how lovely I was. Others had tried, but I refused, fought and ran if I had to. I wanted to wait until I was ready. With Mickey I was ready. I lay back on the bed, thrilled at the heat and softness of his skin against mine. I imagined how the camera would move in slowly for a close-up when our lips finally touched. I didn't want him to ever stop kissing me. This was exciting and intoxicating. Something I was forbidden to do in real life or in the movies, I was doing anyway.

MICKEY AND I BECAME an open secret in Hollywood. We weren't the first younger girl/older man relationship, and it didn't take me long to realize they were a dime a dozen, in all ages and sexual preferences. His being almost fifteen years older seemed normal to everyone around us. At home, and working at the laundry, I was still Anna or Liu-Tsong. Only Lulu knew about Mickey, and as always, she kept my secret. Mickey took me to Hollywood dinners and parties, and promised me we would travel to Mexico to get married as soon as he'd gotten a divorce.

And I believed him.

But months later, at one of the small, out-of-the-way coastal restaurants we frequented, Mickey fidgeted in his seat, looking uncomfortable and nervous.

"What's wrong?" I asked.

He didn't answer at first, looking at me as if he was trying to memorize my face. He swallowed his drink, and finally said, "We can't be together anymore."

I thought he was teasing me at first, but by the grim look on his pallid face, I knew he wasn't. For the first time, Mickey looked older to me.

"What are you saying?" I asked, suddenly feeling sick to my stomach.

"I'm sorry," he kept repeating. "Staying together will be the end of my career. I've been warned by the studio. I'm already hanging by a thin thread as it is."

I looked at him in disbelief.

"You can't do this, not now," I pleaded, swallowing the rest of the sentence, *when you know I love you*.

"I'll never be able to work in this town again," he added, his voice breaking. "I need the work, Anna May. It's not that I don't care for you."

"You can't!" I raised my voice, half rising from the chair. "You've known about all of this, and yet you lied to me for all of these months!" He'd told me he'd make me a star.

"Please, Anna May, don't make a scene."

If he was so afraid I'd make a scene, why did he take me to a public place? Was it because he thought a good Chinese girl wouldn't make a scene in public? It would have been so easy to cry and scream and get him into trouble, but I saw the fear in his eyes and couldn't do it. I wondered if Mickey's courage began to slip away as our plans came closer to reality. He sat there waiting, afraid of looking me in the eyes, afraid of what I'd do. For the first time in my life, I realized that I also held some power over a situation. It was a feeling I would never forget.

Slowly, I sat back again, tears streaming down my face.

"You're a coward," I whispered.

Mickey remained silent, his eyes avoiding mine.

I watched him pay the bill and we returned to the car. The drive was quiet and solemn. I felt sick with hurt and despair roiling in my stomach, but somewhere along the way back, my tears had dried. He stopped the car at the same side street two blocks from the laundry, but he kept the engine running.

He turned to me, and said, "Anna May, I'm so sorry."

"Coward," I repeated, and stepped out of his convertible.

I didn't look back. I couldn't, because of how angry I was. He didn't even turn the engine off, wanting a quick getaway. I walked faster in the opposite direction, hoping that leaving me would one day return to haunt him.

In the end, it had nothing to do with the fact that he was still married, or that I was only sixteen; it was because I was Chinese. He'd been threatened by the studio heads, and warned by his friends that if he married me, the anti-miscegenation law would ruin his career. And just like that, he was gone.

THE FOLLOWING MONTH, I fell into a deep abyss and couldn't find my footing. I'd wake up each morning exhausted, paralyzed, feeling like there was something heavy pressing down on my chest, making it hard to breathe. I'd been swept up in the romance of it all, of movie stardom, and having a worldly man care for me. At least I thought he had. I couldn't return to the movie world where everyone knew about us, the ill-fated affair between the older director and the naive Chinese girl. I was nothing but a cliché. It was so embarrassing I wished I could disappear.

Instead, I found solace working at the laundry again with my family. I didn't want to admit how much I needed them. Lulu was nineteen and the only one who understood what I was going through, while Mary, who had turned eleven, had decided she wanted to follow me into acting. I hovered over the ledger, making sure the laundry's accounts were all in order. I washed, ironed, and folded to keep my mind off Mickey and the movie business. The repetitive work calmed me.

But it didn't take very long before other troubles followed me.

As much as *baba* ruled over his American children, we were told he had a first wife and son in China as soon as we were old enough to understand. Like many men of his generation who had returned to their ancestral villages and married, he now had two families to support. His eldest son, my half-brother, Huang Dounan, saw me in the movie *The First Born* in Tokyo while studying at Waseda University. He wasn't happy about it, and had written a letter to my parents pleading for them to stop me from making any more movies. He called it "daring and disgraceful" for a young girl to parade herself in front of the camera for everyone to see, and told my father that it would lead to no good. While my mother ignored my eldest brother, my father began to seriously focus on finding me a suitable husband before I made another film. At almost seventeen, I was already too tall, and too independent for his liking.

"Perhaps I should have Dounan find you a good husband in China," my father threatened during one of our many heated conversations.

These talks usually took place in the back room of the laundry, while I was working on the books, or in the kitchen of our house behind the laundry. Every time my father entered the room, my heart raced, my body tensed, and it often led to headaches.

Losing Mickey had been devastating to me, but I shivered to think what *baba* would have done if he knew the extent of my relationship with him. Mickey was everything my father insisted was bad about Hollywood, and I could no longer deny it. If he had found out, *baba* would never have been able to marry me off to a good Chinese family. I would be spoiled goods, reinforcing what he already thought about actresses: that we were no more than prostitutes. No matter how much I loved Mickey, he would never have been anything more than a *gweilo*, a white ghost, to my father.

But marrying me off to China didn't frighten me. I knew it was an empty threat because *baba* didn't have the money to send me back to China. Although he neglected to mention that I was helping to put Dounan through Waseda University with the money I earned from acting, I avoided saying anything concerning a husband and marriage.

Instead, I said, "It might help my acting to go back and see China."

My father fumed. "Your acting will drive everyone away!"

"Or keep everyone in school and well taken care of!" I snapped back.

I'd become more brazen since earning my own money. Things were easier for me now that I was contributing to the family. My mother, who sat sewing, looked at me and shook her head as if to say, *don't start*. I had no desire to start anything; this same old argument needed to be put to rest. What about Lulu? She was his eldest daughter, but I'd never once heard him threaten to marry her off.

Granted, she was more indispensable, doing so much at home and at the laundry. Lulu's departure would leave an irreplaceable void not just for the family, but for me.

I sometimes wished I had been the first American-born son my father wanted so badly. It would have allotted me so much more freedom at home and with my movie career. Still, I knew I had crossed the line by throwing the money I made in my father's face. I quickly bowed my head in respect. I could feel *baba* glaring at me. He must have wanted to raise his bamboo stick and bring it down hard across my back.

I looked up to see him walking out the back door, slamming it behind him. My mother shook her head and mumbled, "So stubborn," which could have applied to either of us, before she returned to her sewing. I closed the account ledger and placed it back in the top drawer of the desk knowing our angry arguments over marriage were far from over.

HOLLYWOOD
Breakthrough — 1922

I'd been abandoned by Mickey. I'd had months to live with it, a humiliation I'd never felt before and would never forget. He'd broken my heart in a way that only a first love can. He had been tender and all encompassing as he promised me leading lady roles in movies, and encouraged my dreams of Hollywood stardom. I fell for his lies but where was I now? Completely wrung dry, I woke up one morning no longer sad but angry. I'd grieved enough, and I knew I would never be that innocent and trusting again. I used the anger I felt to pick myself back up again. After months of hiding, I held my head up high and returned to the world of movies.

HOLLYWOOD BECKONED. I WAS still a rising star, with or without Mickey Neilan. Ironically, I was kept busy with new options that seemed so much brighter. While *Bits of Life* was a movie that would be forever tied to Mickey, it also opened new doors for me.

I threw myself back into my acting career. Only when I stood in front of a movie camera did my complicated home life disappear into the magic. I couldn't get enough of it. Anna or Liu-Tsong vanished into thin air to become someone else. I remembered how both my parents had little trust for photos, much less for films. "It traps the spirit," they always said. "How can you trust anything that captures your soul for all eternity?"

I smiled to think of it. I couldn't imagine anything better.

I MADE ANOTHER MOVIE, *Shame*, set in Shanghai with John Gilbert, the long-time matinee idol whose movies I'd watched for years. He was older and very professional. I had to pinch myself to think I was in a movie with him. I received a second billing and didn't have to wait long before I was offered a starring role in *The Toll of the Sea*. This was my first leading lady role, and it sadly resembled what I'd just gone through with Mickey. I immediately felt an affinity with the main character who had been abandoned by her Caucasian lover.

The Toll of the Sea's storyline borrowed closely from Puccini's

Madame Butterfly, and had been hugely successful not only as an opera but as an earlier movie starring Mary Pickford, whom I had admired for years. Excited to appear in something even remotely tied to her, I already felt this particular movie would be a turning point in my career. It was not only the first major film shot in Technicolor but also starred a Chinese actress in a major role. I knew I needed to make the most of it.

The studio had changed the location from Japan to the Chinese coast near Hong Kong. I would play Lotus Flower, who rescues an American man who has washed up on the rocks of the coast. She nurses him back to health and falls in love with him. When a family emergency calls him back to America, he leaves her pregnant and subject to the ridicule of the other Chinese women in the village. When he returns, it's with a new Caucasian wife and with the intention to raise Lotus Flower's son as theirs.

Heartbroken, she throws herself into the sea.

I balked at Lotus Flower having to drown at the end as I read the screenplay by Frances Marion, who was one of the few women screenwriters in Hollywood. Because it was the first silent film shot in Technicolor, it was already gaining national attention. The story itself paralleled so much of the life I'd been living just the year before, it was eerie. All Hollywood knew about Mickey and me. Maybe that was the reason I'd been given the role, since I was ripe to play the jilted lover. I was just thankful my own personal story didn't include an unexpected baby and end with my suicide.

Despite its tragic ending, I was only seventeen and *The Toll of the Sea* was the role I'd been waiting for. It was my chance to show the studio heads and movie audiences who I was as an actress. I knew my performance would have to be heart wrenching and sympathetic, shown by the expressions on my face, the subtle gestures of my body, and the tears I would cry when I learned I'd been betrayed by the man I loved. I knew Lotus Flower's despair, and I was determined to recreate it. For the first time, *The Toll of the Sea* would give me a fair share of screen time, and I was determined to show movie audiences a real Chinese actress who wasn't in yellowface. I wanted to enhance my performance through the clothes I wore and the hairstyles I fashioned. I was excited knowing I'd be able to create a Chinese character from scratch.

"Would it be all right if I made some changes to Lotus Flower's costuming?" I asked Frances Marion after our first group reading.

I liked her; she held her ground, not backing down to the men running the show. She had chestnut-colored hair and beautiful, deep blue eyes. I was years younger but inches taller than her.

She looked me up and down with curiosity. "Depends what those changes are," she answered.

I smiled nervously. I knew I couldn't do anything about the ending, but there were other ways to bring Lotus Flower to full bloom. "I'll show you at our next rehearsal," I said. It would give me two days to gather my thoughts and present my ideas to her.

"Looking forward to it," she said, and was out the door.

MY IDEA WAS TO show Lotus Flower's evolution through the movie by the clothing she wore and with her changing hairstyles. At the beginning of the movie, in all innocence and happiness, I wanted her to wear bright colors of yellow and blues, with her hair in the "virgin-child" cut, to show her youthful happiness and zest for life. Later, when her lover leaves, she would wear darker, drab colors, and her hair would be pulled back into a chignon, like *ma ma*'s, in the *binzi* style of a married woman. As the years went by, Lotus Flower's terrible predicament would be shown reaching a peak by her cutting part of her hair across her forehead to represent the young innocent girl, while the rest remained pulled back like that of a married woman. I wanted to physically show Lotus Flower's dilemma, the belief in her heart that she was married even if she wasn't.

Frances Marion loved the idea and went to bat for me.

The rest I drew from my own recent unhappiness. I carefully dredged up the emotions I'd experienced the year before with Mickey. Then, all I had to do was think about those taunting, bullying boys from the schoolyard of my childhood, along with my family difficulties to make the tears flow on screen without the use of any aids. It was crucial for me to show movie audiences a well-rounded, flesh-and-blood Chinese woman who had never been seen on the screen before. It didn't matter whether she was Chinese or Caucasian; Lotus Flower was simply a naive young woman who had been wronged by the man she loved. Once I was in character, the rest came as naturally as a flowing stream of water.

It was hard to stop when the director called out, "That's a print!"

THE TOLL OF THE SEA made me an overnight success. I was hailed as *"extraordinarily fine,"* while another review said, *"She should be seen again and again on the screen."* One paper had even said I was a *"natural Chinese,"* which was a ridiculous kind of praise. I *was*

Chinese; it couldn't be more natural for me to play who I was. I succeeded in a very difficult role and had stolen the show.

The praise kept coming and Hollywood finally took notice.

THE TOLL OF THE SEA premiered on November 26, 1922, at the Rialto Theatre in New York City. I was mesmerized by the tall buildings and bright lights, but there was little time to enjoy the sights with Lulu due to my hectic schedule. I was mobbed when I arrived at the theater, the flash of the cameras blinding as I stepped out of the car the studio had sent for me. It was a cool, clear evening. I stopped and turned around, wavering, waiting for Lulu to emerge. I had dreamed so long for this moment only to suddenly feel terrified. What if it was all a big mistake, and when the audience saw me up on the big screen, my short career would be over?

"Hey, doll, take a breath and smile for the cameras," a familiar voice cut in. "It's just first-time jitters."

Like magic, Frances Marion was standing next to me, her voice soothing as she waved to the cameras and took my arm. We'd become friends during the making of the film. She had been on set most days for any last-minute script changes and treated me as an equal, not the young, unknown starlet that I was. Frances asked for my opinion concerning Chinese language and traditions and mannerisms. She welcomed my changes and all my decisions concerning hairstyles and dress. I took a deep breath, smiled, and waved.

"Attagirl," she said, "you'll get used to it. After they see your performance tonight, everything is going to change for you. You take my word for it."

Frances was a well-connected, well-respected part of the Hollywood scene. She knew everyone and everyone knew her.

Lulu stood at my other side and I felt protected. "What do you think?" I whispered to my sister.

"There are so many people," Lulu said. "And they're all here to see you, Anna."

I smiled and squeezed Lulu's hand.

Frances turned to me. "Come on, there are some people I want you to meet." She pushed through the crowd and pulled me along with her. I held on to Lulu. I was taller than Frances, but she was a towering force.

Who did she want me to meet? I wondered, relieved to be led away from the onslaught of glaring lights, only to be met by another group of waiting photographers.

"Miss Wong!" someone shouted.

Another voice yelled, "Miss Wong, look over here!"

Frances was good at keeping the photographers back just enough so I wouldn't panic. I suddenly felt like a child again, seven instead of seventeen. The crowd surged forward and it felt overwhelming.

Lulu leaned over, and said, "It'll be okay, Anna, just keep walking."

When Frances stopped, it was before a couple who had their backs to us. She touched the woman's shoulder. "Mary and Doug, I want you to meet a good friend of mine," Frances said.

I smiled shyly when they turned toward us, and swallowed my surprise when I saw who they were. Above all the movie stars I'd already met, Mary Pickford and Douglas Fairbanks were considered real Hollywood royalty. I'd spent so much of my childhood watching their movies at the nickelodeons that it felt like a dream come true to finally meet them in person.

Mary Pickford turned and looked up at me; she was so much shorter than I'd imagined, though her beautiful, dark, and expressive eyes were even lovelier in person.

"Anna May," she said, taking my hand. "Frances can't stop talking about you."

Douglas Fairbanks immediately leaned in. "Ah, so you're the young lady who's stolen the show," he added. "I hear you're on your way up, my dear. Who knows if you'll remember who we are in a year's time?" He couldn't keep still, waving and tipping his hat to people in the crowd, posing for every photographer who came our way.

"Doug, stop. It's hard enough being gawked at without your teasing," Mary Pickford said, calm and reassuring.

"Isn't that why we're here?" he said, smiling for a camera.

I blushed, the heat rising to my face. I was standing with Mary Pickford and Douglas Fairbanks and I couldn't find my voice.

"I've seen all your movies!" I finally blurted out.

"And someday a young actress will say the same thing to you," Frances said. "Come on then, let's go in and find our seats." She glanced back at Mary. "What I wouldn't give for a martini."

"What else is new?" Mary said back to her.

Frances laughed. "The fact that I don't have one in my hand right now," she answered.

"Shall I dispatch Doug?" Mary Pickford asked.

"Nah, I don't suppose it would look too good having a stiff one before the movie begins, much less during Prohibition, but just wait until it's over. The movie, that is," Frances said, and laughed. She seemed right at home.

I liked listening to them talk. They were fun and intimate, and I couldn't contain my joy in knowing that I was part of their world, at least for tonight. I held on to Lulu's hand, stood straight, and walked tall among them as Frances tightened her hold around my arm, and a volley of camera bulbs flashed in unison as we walked into the theater.

LATER, WHEN THE MOVIE ended and the lights rose, Lulu squeezed my hand again while Frances leaned over, and said, "You can't hide now, doll."

Mary Pickford and Doug Fairbanks lavished me with praise. "It was a splendid performance," Mary said to me.

"Bravo, my dear," Doug added. "Get ready, you're going to be a big star after that performance."

I sat, dumbfounded as the audience clapped for what felt like forever. As soon as we stepped outside the theater, a throng of reporters rushed in my direction, camera flashes blinding in the black night, voices yelling out to me.

I couldn't hear a word they were saying.

The crowds pushed forward.

I clung to Frances and Lulu.

"Just keep walking," Frances said.

"You're a star," Lulu added.

This was really it.

Hollywood was finally at my doorstep.

A MOVIE STAR
Backlash—1923

"They're waiting outside again!" Mary said, smiling wide as she rushed in through the back door of the laundry.

She was twelve and thrilled that a group of movie magazine reporters hoping for a photograph or an interview with me had shown up at the laundry every day since *The Toll of the Sea* was released. They called out their questions as soon as they caught a glimpse of me.

"Miss Wong, have you always wanted to be an actress?"

"Look this way, Miss Wong, can we get a quick photo?"

"Tell us what it was like being the first Chinese actress to star in a leading role with a Caucasian leading man?"

I paused, longing to say that it was about time, but smiled and simply waved. I didn't want to say anything that would jinx my happiness. The fact that reporters were even asking me the question meant Hollywood was taking a step in the right direction.

By the end of the week, my father had had enough and was outraged with all the interruptions. He was more determined than ever to arrange a marriage in China for me, eager to stop all the disturbances once and for all. It made him even angrier to see the throng of new customers arriving at the laundry with armfuls of soiled garments, hoping for a quick glimpse of me.

Every morning, *baba* peered through the picture window of the laundry and fumed at the reporters hovering on the sidewalk. "This wouldn't be happening if you were married and settled," he yelled from the front counter. "These people have no right disrupting our business with your movie nonsense. Enough is enough!"

I was in the back room, helping *ma ma* fold the laundry for delivery. She hadn't said much about the reporters, wisely knowing the money I brought in was a great help to the family. "He'll calm down," she said.

"I want to be an actress too," Mary said. She'd seen all my movies and cried when she couldn't go to the premiere of *The Toll of the Sea*.

"Don't let your *baba* hear you," *ma ma* said.

"Why?" Mary asked.

"Because life isn't always about what you want," my mother explained, looking directly at me as she spoke. "We're not *gweilo*, those white ghosts, we are Chinese, and the Chinese believe the needs of the family always come first. The needs of the individual are a Western belief."

"Aren't we American too?" Mary asked.

I could have hugged my little sister right then and there. I tried not to smile at her question, but it irritated me to no end when my parents constantly held their strict Chinese beliefs over everything I did. I never heard my parents say that the money I made from acting was a bad thing, especially when bills needed to be paid. I felt smothered by their beliefs that we could only live and breathe as Chinese even though we were born and raised in America. Didn't it play right into the hands of those who considered us Chinese, and therefore not American? It took everything I had to keep silent. I was already fighting with my father nonstop; I didn't need to have my mother angry at me as well.

Ma ma turned to my sister, and simply said, "We are Chinese from the inside out. We were born of a culture that has generations of teachings, and those teachings will continue to guide us no matter where we live."

Mary knew better than to say anything more.

When *ma ma* returned to her folding, Mary quietly made her way to my side and whispered in my ear, "I still want to be an actress."

I smiled at her. "Then you will be," I whispered back.

Nevertheless, I also understood what my mother was saying. No matter how American we were, our Chinese culture and traditions were ingrained in us from birth and would forever be a part of who we were and how we lived our lives. As much as I fought against it, I was in a no-win dilemma. I'd been in a hopeless relationship with a Caucasian man who couldn't marry me due to the anti-miscegenation laws that prohibited mixed-race marriages, and I couldn't imagine marrying a Chinese man who expected his wife to stay home and obey his every whim. There was also the practical side: What would happen to my career and the money I earned? Would my "husband" take possession of everything I had worked so hard for? Not that *baba* had an easy task finding a husband for me. I was already too spoiled and indulged living in America, too independent and brazen compared to the hardworking, obedient Chinese women born and raised in China. Not to mention, I was an undesirable actress.

INCREASING TENSIONS BEGAN TO haunt me. The following week, I could barely get out of bed. I felt listless and empty. The heavy weight pressing down on my chest had returned, and all I wanted to do was sleep. The anxiety of the past weeks circled my thoughts and invaded my dreams. I was finally the leading lady in a successful movie that had garnered glowing reviews, but I had no idea what would happen next. I was on my own learning a complicated business. Did I have a long-term future in Hollywood? Suddenly, my resolve disappeared. I felt like I was climbing a ladder with *baba* holding on to my leg and pulling me back down, telling me it was for my own good, and that my true fate in life was to be married and to have a family, not making a spectacle of myself in the movies.

What bothered me most was I knew there were also positive sides to being married in Hollywood, while remaining a single woman limited my career. Marriage to the right person, such as a well-known actor or director, helped to continue the Hollywood mystique. I had just turned eighteen, but fans and movie magazines alike constantly questioned my marital status, wanting to know whom I was dating. I watched how Sessue and Tsuru, and Mary and Doug used their marriages to enhance their popularity by throwing parties at their beautiful mansions called the Castle and Pickfair. Movie magazines loved taking their couples photos, while detailing their lavish cocktail and dinner parties where they entertained other movie stars, directors, and important studio heads. Fans loved reading about glamorous parties, along with occasional scandals of romantic trysts, marital breakups, and drunken frolics in one studio head's marble fountain (a scaled down version of the Trevi Fountain in Rome). Meanwhile, I lived at home with my parents and my siblings, in the crowded house behind the laundry where I still worked.

OVERNIGHT TRAIN TO SACRAMENTO
1960

Out the window, the sun is setting and the light has dimmed, leaving everything in shadows. I close the notebook. We should arrive in Sacramento very early in the morning. My head is swimming in the past. It almost hurts to remember the girl I was back then. It's equally frightening to realize how young I was while navigating through my family life, the movie business, and those spineless early lovers. How did I do it?

A year after he left me, I heard Mickey finally divorced his wife and quickly married Blanche Sweet, already a well-known, respected actress his age. Somewhere down the line, they divorced, too, and his movie career began to wane just as mine began to rise. It was the best revenge, if one was looking for it, and I was. Ironically, over the years, I still think about Mickey, who passed away two years ago of cancer. While traveling, if I saw something that reminded me of him, I'd buy it and give it to him when I returned to Los Angeles. He was my first love, and the only one who remained tied to me by an invisible thread through life. It's the only explanation I can give for forgiving him.

I still wonder if my early lovers—Mickey, and later, Tod Browning, another older director—ever regretted their cowardice, having seduced and then abandoned a teenager who knew so little of the world. Did they believe I was really like the characters I played, the sexually available *Oriental femme fatale* who needed to be taught a lesson in the end? I was just a girl dazzled by their glamour and attention, by the fact that being with Mickey and Tod meant I was part of the Hollywood crowd. I would have followed them anywhere. If I had, where would I be now? Married or divorced with children, both of us unable to work in Hollywood ever again.

And suddenly, I can't breathe.

I sip some water and stare out the window, watching the world flicker by.

THE TRAIN LURCHES FORWARD. What I really need now, I fish out from my handbag: the silver flask given to me by Douglas Fairbanks. I once admired his, only to have him gift me one of my own, engraved with my initials AMW.

"Wouldn't want you to mistake it for mine," he'd said.

He liked to be called Doug, and he knew how to have fun. I can still see him doing handstands and vaulting over sofas at parties, always the swashbuckler showing off his dexterity. I once wanted what he and Mary Pickford had more than anything in the world, a marriage made in Hollywood, a leading man, something I was forbidden to have if he was the wrong color. In the end, even the "golden couple" had their problems, and their marriage ended in divorce. It was hard to blame Mary, for being married to a man who was a perpetual boy must have been difficult. But Doug was great fun and always kind to me. If it weren't for him, I would have never gotten the role as the Mongol slave girl in *The Thief of Bagdad*.

I pour the vodka into the cap and toss it back, swallowing the sting down my throat. I know Dr. Bloom won't be happy with me, but he isn't here now. Sip after sip from the flask, and the hum of questions I've been asked by reporters over the years return like the buzzing of mosquitoes near my ear. The days of Louella Parsons and Hedda Hopper are long gone. They had class, knew what secrets to keep and what to let out into the world. It helped if you stayed on their good side, which I somehow managed to do. Nowadays everyone wants a scoop, not caring to know the entire truth about a person. Hollywood, after all, is a world of secrets and lies. The lines often become so blurred you no longer know the truth from the myth. I close my eyes and a flurry of questions returns.

"Where did it all begin?"

I take another sip of vodka and smile.

"Did you always want to be an actress?"

I take another sip.

After a while, they become braver. "Was it difficult being a Chinese actress?"

"It wasn't difficult for me," I answer, "but it was apparently difficult for Hollywood."

I laugh, take another sip.

And then the question that never fails to be asked, the albatross on my back. "Why have you never married? What did your family think?"

I pour another, tip the cap back. Where do I begin? How much do I reveal? My father spent years trying to marry me off, I want to say, but even tipsy, I've become polished in the fine art of the interview. Be selective. Take control.

I smile and say, "Yes, I've always wanted to be an actress. The movies were love at first sight for me. Let me tell you how the romance began . . ."

THE THIEF OF BAGDAD
Stardom—1923–1924

"Again!" Mary yelled out happily.

"Yes, again," Lulu agreed.

"Okay then," I said, when one song ended and another began.

The music of Willie "The Lion" Smith, Duke Ellington, and Louis Armstrong blasted from the radio as we danced and bumped into each other in the thick, breathless air of our crowded bedroom. We were all sweating and couldn't stop laughing as we grabbed on to each other so we wouldn't fall. Lulu and Mary wanted me to teach them all the latest dances—the Charleston, the Lindy Hop, and the shimmy.

The 1920s had roared right in, and with it, a new way of thinking and living that I fit right into. It gave me a chance to reinvent myself, to become whoever I needed to be to show that I was just as Western as the next girl. I easily transformed myself into a twenties "flapper," from head to toe. As an actress, there was nothing I loved more than inhabiting another character. It was time to revolt against the stale and conservative notions of the "Gibson girl," with her long hair, long straight skirts, and high-collared buttoned shirts.

"That's a nifty song," Mary said, using the latest lingo.

"It's the cat's meow," I added, and we laughed.

The "roaring twenties" couldn't have come at a better time for me. I happily revolted against everything that was holding me back. Being a flapper also freed my thinking, from fashion to hairstyles to letting go of old constrictions. I cut my hair short into a "bob," and later, I adopted the "shingle cut," slicked down with a curl on each side of my face. I also realized how hats could enhance a look, and wore a bell-shaped cloche that bolstered the flapper effect.

The latest styles complemented my new outlook. I was completely at ease wearing light, loose dresses with dropped waistlines, their hems falling just below the knee, and stockings made of a new material called rayon that rolled over my garter belt. It made dancing the Charleston and the jitterbug so much easier. Much to my parents' horror, I also started wearing makeup—rouge, powder, dark eyeliner, and bright lipstick—something that was only worn by those they considered loose women. It was a new attitude, a new way of looking at life in which each moment was embraced with spontaneous joy. I was determined to navigate this new world, even if my traditional Chinese upbringing remained a step behind, jabbing me in the back with a pin just like that boy in school did all those years ago.

"Again!" Mary said, after another song ended.

Lulu fanned herself. "That's enough for me," she said.

Mary looked my way.

"Me too," I said, laughing, and pulled them both down onto the bed with me.

"Can we go for a drive then?" Mary asked, sitting up.

To add to my newfound sense of freedom, I'd bought a Willys-Knight six-cylinder roadster.

"It's late," I said. "We'll go tomorrow."

Mary nodded and dropped back down on the bed.

ALONG WITH MY NEWFOUND flapper attitude of truth, freedom, and recklessness came the constant partying that involved drinking, smoking, and dancing, all of which I excelled in. There were parties every night if I wanted to go to them, and for a while, I did. I felt like so many of the restrictions in my life had been lifted. I was too old for my father to rein in, so he showed his displeasure with an impatient grunt, or with a sharp remark just as I was leaving the house. *Did you forget to balance the books again?*

A few weeks after the dance lessons with my sisters, as I shook and shimmied at the Commodore Club after a cocktail party at Mary and Doug's, my head began to throb, the room spinning in a haze of bright lights and cigarette smoke. I suddenly stopped in the middle of the crowded dance floor, reminded of when I suffered from St. Vitus's dance, and I couldn't stop moving, my arms and legs flailing involuntarily. I was doing some of the very same moves, only now it was all the rage.

"Come on, then," someone said, leading me off the dance floor. "You've had enough to drink for tonight."

I remember laughing. Or was it crying?

NOT LONG AFTER, I was involved in a car accident. Fortunately, no one was hurt except for my car. It shook me up enough to calm me down. My flapper phase had strengthened my belief that I could change my persona by changing my clothes and hairstyles—something I'd tested successfully in *The Toll of the Sea* when I set myself apart from the rest of the actresses I was competing against. I was Chinese in a Western world; I had to look for ways to be recognized as an *actress*, and not simply judged for being Chinese. With the help of studio publicity, I made a series of photographs dressed as a flapper, which created a more sophisticated persona. In the movie magazines, I showed my fans that remaining independent was what being a flapper was all about.

ALTHOUGH THE REVIEWS FOR my next movie, *Drifting*, were positive, the film failed at the box office. It was also the beginning of another intense relationship, with director Tod Browning, who was almost twenty-five years older than I was. Again, no one outside the movie business could know what was going on in my private life. In a tough, cutthroat business, who you were seeing was always gossip fodder, but interracial love affairs, as well as homosexuality, stayed within the Hollywood community's code of secrecy. Tod, like Mickey, professed his love and commitment, showering me with attention and promises of movie stardom, all of which I craved. But in the end, Tod was as much a coward as Mickey. He wouldn't risk his career for our relationship. I was eighteen and had already been abandoned by two older lovers who were too frightened to claim me as their own.

While my personal life was once again collapsing around me, my career continued to soar, featured in movie magazines throughout the US and in Europe. My love of fashion was becoming a real asset. I instinctively knew how to use what I wore and how I looked to set a scene. I easily transferred it all to film with the same dramatic flair as my studio photos.

I NEXT PLAYED A flamboyant role in a Douglas Fairbanks movie called *Honky-Tonk Girl*, which led him to choose me for his next big movie, *The Thief of Bagdad*. By then, I knew Doug well enough to know that life for him was one big party after another, while Mary Pickford was the solid, sensible one. After my less than respectable role in *Honky-Tonk Girl*, Doug made it his mission to convince *baba* that *The Thief of Bagdad* was going to be completely different. He showed up at the laundry one afternoon, smiled wide, and promised my father that if he consented to my being in the movie, I would be watched and protected on the film set at all times.

"No one is going near Anna May without going through yours truly first," he said, flashing an innocent and charming smile at my father, despite knowing of my unhappy affairs with Mickey and Tod.

"Do I have your word?" *baba* asked.

Doug dramatically placed his right hand over his heart. "I promise you, sir, your daughter will be kept safe with me."

Baba watched Doug, considering him for a long while, until he nodded.

I was making one movie after another, and though *baba* couldn't stop me from being in *The Thief of Bagdad*, Doug knew that showing him respect went a long way. In the next moment, Doug lunged forward and hugged my father enthusiastically. I caught the look of surprise on *baba*'s face, followed by the trace of a smile.

IN *THE THIEF OF BAGDAD*, I played the part of a Mongol slave who betrays her mistress. It was a big production, and I had to make a big impression. I knew my role would be brief, so I needed to make it unforgettable. My hair was cut in my trademark "virgin-child" style with a costume that was scarcely more than a two-piece bathing suit, a skimpy top and bottom that revealed ample areas of bare skin on my upper body and legs. I knew I had to wear the costume if I wanted the role, and I wanted it. Doug was bronze and bare-chested throughout most of the film, and audiences were given an eyeful of both of us. It was something rarely seen in American movies. I didn't allow myself to think of *baba*, or my family, as I transformed myself into the slave girl.

It wasn't me, I kept telling myself.

It wasn't me.

I was acting.

THE THIEF OF BAGDAD was a worldwide hit, and brought me a newfound recognition that I hadn't expected. Suddenly, I was being written about in movie magazines all over the world, from Britain, France, and Germany to Japan and Australia. At nineteen, I found myself a fully established movie star in Europe, where scantily clad actresses were readily accepted as part of the entertainment. America and Americans were much more puritanical in their thinking, as were, to a greater degree, my traditional Chinese parents and the critics in China. No matter how much I prepared myself, I knew I would never win this argument.

Baba was enraged, and nothing or no one could change his mind. While I was gaining fame in the United States and Europe, I was also disgracing my family name. My father blamed Doug for his "losing face."

"The man is a liar," my father roared. "He said he would protect you!"

"Protect me from what?" I asked, trying to keep my voice calm. "I was just playing a character in a movie. It has nothing to do with me, or our family."

"It has everything to do with our family!" my father shouted. He stood and retrieved a Chinese movie magazine he'd bought, slapping it down hard on the kitchen table. "The critics in China are calling not just this movie, but all your movie performances, disgraceful and degrading. You think only of yourself, and not of your family or your ancestors. You have shamed our family name! You have shamed our motherland!"

I could feel the sting of my father's words like a slap in the face. Who cared what the critics in China thought? All my resolve to stay calm and composed flew out the door. I was so angry and hurt, I wanted to scream.

"We live in America," I yelled. "I'm getting great reviews here in Hollywood, not to mention all over Europe and Australia. If the Chinese critics think I'm nothing more than a disgrace and disappointment, then so be it. They're too far away to make any difference to my career!"

Baba shook his head. "You always have to learn the hard way!" he said. "You don't see beyond what's right in front of you."

I lowered my voice to a menacing whisper. "You have no idea how difficult it has been for me. If you did, you would respect my acting career, just as much as you do my monthly checks."

My father was a tall man; I'd gotten my height from him. He straightened to his full height and looked down at me, the vein by his temple throbbing, his voice threatening.

"You expect me to respect you when you play prostitutes and madwomen. Have you no shame? It's not too late, Anna. Leave this movie business now! You can still have a good marriage, a fulfilling family life."

"I have a fulfilling life!" I said, angrier than I'd ever been.

I didn't say another word. I had worked so hard, longing for this kind of fame since I was a young girl. I was realizing my dream and for the first time, I wasn't afraid of my father. I matched his stare and refused to acquiesce in the face of his fury until he was the one to turn away.

Baba cleared his throat. "If you don't end this frivolous, demeaning behavior, Anna, I don't know what will become of you. You will be worthless in the eyes of your family and our ancestors."

I turned and walked away. There was nothing else for me to say.

WHEN I QUIT HIGH SCHOOL at sixteen, it wasn't without a plan. I gave myself ten years to become successful in the movies. If I failed, I would still be young enough to find another direction. Less than four years later, I had achieved more than I could ever have dreamed of: major film roles, my photos on the covers of movie magazines around the world, enough money to both help my family and save for the future.

And still . . . trailing me, there would always be that obedient Chinese daughter who winced and cowered at my father's every word, each an invisible papercut that quickly added up to a serious wound. As much as I wanted to make movies, I also needed the support of my family. I never imagined that I would have to choose between them and my career. All the superstitions and traditions that I was raised with were so ingrained in the way I looked at life that it seemed I would always be at odds not only with my father but also with myself.

I was on the verge of becoming a Hollywood movie star, yet living in two separate worlds. This was America, I reminded myself. Why couldn't I have both?

LATER THAT NIGHT, it was Lulu who whispered to me when we were back in the quiet darkness of our room. Mary was already fast asleep.

"What will you do?" she asked, lying in the twin bed right next to me.

I felt anxious, my stomach churning, but I tried to remain calm. "I don't know yet," I whispered.

"You should follow your heart," Lulu said. It was the first time she voiced her own opinion concerning this battle *baba* and I were waging.

"You think so?"

She turned to face me. "Yes, I do. You've come so far, and you're such a good actress," she whispered.

At a loss for words, my heart filled with gratitude. I didn't realize how much I needed Lulu's encouragement until my tears fell. I was glad all the lights were out, with only a sliver of moonlight through the parted curtains. It was always a struggle with *baba,* and like *ma ma,* Lulu had learned the fine art of watching quietly from the sidelines as we battled it out. I never knew what she really thought. As the eldest daughter, she'd been handed the role of being dutiful and responsible, which she always was. But what was underneath it all? What did she really want in life?

"Thank you," I finally said. Then I asked my sister something I should have asked a long time ago. "Lulu, what do *you* want to do?"

There was a long pause, and I thought she might not answer. "For now, I want to help at the laundry," she said. Then added, "But not forever."

"No, not forever," I echoed. "Just until you decide what you'd like to do next . . . or, *marry and have a family of your own,*" I mimicked *baba*'s voice.

We both began to laugh, trying not to wake Mary.

Lying next to Lulu, I realized just how much she was tethered to our family—as we all were—but rather than fight against *baba* like me, she seemed to embrace it. Lulu could already run the laundry as competently as my father. She was naturally maternal, looking out for me from the time we were bullied at school and covering for me every time I skipped Chinese language school to go to the movies. More recently, although she didn't approve of my ill-fated love affairs, she still shielded me.

I wanted so much more for Lulu. Most of all, I wanted her to see that there was a life beyond the laundry. But right now, I wanted nothing more than to hug her for not abandoning me. Instead, I reached over and took her hand in mine, giving her our familiar and comforting squeeze. Our hands stayed together across the narrow divide between our beds until we fell asleep.

1400 NORTH TAMARIND
Fame and Fallout—1924–1926

By 1924, my face was on the front cover of movie magazines around the world—*Picture Show*, *Silver Screen*, the French magazine, *Mon Ciné*. Well-known in Europe after my two films, *The Toll of the Sea* and *The Thief of Bagdad*, were showed to appreciative audiences, I'd had my first taste of major Hollywood stardom, and I couldn't wait for whatever was coming next.

But with my newfound fame, I also made a novice mistake. I signed a deal with boyishly charming Craig R. Woods, an independent producer who had worked on several MGM films, to start "Anna May Wong Productions." I was thrilled at the thought of making films based on Chinese myths. I should have been suspicious, but Hollywood was crawling with "credible" producers.

"Together, we'll bring the real world of China to audiences," Craig promised, as we sat in his Sunset Boulevard office.

I was ecstatic.

When months went by and all I heard was excuses for the production delays, I began investigating. Craig had no idea I'd balanced the books at the laundry for years and knew my way around a business ledger. When I found out my so-called business partner was using the company finances for his own gains, I quickly had the company dissolved and a lawsuit brought against the smooth-talking thief. Shaken, disillusioned, and heartbroken about what might have been, I vowed to stay focused on my acting.

THROUGH IT ALL, my fame and recognition made little difference at home. Like my siblings, I was expected to respect my parents (and still do the accounts at the laundry), even as young girls everywhere copied my virgin-child hairstyle, and fans near and far embraced my innovative style of combining Chinese clothing with Western dress. All I hoped for was some peace at home after the demise of my production company. But the following week, when I returned from a lackluster screen test I'd had for a new MGM movie, my father was once again angered by an article he'd read about me in a Chinese newspaper. He demanded that I get married and settle down. It was exhausting. I'd endured so many of his rants that I didn't even fight back. I no longer believed he could find a suitable husband for me in Los Angeles, or in China. Fortunately, I had finally saved enough money to buy a place of my own. It was time, and *baba* had left me no choice but to leave home.

I QUICKLY LEARNED THAT being Chinese meant I wasn't allowed to buy a house in upscale areas like Beverly Hills or Hancock Park, where other movie actors and actresses lived. When real estate advertisements featured "exclusive" neighborhoods, what they really meant was "restricted" to anyone whose skin was a different color. What did I expect? I couldn't kiss a Caucasian actor onscreen, much less marry one. I couldn't take a trip to Mexico after the success of *The Thief of Bagdad* without filing multiple forms proving my citizenship so that I could reenter the United States. And I couldn't keep what I earned from my acting career if I married because then my assets would also belong to my husband. It felt like all I did was fight to stay afloat.

When I finally found a charming bungalow in the 1400 block of North Tamarind, I was just shy of twenty years old. I had at last stepped out of the shadow of my father. I loved the peace and quiet that having my own place afforded me. I filled it with Chinese artifacts I'd begun to collect after seeing them used on early movie sets—cloisonné vases, brush paintings, and a large black lacquer screen inlaid with mother-of-pearl cranes, which I used to separate my living room from my dining room. Now I had the privacy and the freedom I longed for, away from constant arguments with my father in a cramped, noisy house with all my siblings.

ONE OF THE FIRST visitors to stop by was Frances Marion with two bottles of bootlegged gin as my housewarming gift. She was one of the few people in the movie business who was known for her loyalty to the actresses she worked with. We sat in the small, fenced-in backyard smoking and drinking the night away.

"How does it feel being the woman in charge of her own household?" she asked. She offered me a cigarette, then lit another for herself.

"Freeing," I said, and laughed.

"I bet! I can't imagine being bossed around by my father the way you've been, and mine wasn't easy. When he actually liked my second husband, I should have known that we'd end in divorce!" Marion poured us each some gin, followed by tonic water and an ice cube.

I sipped my gin and tonic. "It's never been that simple. We Chinese are born into beliefs and traditions that are ages old. It's in our blood, a part of who we are. My father believes in carrying on traditions."

"What about you?"

I looked away for a moment and poured more gin into my glass. "Even though I've constantly defied my father, and many of the traditions he expected me to honor, I'm still torn by the choices I've had to make."

Frances sat back and drew on her cigarette. "But would you really get married because he tells you to? Not that I'm one to talk. I'm hoping 'three's a charm' with Fred, but it helps he's an actor and always away filming cowboy movies."

I was torn about that too. Although I played the modern Chinese girl who didn't care for traditions or what my parents thought, I really did. The air was warm and the crickets were just beginning their nightly symphony. Frances was not only my mentor but a good and trusted friend, even if she questioned what I was up against. It all seemed absurd now as we lazed on our lounge chairs and sipped our drinks.

"Does it look like I have surrendered?"

Frances laughed. "That's my girl!"

BUT NOW THAT I lived alone with too much time to think, all the conflicts that stirred inside me began to rise again. I drank to keep my internal anxieties submerged. I'd always felt pulled in different directions, trying to balance the two very different lives I led, which felt even more apparent now that I was on my own.

I was between movies, and as the days turned into weeks, I felt a deep longing for everything I'd left at North Figueroa Street. I missed Lulu and Mary, how we gathered in our small upstairs bedroom when I was home to play card games, or listen to music, and our noisy family dinners around the old kitchen table. Even my baby sister, Marietta, who had died before she was a year old, was alive in my memory again. A low, humming misery grew louder every day, so I drank to dull my loneliness and to help me sleep.

WHEN LULU AND MARY came to visit, I wanted to know everything that was happening at home. It all came out in a torrent. What was *ma ma* sewing? Who was keeping the books for *baba*? How were James, Frank, and Roger doing in school, and how was little Richard?

Lulu laughed. "Calm down," she said, taking off her coat. "Let me answer one question at a time."

I swallowed my eagerness. "Just wondering," I said.

I felt Lulu's gaze return to me even as she wandered around the living room, looking at all the artifacts I'd bought.

"I think *baba* misses you," Mary said.

I was happy to hear that. "Why do you say that?" I asked.

"He keeps saying how quiet it is since you left," Mary answered.

I laughed so hard that I couldn't help myself when my laughter turned to tears. My sisters gathered around me.

"Anna, what is it?" Lulu asked, hugging me.

I held on to her tighter. "I miss home," I whispered in her ear.

"Then come back," she said.

After all the arguments we'd had that shook the foundations of our family, could it be so simple? I thought. I held my sister tighter and felt more at ease knowing I could.

NOT LONG AFTER, it was *baba* who unexpectedly invited me back home, but first he would build a separate house for me behind the laundry. I was wildly happy that he understood I was no longer a young girl and needed my own place as much as I needed my family. Having bought a house and lived on my own, I sensed he finally saw me as an adult who could make my own decisions. But more importantly, I was surprised and gratified to know that we'd come this far.

I SOLD MY HOUSE and moved back to North Figueroa Street. With my home life calmer, I concentrated again on my career. After my success in *The Thief of Bagdad*, I made several movies, one after another, while waiting for a leading lady role that would finally portray a Chinese female character with authentic flesh and blood, instead of the unrealistic stereotypes that I was constantly asked to play. Despite a drawer full of rave reviews for *The Toll of the Sea* and *The Thief of Bagdad*, I was only offered minor, degrading parts: Chinese women who were weak and fragile, or women who were so evil and manipulative, they had to suffer and die by the end of the movie. The studios had a *real* Chinese actress available; why wouldn't they use me?

I was so tired of playing second or third-billing movie roles simply to add *Oriental* atmosphere. Lulu was right all along; I was treated as an object used to decorate the room. Apparently, I'd never be able to garner the large financial contracts that leading ladies like Gloria Swanson, Norma Talmadge, or Lillian Gish were given because I was too Chinese to play a Chinese leading lady. Yet I wasn't about to give up. I was determined to fight for roles with more depth. I knew I was good, better than some; I just needed to find the right person who wasn't afraid to break the rules.

I began to travel more for work, filming *The Alaskan* in Canada, followed by *Peter Pan*, in which I was cast as the Indian girl, Tiger Lily. It was a major Hollywood motion picture with a large and extravagant publicity campaign that I'd never experienced before. I performed a memorable dance scene in a clearing before I led the "Lost Boys" on an attack against Wendy and the British. It was beautifully filmed by cinematographer James Wong Howe, who I thought was brilliant. When he released the still shots from that scene for publicity, my photos were seen everywhere—in movie magazines, on cinema posters, and reprinted as postcards—both here, and around the world. It bolstered my growing international fame, which had begun with my scantily clad image from *The Thief of Bagdad* as I cowered before a bare-chested, sword-waving Doug Fairbanks.

I dared to hope. Again.

HOLLYWOOD
Still Photos—1926–1927

"Turn slightly to the left," I was coaxed by the photographer. "Now, lift your head just a bit and stare into the camera. Show me those big, beautiful eyes of yours." My hair was long and full, cascading down my back, so different from the virgin-child cut I usually wore.

I turned and looked directly into the camera. Lounging by the swimming pool at the Hearst Castle, I wore a bathing suit made of thin fabric, my arms and legs completely bare. *What would baba think?* I thought, even as I heard the camera click, click, clicking.

"That's it. That's the shot. Beautiful!" the photographer said.

IF I COULDN'T BE a leading lady in the movies, I could still remain a significant presence in Hollywood by releasing a series of studio photos that would keep the momentum going. Since the photos from *Peter Pan* had appeared in all the magazines, fans clamored for more. Before I knew it, famous photographers were offering to work with me. Clarence Sinclair Bull took publicity shots, while Ruth Harriet Louise, who worked for MGM as their studio photographer, took close-up headshots, along with some risqué photos baring my arms and legs for *Theatre Magazine,* and British photographer E. O. Hoppé's hand-colored images of me were made into postcards.

I was reminded of how I used to stare into the mirror when I was young, always trying to recapture an expression that I'd seen in a movie. A still photo gave me creative control, and allowed me to set a scene and achieve the tone I wanted to capture through a gaze or a smile. Also, my hands and long, tapered fingernails provided another focal point and helped to accentuate the clothing I wore. The studio photos gave me a sense of power and independence I'd never had before.

Once in a while, I'd get lucky and meet someone like Alla Nazimova, who allowed me to watch and learn, or Frances Marion, who listened to my input on a script. Mostly, I had no choice but to do as I was told. Now I was certain that, with the right photographer, and by donning an array of different fashions and hairstyles, I had the opportunity to show my fans that I was a woman of many sensibilities. In my still photos, I began to widely explore the concept of wearing both Western and Chinese clothing, revealing my two very different personas. While I wore a Chinese *cheongsam* and silk embroidered jacket in one photo, the next might show a take-control Western woman dressed as a flapper, or in a bejeweled evening gown, or a culotte outfit that was billed as the first business suit for women. I even designed a jacket made from *baba's* old wedding coat that was one of my prized possessions.

The idea of using fashion to further my Eastern and Western identity became a wonderful distraction between movies. Unlike my film roles that rarely varied from *Oriental* caricature, my studio photos proved that the real Anna May Wong lived in both worlds.

It wasn't long before my studio photos paid off. While I wasn't getting any leading lady offers, supporting roles in movies kept coming. When my photos began to grace the covers of international magazines, I was gradually being considered as a serious actress who had the looks, personality, and talent to add to any film. I'd already gained a large global following, helped along by the studio photos and my growing list of film roles. I was everywhere on the newsstands and the drugstore racks, but I feared that I would never achieve movie stardom without a lead role.

WITH MY BUSY MOVIE schedule, it was easy to ignore my father's renewed contempt for my career, amplified by what the Chinese movie critics were writing about me. Our truce had ended. I still didn't care if they thought my performances were degrading, or that I continued to play vile, scantily clad women in the movies with no regard for the shame I brought to my family and to China. My father couldn't see beyond how I appeared in the eyes of the Chinese in China. He pushed harder, insisting that marriage was the only respectable way for me to live my life. Again, I swallowed my resentment. I was living the life I wanted to. I could have countered his verbal attacks, but what good would it do? I chose to avoid more arguments and concentrate on keeping the peace at home.

"*Baba*, China is six thousand miles away," I tried to reassure him. "My star is rising here in Hollywood."

He balked. "China is our homeland," he said. "One day your careless behavior will return to haunt you."

"Is it so hard to be happy for my success?"

"Not when it brings shame to our family," he said.

"Won't you try?" I asked, my voice almost a whisper.

My father sighed. "If I have to try, Anna, then it isn't real happiness," he answered, not unkindly.

There was no appeasing my father. I couldn't understand this *shame* he kept throwing at me. Why couldn't he understand that I was showing the world a real Chinese actress onscreen? Not the yellowface caricatures they presented. Why was Japan so proud of Sessue Hayakawa's success in American movies, while I gathered only disdain from China for my work? While Sessue was able to play the villainous matinee idols, I had to take what roles were offered to me. I didn't have a choice. I was intent on changing the way Hollywood portrayed Chinese women in the movies, but it would take one step at a time.

HOLLYWOOD
Disillusionment—1926–1928

No matter what *baba* thought, movies continued to grow into America's favorite pastime. Audiences, young and old, were seduced by accounts of extravagant movie premieres. Flashy opening nights were attended by their favorite movie stars, shown on towering billboards, with photo spreads in all the movie magazines.

In January of 1926, I joined Norma Talmadge and Charlie Chaplin at the groundbreaking ceremony for Grauman's Chinese Theatre. It was the talk of the town, a theater that would seat more than two thousand moviegoers, a spectacle built by showman Sidney Grauman. Reporters from newspapers and movie magazines flocked to the event. I wore a full-length Chinese silk coat to shovel dirt with a gold-plated spade. As the light bulbs flashed, I stood straight and tall, smiled for the cameras, and waved to the crowd, once again lending an air of legitimacy to the "Chinese" theater.

A year later, the box office opened, a replica of a pagoda with a jade-green roof made of bronze, flanked by tall columns and a huge stone dragon in relief on the wall behind it. An excited crowd of movie fans anxiously awaited entry to see the entwined silver dragons at the center of the theater's ceiling. Ushers and usherettes wore outfits replicating ancient Chinese costumes. As a publicity stunt, actors and actresses were asked to immortalize their hand and footprints in wet cement outside this new mecca of the Orient. But although I was the only Chinese actress in Hollywood, I wasn't even invited.

NOT LONG AFTER, I met Frances Marion for lunch at The Brown Derby, the most popular new restaurant where studio heads gathered with movie stars for business and pleasure. We drank martinis and ate their famous Cobb salad. The warm interior and secluded booths provided just enough privacy for many kinds of negotiations.

"Sidney's a buffoon!" Frances said. "He can't see anything beyond his own shadow. You were the only genuine Chinese at that circus of a theater, and he doesn't include your handprints!"

I laughed. It did sting not to be invited, but it was nothing I hadn't experienced before. "Just add it to the list," I said.

"You can always return to the vaudeville circuit," Frances teased.

"Done and dead," I said, with a laugh.

When I wasn't making movies, there was always the constant struggle of staying in the limelight. After my freewheeling flapper phase, I had briefly toured on a vaudeville circuit with other silent movie stars, including Phyllis Haver, Cullen Landis, Helen Holmes, and Bryant Washburn. We sang and danced, and performed short skits. It started out well in Texas and New York but failed miserably by the time we reached Kansas City. Due to the lack of ticket sales, we ended up performing for no pay and scurried back to Hollywood soon after. Despite the financial mess, I did learn a great deal about stage presence, and how to project my voice while performing live.

"What are you working on?" I asked.

Frances exaggerated her tiredness. "An adaptation called *The Son of the Sheik*, starring Valentino."

"Sounds exciting," I said.

"I hope it'll be."

I looked around the restaurant, trying to spot the tables in negotiation.

"Table toward the back," Frances said.

"How can you tell?"

"Besides their serious demeanor, they just ordered another round of drinks," she said, laughing as both of us reached for our martinis. "It'll take at least three drinks to get through the Hays Code," she added.

I cringed at the thought. The Hays Code was the informal name for The Motion Picture Production Code, the moral guidelines for moviemaking set up by Will H. Hays, a Presbyterian elder and president of the Motion Picture Producers and Distributors of America. Though not yet officially adopted, a list of rules that included the

"Don'ts" and "Be Carefuls" when making a film had already been set up by the MPPDA.

"Can't be easy for you to write scripts around all those rules."

"Let's just say the list begins with the line: No picture shall be produced which will lower the moral standards of those who see it," Frances said, and laughed.

"That's setting a pretty low bar here in Hollywood," I said, with a smirk.

"Try writing around no profanity, no suggestive nudity, no drugs, no sex perversion, no seduction or rape, no white slavery, no interracial relationships, no excessive or lustful kissing, and no men and women in bed together . . . no damn storyline!" Marion stopped to take a breath. "It's exhausting!"

I nodded. It *was* exhausting, a clear reminder of what I'd already been up against. Along with moviemaking's new code of conduct, the big studio heads were ruthless, locking their actors and actresses into ironclad contracts, dictating what their screen names would be, deciding what movies they could and could not make, who they should love, and should marry to spike publicity. I couldn't help but think how similar it was to my home life, and of how *baba* would fit right into the Hollywood studio system with his demanding ways.

The studios had no use for those who didn't follow the rules, and could make or break a career in an instant. As I became more ingrained in the system, I tried to sympathize with what Mickey and Tod were up against being involved with a Chinese girl, but it was hard to forgive grown men who knew exactly what they were doing.

Even if I'd been slighted and relegated to senseless roles, I was lucky to hold a distinct niche in the movie business. The

Orient continued to draw audience interest, stirred by the exaggerated mystery and dramatic intrigue perpetuated in popular movies, which provided me with roles in *A Trip to Chinatown* and *The Silk Bouquet*, among others. While most roles left me with a bad taste, I continued to work hard, aware that I must always straddle two worlds—Chinese and Western, family and career, love and marriage—while I kept moving forward, hoping to find my way.

BY THE END OF 1927, I was twenty-two years old and had been in the movie business for eight years. I had acted in three major movies and dozens of other films, taken hundreds of photographs, and gained a worldwide audience. But still, in film after film, I was cast in small and inconsequential parts with no substance. I was tired. I felt my career had stalled and would never improve as long as the anti-miscegenation law remained in place. If I couldn't kiss the leading man, I would never be the leading lady.

After a string of awful roles, I was happy to get a part in *Mr. Wu,* starring my old friend, Lon Chaney. As the maid, at least I wasn't subjected to death this time. Instead, during our breaks, I had to teach the lead actress, Renée Adorée, how to use chopsticks and speak a few words of Cantonese to match her yellowface.

While the films I was offered continued to be depressing, my studio photos were keeping my popularity high. I also began seeing cinematographer, Charles Rosher, who was a member of the Uplifters Club located in Rustic Canyon near Pacific Palisades. The Uplifters began in 1913 by a group of wealthy businessmen, actors, directors, and producers who were members of the Los Angeles

Athletic Club. They eventually purchased a large swath of secluded canyon property where the members built a large clubhouse surrounded by their private cabins and called it the Uplifters Ranch. Charles owned one of the cabins and I began spending most of my free time at the Ranch with him. He was fun and we had a good time together without the angst of my early relationships. I also relished the amenities at the ranch: the Olympic-size swimming pool, tennis courts, horseback riding, and polo field. The *Oriental* beauty they made me out to be was really a tomboy at heart. As a child, I'd been passionate about sports and continued to play tennis and swim whenever I could. At the ranch, I enjoyed it all. I spent so much time there with Charles, I became a regular and the members named a garden after me. It was a bright light among all the dreary films I was making.

The Uplifters Ranch was also a popular getaway for many Hollywood stars. I was often in the company of good friends there, dining with Lon Chaney, Mary and Doug, Hal Roach, and Clark Gable. We sang and dance and performed occasional skits together for fun and entertainment. I also happily met many German expatriates and international members that led to dinners and parties with Lon and Frances, German actor Emil Jannings, and Sojin Kamiyama, whom I'd known since we made *The Thief of Bagdad* together. Sojin and his wife threw wonderful dinner parties always populated with interesting German and European actors and actresses.

On one evening at a lovely dinner at Sojin's, I'd drunk a bit too much champagne and was easily persuaded to sing a ballad that had been written for me by a young composer I'd met a few years earlier:

I'm Anna May Wong
I come from Old Hong Kong
But now I'm a Hollywood star
I'm very glad
Dream in the nap, Bagdad
I look oriental
I am kind to other players
I make them smile
Good luck to China
As there is nothing more
I can do to become beautiful . . .

"That was beautiful," Sojin said, pouring me another glass of champagne.

"And true," I said. "There's nothing more I can do."

Sojin smiled. "You have more fans than you realize, Anna May. Perhaps you should leave Hollywood for a while and go where your fans might appreciate you more, give you the praise you deserve. Emil will be returning to Europe soon; it might not be a bad idea for you to visit too."

"You really think so?"

"I do," he said. "Go where you're wanted."

MY POPULARITY ABROAD WAS at an all-time high. British and Japanese film magazines were giving me full-page coverage. Even China's *Liangyu Huabo*, Shanghai's most popular women's magazine, edited by Wu Liande, featured me on the cover. But that did nothing to soften China's disdain for my next performance. *The Chinese Parrot*, which did well in England, angered the Chinese critics, who criticized me once again for playing a prostitute in a scene in which my back was bared. If I didn't mind skirting the motion picture guidelines and tastefully showing a bit of flesh, why should they?

I made three more films at the beginning of 1928, and after having to teach Myrna Loy in yellowface to use chopsticks once again in *The Crimson City*, I'd had enough! Charles and I had parted as friends, and Sojin's advice to venture out to more open-minded audiences made perfect sense. I finished all my other movie obligations and decided to accept a movie offer in Germany that came through my European representatives. If Hollywood put the brakes on my movie career simply because I was Chinese, then it was time to pack my bags and leave. I had a large following in Europe and the idea of traveling freely, unhindered by family responsibilities, was a huge lure.

WHEN I TOLD MY family I was going to Germany, my parents weren't happy with my abrupt career change, advising against something so uncertain. It was too far away, and I didn't know the language, they lamented. After many family discussions, I was still determined to go and refused to back down. Whatever my parents thought, they knew me well enough to know that I wasn't going to change my mind. To ease their concerns, it was agreed that Lulu would go with me. I'd already begun the paperwork for us to travel abroad. I also promised I would return right after the film was completed if I wasn't happy. As

I hoped, they instantly relaxed knowing Lulu would be at my side. She would provide a steady, calming influence against all their fears of my stepping recklessly into dangerous and foreign territory. I was simply happy that Lulu would have the chance to get away from the laundry and see the world.

MARY, WHO HAD JUST turned seventeen, was despondent that she had to stay home and finish her last year of high school. She still had high hopes of following in my footsteps and pursuing an acting career even as I gently tried to dissuade her. She was so sweet-natured and trusting, I knew Hollywood would swallow her up. So far, her only experience was watching me in films. She had no clue as to the persistence and thick skin required to get any roles.

I felt Mary's eyes on me as I pulled my suitcase out of the closet in our childhood room. "Acting isn't an easy life," I said.

"I don't mind working hard," she answered. She sat on her twin bed, fingering her pale yellow chenille bedspread.

I smiled. "It's not just about being a good actress. It's a business, and there are so many other aspects of Hollywood that make it very difficult to be an actress, especially a Chinese actress."

"Like what?"

Where do I begin? I thought. I was constantly reminded that my success in *The Toll of the Sea* and *The Thief of Bagdad* meant very little to the men running the studios. There were few parts for a Chinese girl who didn't take risks, and I didn't see my younger sister as a risk-taker; none of my siblings were. It was a world that could easily wring her dry and toss her aside. How could I explain that we would always be confined by the way we looked? I didn't want to tell Mary that I'd become the standard for the *Oriental* beauty in films. Even with my successes, I was still window dressing.

Instead, I said, "You're smart and talented. Don't be like me. Finish high school first." I hoped upon hope she would fall in love with someone, or something else, in the next year, but the ironic echo of my father's advice to me rang in my conscience.

AS THE DAYS GREW closer to our departure, I began to worry about how Lulu and I would get along in the months ahead. Lulu became ever more efficient, making sure I was packing wisely and that everything we needed was accounted for. She was becoming more and more insufferable, too, right up to the night before we were to leave.

"Do you have your papers?" Lulu asked.

They were the first thing I had packed, knowing she would ask. I pointed to my handbag, annoyed, and returned to packing my suitcase.

"You remember what happened the time you forgot."

I placed a sweater on the bed. "Yes, how could I forget?"

It was only that one time, but Lulu never let me forget it. I was on my way to New York, only to realize I'd forgotten my identity papers just as I arrived at the train station. I frantically searched through my possessions, remembering I'd left my papers on top of my bedroom dresser. Right down the block from the train station was a huge billboard with my face on it, advertising a movie I was starring in. Still, I couldn't board the train without my identity papers and was left with no choice but to catch a later train.

I REACHED FOR MY handbag, pulled the papers out, and held them up in front of Lulu.

"Now, let me see you put them back into your handbag," Lulu said.

I exaggerated every move, clicking my handbag closed.

Lulu smiled.

We left Los Angeles for Berlin on March 28, 1928.

SACRAMENTO, CALIFORNIA
1960

I wake with a start. For a split second, I'm not sure where I am, but the click-clacking of the train brings me right back to my small compartment. The cabin is bathed in a hazy gray just before daylight, the sharp edges of the small space just coming into focus. My silver flask is perched, almost empty, on the petite side table. The sound of muffled snores comes from the train compartment next to mine. I had dozed on and off through the night, not bothering to have the seat converted into a fold-down bed. I'd taken out a pillow and blanket from a small closet and found myself reading snatches of the notebook every time I woke. I must have clicked off the overhead light sometime during the night with my notebook lying open across my stomach.

The train slows and stops in the middle of nowhere from what I can see, a moment of rest before we continue on to Sacramento. Half an hour more, I tell myself, closing the notebook and putting it on the table.

I close my eyes against the growing light.

SLEEP DOESN'T RETURN, only memories. This is what I feared, the past rising up and overwhelming me. It's a wonder I made it through those early years battling with my father, struggling with St. Vitus's dance along with the relentlessly dark moods that have continued to follow me throughout my life. What would have happened if I hadn't succeeded in the movie business? Marriage and a family like *baba* wanted, living an ordinary life as someone's wife? What would it have been like to have no early struggles with my father? Our relationship would have taken on an entirely different tone: easier, yet far less challenging. And lord knows how I love a good challenge.

Still, my father's presence has returned, and he feels very close to me again. He has been gone since 1949, dying of heart failure at the age of eighty-nine. Even with all of our conflicts, I was devastated by his death. Despite the many harsh words we exchanged through the years, I hear only the ones that mattered most: the whisper of his voice comforting me when St. Vitus's dance had taken over my body.

You're strong, Anna, you can do anything. I know you'll be okay.

I've carried those words with me through the years like a good luck charm. I don't know, *baba*, I want to tell him, some days have been better than others.

When I open my eyes, the train compartment is filled with morning light.

IT DID TAKE STRENGTH to leave Hollywood behind. I had proven that I could act with the best of them, and yet, at twenty-three, I was tired and needed a change. I accepted a movie offer in Berlin. While so many European actors and actresses were flocking to Hollywood, I bucked the trend and headed to Europe.

I wanted to make movies based on the strength of my acting ability instead of the color of my skin. Europe was also more accepting of interracial relationships in everyday life and as part of society. This was the kind of personal freedom I longed for, and I had Josephine Baker's experience to look to for inspiration. She'd grown up a poor Negro girl in Missouri, and when America rejected her talents because of her ethnicity, she found fame and adulation in Europe. Against all odds, I was willing to take the chance, both for my professional career and for my emotional health. I saw Europe as the birthplace of an older, much wiser Anna May Wong.

PART TWO

I think I left America because I died so often.
Pathetic dying seemed to be the best thing I did.

—Anna May Wong

A CIRCLE OF CHALK
1928-1935

EUROPE
Berlin, Germany—1928

Der Zug auf Bahnsteig sechs nach . . . an announcement in German boomed over the loudspeaker in the great, open hall of the Hamburg train station. It made Lulu and me feel even smaller and more inconsequential than we already did. People hurried by us, and we didn't understand a word of German as we stood like two orphans left with our luggage on the crowded platform. We hesitated to board the waiting train, uncertain if it was the right one that would take us to Berlin. For the first time, I wondered if I'd made a mistake coming to Germany as I watched Lulu slowly edge closer to a group of middle-aged Germans who were deep in conversation.

"What are you doing?" I asked.

Lulu turned to me. "Listening for someone to mention Berlin," she answered.

It made perfect "Lulu" sense, practical and efficient.

I began to do the same.

When Lulu heard a woman say Berlin, she stepped closer and smiled, pointing to the train in front of us. "Berlin?" she asked.

"*Ja*, Berlin," the woman said, looking at us wide-eyed. "Berlin," she repeated, nodding and nodding, gesturing toward the train.

Only later did we realize how unusual it must have been for her to have two young Chinese women suddenly approach her. By the time we arrived in Berlin, we'd read in our guidebook that only a handful of Chinese lived there, with no more than thirty Chinese women in the entire city. I'm sure that woman in the train station now had a story to tell her children and grandchildren for years to come.

I WAS MESMERIZED WITH Berlin from the moment I stepped out of the train station on a glorious April afternoon. The Weimar Republic of the past decade had turned its capital into one of the most modern and vibrant cities in the world. All my earlier fears dissipated when I walked down the famous Kurfürstendamm, one of the most elegant shopping avenues in the bustling city, that stretched from the Kaiser Wilhelm Memorial Church in Charlottenburg to the district of Grunewald, lined with stately buildings, cafés, clothing shops, cinemas, and grand theaters with dance halls downstairs.

The city pulsed with energy, alive with art and literature, philosophy and theater, film and music, particularly the jazz performed by Negro musicians. It all set the tone for the Berliner's attitude of letting go and improvising, where everyone and everything was accepted, including outcasts who flocked to Berlin from more conservative and less open-minded countries—a group in which I could now include myself. I had already developed quite a reputation in Europe through my movies, photos, and movie magazine articles. I was seen as a free-spirited, modern-thinking flapper who smoked, drank, drove, and remained unmarried. Berlin was the bastion of innovation and freedom of expression. It was where the exotic and the erotic reigned without fear, and where one's body was to be revered, no matter who you gave it to. Suddenly inhabiting such an open and vibrant world was dizzying.

Lulu and I were also Chinese, rare entities in Berlin, and quickly embraced because of it not only socially but professionally. My first German film was *Song*, a movie produced and directed by Richard Eichberg. On the set, I met up-and-coming photographer Lotte Jacobi, whose still photos of me soon found their way into movie magazines across the continent, thus repeating for *Song* the success James Wong Howe achieved with his stills from *Peter Pan*. I was suddenly seen everywhere in Europe, where there was a deeper sense of appreciation for art and beauty. I relished my new, unrestricted life, and began taking German lessons, realizing how important it was to know the language if I wanted to communicate with other directors, actors, and actresses while I continued to make movies in Berlin.

When I wasn't filming, I explored the city with Lulu, who loved the German cream cakes and the heavy rustic bread served with cheese and meats for breakfast. "We better walk off what we just ate," I teased her, only to laugh when Lulu piled meat and cheese between slices of bread to take along for lunch.

We went to the Brandenburg Gate first, one of Berlin's most famous landmarks, and beyond it the boulevard of linden trees that led to the royal City Palace. Lulu preferred the Charlottenburg Palace, with its fine china and beautiful paintings, situated in the middle of the manicured gardens right near to the river Spree. I indulged in the theater and opera and the café society, where artists and writers formed intellectual circles that eagerly welcomed me to their gatherings. At a private party, I met the philosopher Walter Benjamin, who'd just returned from Moscow and Paris and was now writing essays for *Literarische Welt*. I feared he might be the type of scholar who had no use for a Chinese-American actress. Instead, he described our meeting in a magazine piece as having been "dazzled" by my beauty. I suspect that meeting a Chinese woman was a new experience for him, too, but we became instant friends and met whenever possible for meals and conversations.

It wasn't long before German photographers began lining up to shoot portraits of me. Lotte Jacobi's photos had also found their way into French and British magazines, and photographers from all over the continent began jockeying to snap my image. American editors quickly included the pictures in their magazines, and Edward Steichen provided more photos to *Vanity Fair*, which were seen far and wide. More postcards were printed, and my image soared to all corners of the world. In Europe, nudity was an expression of beauty, not to be suppressed as in the United States. I did bare my breasts in a few shots, although I knew Lulu would have been horrified if she were there with me.

"Oh, Anna, why would you?" she asked when I told her later at the hotel.

"Why wouldn't I?" I snapped, though I couldn't look her in the eyes.

Why couldn't my sister just be happy for me?

"It's different here, Lulu," I added. "No one cares what you wear or don't wear. It's all about art. You need to let go of all the old-fashioned ideas we grew up with."

"It's not that simple," she said.

"It is that simple," I said, tired of having to feel guilty about everything I did.

"What would *baba* say," she muttered to herself.

I pretended I didn't hear her. I didn't want to fight, and frankly, I didn't care what my father would say. It seemed such a natural part of this newfound expression in Berlin. More than that, I felt a real sense of freedom for the first time in my life. *Baba*'s judging presence was far away, and the European sensibility of openness and acceptance was exhilarating.

It was exactly where I wanted to be.

EUROPE
Paris, France—1928–1929

In June, after I completed filming *Song*, Lulu and I went to France. If Berlin was the city of intellect and innovation, Paris was the city of light and enchantment. As in Berlin, few Chinese lived here. Those who did spoke Mandarin and came from Northern China for business or to study. Lulu and I were immediately embraced by the French, just as we had been by the Germans. But in France, the acceptance felt deeper, more ingrained in their history with an established appreciation of the Orient that dated back to the silk trade in the eighteenth century. We were readily perceived as part of that *Oriental* mystique, rare and exotic in mind and body. In America, our difference had isolated us and held us back, while in France we were held in awe.

The first three days after we'd arrived, Lulu and I walked for miles down the narrow streets of the Marais, and the wide boulevards of Montparnasse, stopping in front of stately and majestic buildings and charming shops. We strolled through the Tuileries Gardens, the Musée du Luxembourg, along the Champs-Élysées to the Louvre. In front of the Notre-Dame Cathedral, we were stopped to pose for photos.

"They look at me as if I'm a rare piece of porcelain," I whispered to Lulu.

"Handle with care," she said, and we both laughed.

We paused in the middle of the Pont Neuf as we crossed over the river Seine, watching the barges glide by and the artists painting. It was still beautiful, despite the water rats scurrying to and fro. No wonder Paris attracted writers and artists seeking inspiration. People filled the streets at all hours, crowding into cafés and restaurants where there was no such thing as Prohibition. They could sit for hours nursing a glass of wine or Pernod or absinthe, watching life flowing in front of them.

We enjoyed the open-air market at Les Halles, a maze of stalls where pigs and hares, chickens and geese waited to be butchered. Flies buzzed with euphoria over moist blood dripping from naked carcasses. Lulu flinched from the scattering rats and screeching cats in the alleyway behind the market, fighting over the bloody entrails.

I took Lulu's arm and led her toward the bright and colorful fruits and vegetables stacked high in wooden crates, the sweet-scented flowers with dirt clinging to their stems as if they'd just been plucked from the earth.

Lulu relaxed, and whispered, "It's like a beating heart; everything is so alive."

Like so much we had experienced in the weeks we'd been in

Europe, there was a balance between the beautiful and coarse, the soft and the hard, the polite and the rude.

"Yes," I said, "it is."

This is what I hoped Lulu would experience, the urgent hum of life outside of the laundry. I loved listening to the smooth flow of the language and was determined to begin studying French, too, along with German. We were both captivated by Paris now, enjoying long lazy lunches, evenings at the theater, and nights in jazz clubs.

ON OUR FIFTH NIGHT in Paris, Lulu was tired and returned to the hotel after the theater, while I was taken to a late dinner at La Coupole by George Fritzgerald of the French magazine, *Pour Vous*. Since its opening the year before, La Coupole had become the most popular brasserie in Paris with its beautiful and modern art deco design: straight lines, tall pillars, and geometric shapes. It teemed with the Paris elite, the wealthy and the well known, and all those who hoped to see them.

We pushed through the noisy crowd waiting outside, and stepped inside the exquisite room filled with delicious aromas. As I looked around, I heard someone yell, "Frizie! Frizie! Over here!"

George stopped when he saw who had called to him, then took my arm and said happily, "Come this way, there's someone I want you to meet."

Mystified, I followed George past the bustling banquettes toward the back of the restaurant, and there she was, seated at a round table surrounded by friends and admirers, her large, dark eyes even more striking in person. She was wearing a gold sleeveless low-cut silk dress that shimmered against her bronze skin. Her short hair was slicked close to her head and held with a diamond clip while large art deco diamond earrings glimmered at each side of her lovely oval face. Although I'd seen her image in hundreds of magazines and newsreels back home, she appeared even more dazzling in person holding a glass of champagne.

"Frizie, what have you been up to?" she asked, smiling.

"I have a very special dinner companion I'd like to introduce you to," George said. He ushered me forward. "Josephine Baker, meet Anna May Wong."

I felt a warm rush of joy. All the background noise, the voices, the laughter, the dishes clinking seemed to recede.

"*Enchantée*," I said, "I'm so happy to meet you." I reached across the table to shake her hand, more excited than I let on. Lulu and I had hoped to see her show *La Folie du Jour* at the Folies Bergère, but were disappointed to find it was sold out through the summer.

Three years earlier, Josephine Baker had left America to find stardom in Paris. Her stage revue, which included singing, dancing, and her comic antics, was a smashing success. I couldn't help but follow her career, which mirrored mine in so many ways. America had denied us both respect and access to any kind of real success because of the way we looked, and the color of our skin. But now, Josephine Baker was known everywhere in Europe and in America too. I could only hope that Anna May Wong would follow in her footsteps.

Josephine half stood to take my hand in hers. "*Enchantée*," she said, with a radiant smile. "Please, please join us," she offered. Her guests were already scooting around the table so I could have the seat next to her. "Frizie can interrogate you later."

"Of course I can," George agreed. "I already have my story right here, the two most beautiful and exotic women in Paris dining together."

"Ah, you've always had a way with words, Frizie," Josephine said, blowing him a kiss across the table.

Compared to other actors and actresses I'd met over the past few years, Josephine Baker was special. It seemed we already knew each other, bonded by our adversities. She was a fighter, brave and innovative, and I so admired her courage. I knew exactly what brought her here and selfishly wanted the same for myself. She smelled of jasmine and cigarette smoke. A waiter quickly poured me a glass of champagne.

"I'm so happy to finally meet you," I said, keeping my voice steady. "I've followed your wonderful career all through Europe."

"And I've followed yours," she said. "It's hard not to miss your lovely face on every other magazine at every corner *tabac*."

"With your face on all the rest," I quickly added.

Josephine laughed. "We've taken over Paris, haven't we?"

"Pretty much," I answered. I sipped my champagne and smiled.

"We've also fought quite the battle, haven't we?" she said, and beamed. "And look where we are now? Adored by countries that aren't our own."

After so long, I felt I was in the company of someone who truly understood. Josephine filled both of our glasses with more champagne just as platters of raw oysters and shellfish on ice arrived at the table.

"Why can't America be more like Europe?" I asked. It was a question I'd asked myself over and over since arriving in Berlin.

She sipped her champagne and turned serious. "America is an

infant compared to Europe. They spurn us because they have no idea how we fit into their world. Here, we're embraced for our differences; there, we're feared because of them."

"Easier to deny we exist by denying us any rights."

"Damn idiots," Josephine said.

I couldn't agree more. I'd read that she'd had a tough childhood, striking out on her own when she was very young, working for white families as a nursemaid at the age of nine. Her childhood horrors certainly outweighed mine. *Was it more painful with a family, or without?* I asked myself. My family made my life difficult in so many ways, but also gave me comfort and familiarity when I needed them most.

"Is it ever too much?" I asked.

"Always," she answered. "But we do what we have to do. I can't imagine anything else. Can you?"

Could I? Again, I imagined myself married with a family like *baba* always wanted and being utterly unhappy. Or, modeling fur coats and working in the Ville de Paris department store like I did when I was young, only now, I'd be the manager and selling Chanel dresses that I could never afford to wear. Or, I'd be an extra in the movies for the rest of my life, always in the background and never shimmering to life on the screen. I wanted none of it.

"No," I said, "I can't."

I looked around at the admiring faces glancing in our direction. It was astonishing to think that a Negro and a Chinese woman were the center of attention, the belles of the ball. Josephine leaned over to the thin, mustached man on the other side of her and whispered something that made him laugh. For a moment, I wondered if it was at my expense. I lit a cigarette and drank down more champagne.

Josephine turned back to me. "The count thinks you're very beautiful." He nodded and smiled. "If we weren't engaged," she said, "I'd be jealous."

"But you needn't worry," she added, "you'll do just fine, both here in Europe and back in the States. First and foremost, just be true to yourself. Americans can't resist us for long, try as they might. We're forcing them to see life in a new way, to see it in color. They think we're exotic savages, but we know we're just like them—only infinitely more interesting!"

We both laughed. And just like that, it all made sense. I had never wanted to do anything else but act, no matter the hardships and disappointments. *My* career, *my* success, had to be for me first. Was that how Josephine Baker saw her career?

"Is that the way you've gotten through it all?" I asked.

Josephine shifted closer. "If I wasn't doing this for myself, I'd be changing diapers or scrubbing floors back in Missouri. Just remember, the others are ordinary and bland compared to us," she said, leaning even closer. "We're adored here. That's what we need to remember in our most difficult times. We're doing this for ourselves now, but also for all those who will follow after us."

I nodded. Josephine had fortunately found her heart and home here, but I was just visiting. I couldn't imagine achieving the same kind of adoration and freedom back in Hollywood that she possessed here in Paris. I felt a moment of dread.

"Yes," I answered quietly.

When Josephine saw that I'd suddenly turned serious, she reached out and took my hand. "It's only the beginning, you'll see." Then she crossed her eyes and stuck out her tongue to make me laugh, as she did for her audiences every night. She was smart and irresistible and it was easy to see why Josephine Baker had captured Europe.

She had certainly captured me.

That was a magical night at La Coupole. We ate oysters and langoustines with the champagne, beef filet with glazed carrots, and lamb curry with red wine. For dessert, Chantilly glace with brandy and whiskey, and even more brandy until the wee hours of the morning.

LULU AND I WERE invited the following evening to Josephine's show at the Folies Bergère, where we sat in special guest seats near the stage. Even my usually reserved sister laughed, wide eyed with amazement, as Josephine danced bare breasted in her famous skirt of sixteen bananas. We both stood to clap, having loved every moment of *The Sauvage*. We dined with Josephine and the count afterwards, constantly interrupted by admirers who stopped by her table. When they recognized me, I heard whispers of "Anna May Wong" floating through the restaurant.

Josephine nudged my shoulder. "See, I told you. It won't be long now until you knock me to the wayside," she teased.

"Fat chance," I said, and laughed.

Josephine was scheduled to take her revue to Berlin at the end of August. I was on my way to London to make another film, and then returning to Germany at the same time for the premiere of *Song*. We made plans to see each other again, no matter how busy our schedules were.

EUROPE
London, England—1928

Our brief and charmed stay in Paris ended much too soon, but I couldn't complain. I was off to London to begin filming *Piccadilly*, directed by E. A. DuPont. After Berlin and Paris, I wondered if London might be too quiet, and perhaps too proper. In fact, I found myself delighted to be back where English was the spoken language and a calmer way of life prevailed. I rented an apartment at the Park Lane Hotel in the Mayfair District, and for the first time in ages, Lulu and I felt as if we had a stable home, one where we could settle down for a couple of months and entertain friends. The apartment was high ceilinged and elegant, yet comfortable with ample space, and both of our rooms overlooked Hyde Park. I took to having interviews with journalists in the front room, where there was a lovely fireplace and large windows that let in lots of light. I always made sure my latest interviews, along with my most current photos, reached magazines in the States, and in China, by sending them to editors and journalists I knew, showing the success I was having in Europe. It was a constant worry of mine that I was losing all my Hollywood connections now that I was in Europe.

Paul Robeson and his wife, Eslanda, were among our first visitors. I'd met him during our first few nights in London and we became fast friends. Paul and Essie were college sweethearts who'd married just a year after they'd met. She was an amazing woman in her own right, beautiful and smart, a graduate of Columbia University. Essie was not only an analytical chemist but an author who had recently published a biography of her husband. She was also Paul's agent and business manager, the driving force behind his career. They were both politically active, and two of the most interesting people I knew.

Despite his stellar academic career and a JD degree from Columbia, Paul resigned from his job at a law firm because their legal secretaries refused to work with him. Undaunted by their racism, and gifted with a magnificent voice and stage presence, he turned his talents to a successful theatrical career, artfully managed by Essie. His heart-stopping West End performance of *Show Boat* thrilled London audiences nightly.

Over cocktails, we often found ourselves talking about growing up in our respective homes, New York and Los Angeles. In his rich, deep voice, Paul told me about walking into popular and expensive New York restaurants and hotels back when he was a college student, just to see how long it would take before he was asked to leave.

"The Plaza," he said with a grim smile. "I never made it farther than the front entrance. The doorman wouldn't let me set foot inside."

"That's right," Essie added. "He damn near lost his shoe when the door slammed!"

"But I survived," Paul said, "only to be refused a table at the Savoy just last week, right here in London." He sighed audibly. "You'd think a standing ovation at Theatre Royal might be worth a little something? Even for a Negro?"

Appalled but not surprised, I shook my head in sympathy, then sipped my martini and told them the story of how frightened I'd been as a child the first time I laid eyes on a yellowface actress. "I really thought she was a monster," I said.

"She was," Essie said. "Just like these blackface actors. But you and Paul are on your way to changing all of that!"

"Here's to the real deal!" Paul said, lifting his glass.

We toasted each other, wishing it were true.

We were like magnets, attracted to each other because of our Americanism, even as we relished Europe's open acceptance of us. Here, we were mostly treated like anyone else. And as with Josephine, it was so easy spending time together because it allowed us to hold on to what we'd left behind.

I WAS MOBBED BY frenzied fans in London in a way I wasn't in Berlin and Paris. It was hard to leave the flat without hordes of fans and press waiting when we went to concerts, or to the theater. I hadn't expected it from the more reserved British, but it was uplifting to know I really had made an impact here, just as Josephine had predicted. Women were imitating me, wearing embroidered coolie coats to the theater, cutting their hair short with bangs like mine, and tinting their faces ochre to resemble my complexion. I had never experienced anything so extreme before and I wasn't sure what to do with this kind of adulation. Lulu remained amused by it all, writing home weekly to tell them of our experiences.

PICCADILLY WAS MY FIRST leading role since *The Toll of the Sea*. While the story contained many of the same racial overtones I'd dealt with in Hollywood, and culminated with my death at the end, there was also a strength and depth to the character of Shosho, a Chinese girl who rises from working as kitchen help to become the star performer at the Piccadilly Club, finding love with the Caucasian club owner along the way. It was a role unlike all my supporting roles in the States. This was why I had risked coming to Europe: for the opportunity to play a real flesh-and-blood Chinese woman, an opportunity Hollywood continued to deny me.

When I wasn't busy filming *Piccadilly* at a studio outside of London, Lulu and I ventured down the Thames to the real Maidenhead and Limehouse Districts where the story was set. It was where the sea-trading Chinese had originally settled and started a Chinatown. I'd read all about the area, and seeing it made it easy to imagine what it was like during the eighteenth and nineteenth centuries, when the surrounding docks and wharves of Limehouse Basin played an important role in London's international trade. It had been a busy dock during the day, made infamous for its gambling and prostitution, along with fights and murders, after the sun went down. The area was populated by the poor and the down on their luck, crammed into makeshift houses in the squalid slums where Charles Dickens found some of his greatest characters. Later, ships brought crews from all around the world, establishing communities of foreign sailors, including the Chinese with their opium and tea trades.

When Lulu and I stepped off the boat, it was a gray day, the wind blowing miserably, the waves reaching up and splashing against the stone wall. We hurried up the steps to streets lined with rows of two-story brick buildings that once were the seamen's hostels and public houses. Just as I envisioned the sordid world of opium dens, drinking establishments, dance halls, and slums, I could well imagine my character Shosho walking down these narrow streets, contemplating her future. No wonder Arthur Conan Doyle later had his most famous character, Sherlock Holmes, go to Limehouse in search of opium. It was ripe for intrigue.

WE WALKED DOWN THE narrow causeway where the first Chinese community had settled. Dark and dingy two-story brick buildings that appeared to house apartments upstairs and storefronts and restaurants downstairs lined both sides of the road. We were delighted to see Chinese characters written on their front windows, reminding us a bit of home. Chinese school had paid off for Lulu, who could read almost everything. Unlike our Los Angeles Chinatown with its crowded streets, this quarter was much smaller and eerily quiet. We stopped for tea and learned from the shop owner that a different Chinatown was located on Pennyfields and Ming Streets, its Shanghainese community distinct from this Cantonese neighborhood.

A short walk led us to a newer street with similar two-story brick buildings housing stores, restaurants, laundries, a few pubs, and a number of Chinese social organizations that reminded us of Los Angeles. I found it fascinating that the Chinese communities had separate settlements so far away in England.

"I wonder what *baba* would think," Lulu said.

She appeared as interested as I was in seeking out Chinese locales in London. So far, nowhere else we'd visited in Europe felt as close to the life we'd left behind.

"He'd want to know where the best Chinese restaurant was," I answered.

Lulu laughed. "Or the best laundry," she added.

"Right there," I said, pointing to a laundry just across the road.

We peeked in, hoping to see a Chinese family hard at work, only to see an old Chinese woman alone at the counter. Peering at us, she shook her head and turned away.

"So much for friendly and accommodating service," I said.

It was the first lesson *baba* taught all of his children from the moment we set foot in the laundry. It was important to treat our customers the way we hoped to be treated. Never behave in a way that would disgrace our business or our family.

"*Baba* would have raised his bamboo stick over us if we were that unfriendly," Lulu said, laughing.

We spent the morning exploring the narrow streets, finding comfort in seeing so many Chinese businesses and hearing Cantonese conversations. At one of the restaurants we stopped for lunch, eating sad versions of our usual noodles and dumplings but feeling happier and less alone among the familiar scents and sounds of home.

WITH NORTH FIGUEROA STREET a world away, Lulu became more relaxed and lighthearted during our four months of travel. I glimpsed another person I didn't know growing up, a young woman who was carefree and filled with curiosity, not anchored to family responsibilities at the laundry, or to keeping the rest of her younger siblings out of trouble. I'd always been stubborn and troublesome in my father's eyes, but Lulu was there to watch over me. After discovering Europe together, I was already sad to think she would be leaving in a matter of weeks and returning to Los Angeles.

WHEN LULU SAILED HOME in late July of 1928, I was completely on my own for the first time in my life. It wasn't being alone that was frightening; it was the realization that this new loneliness couldn't be easily filled with casual friends or late-night parties. I couldn't simply replace my sister with someone else. We were connected by a seed long planted, deeply rooted in our history together that no one else shared. She knew me better than anyone, a rose, not without its thorns. It was this belief in family and culture that *baba* had drilled into me. Even in my most rebellious moments, I always knew I had my family to return to in Los Angeles. But now, for the first time, I was alone and very far from home.

By late afternoon on the day Lulu left, the sky had darkened and rain was likely to follow. I sipped a Scotch and smoked as I stood by the apartment window, watching people stroll the manicured paths of Hyde Park across the street. Couples arm in arm, nannies pushing prams, an older woman clutching a bouquet of flowers. Life went on. I dropped my cigarette into the Scotch, grabbed my handbag, closed the door to Lulu's empty room, and stepped out into this new life of mine to take a walk.

When I returned, I found a note from Gregory St. John, a young playwright, who wondered if I'd join him for Sunday roast the next day. The thought of a plate of beef with roasted potatoes, carrots, and Yorkshire pudding sounded like just the kind of comfort I needed.

I STAYED IN THE apartment at the Park Lane Hotel until I finished filming *Piccadilly* and completed the string of interviews I

had planned before my return to Berlin. I liked the apartment im-
mensely, made more my home over the past month with my books
and a few Chinese vases I'd bought in Limestone, along with a
beautiful Chinese embroidered throw that lay over the arm of the
sofa in the sitting room. I packed the throw but left everything else. I
hated to leave it all, but I was still under contract with Richard Eichberg and was scheduled to be back in Berlin by the end of August for
the opening gala of *Song* at the Alhambra Theater.

Happily, a letter arrived from Lulu before I left London. She
had sailed safely back home and was eager for news. *I miss you*, she
had written. *I didn't have you there aboard ship to get us into any trouble, so it was nothing but calm seas. Let me know what has been going
on since I left. Nothing has changed here, and I've stepped back into my
old life as if I'd never gone away. But I did, and it makes all the difference in the world. I wish you nothing but success at the opening gala for*
Song, *and remember, if you have trouble boarding the right train back
to Germany, just listen carefully for the person who says, "Berlin . . ."*

Only rarely since I'd left Los Angeles had I ever felt so homesick.

THE TRANSCONTINENTAL RAILROAD
1960

Not long after the train leaves Sacramento for Chicago, there's a
knock on my cabin door. It's the same porter I'd given my bags to
when I switched trains earlier on the platform. He smiles wide and
takes off his cap.

"Just checking to see if you're all settled in," he says. "My name's

Joseph. Anything you need in the next handful of days before we reach New York, you just let me know."

He's an older, nice-looking man, graying whiskers, skin two shades darker than Josephine's.

I smile. "Thank you, Joseph," I say. "I'm fine right now."

He lifts his hand and tells me there's one more thing before he disappears back out into the corridor to an awaiting cart. A moment later, he returns carrying a tray with a bottle of water and a glass. "You might like this," he says.

"Thank you," I say again, and smile.

He fingers his cap and remains standing awkwardly in the doorway. "Just want to say, I'm a big fan, Miz Wong. Saw *Shanghai Express* a few times. Any movie with a train in it has my attention. But you were even better."

I laugh. "Thank you, Joseph. That's the nicest compliment I've ever received."

He nods, embarrassed, and steps back into the corridor, closing the door quietly behind him. And then he's gone, his cart rattling off to the next cabin.

My compartment is larger and more spacious than the one on the first train, with two fold-down beds above the seats facing each other, a decent-size washroom, and a closet. My home away from home until I reach New York. I unpack, settle in, and place the notebooks on the table under the window.

WHEN THE TRAIN REACHES Donner Pass, I stop reading, close the notebook, and put it down. For this stretch of the train ride, I want to be more attentive, to pay homage to the laborers who made it all possible. Outside the window, the landscape has changed to a mountainous terrain, and the train moves more slowly along a tree-lined slope as we begin our ascent through the high Sierras toward Reno, Nevada. We'll stop shortly at the Truckee train station near Lake Tahoe before we continue on.

Towering pines shade the sunlight, and slivers of blue sky peek through the branches. It's beautiful, but I know that what appears so serene now was once fraught with drama. I lean back, gaze out the window, and remember *ma ma* telling us when we were young that my grandfather's best friend, whom he considered closer than a brother, had journeyed from Taishan to work on the railroad. He was in search of a better life, certain he would find it once he was in America. "No one ever heard from him again," my mother said. It broke my grandfather's heart to lose his closest friend, but it didn't deter him from immigrating the following year, and eventually opening two grocery stores in the Gold Country. He searched for his best friend for years but to no avail, finally giving him up for dead.

I think of how important the Chinese were in the completion of this railroad, and how little credit had been given to them during their lifetimes. Almost a hundred years later, very little has changed.

Soon, the train's whistle blows as we enter the first of the several tunnels blasted through the mountains of solid rock by the Chinese railroad workers. The cabin goes completely dark for a moment before a light flickers on, and all I see is blackness outside the window, perpetual night as we move deeper into the belly of the mountain. And in that blackness, I can almost smell the damp mineral wetness of earth and rock, and experience the claustrophobic feeling of being trapped in constant darkness like the workers who blasted and chipped away at the mountain. I imagine it's what one kind of hell feels like, the perpetual cold and darkness, barely able to see your hand held out in front of you, lit only by the dim glow of the flickering oil lamps.

The prize of their survival only meant they'd have to blast through another mountain, and another after that, provided they hadn't lost a limb or their hearing or their minds from fear. Some Chinese workers were assigned to create roads, dangling from ropes over the cliffs to plant dynamite, while others laid the hundred miles of railroad tracks over mountainous terrain that rose to seven thousand feet. And still, they kept working and dying, hoping to find a better life in America. Has the ghost of my grandfather's best friend remained in these mountains among all the other men who died? It was an amazing feat, and I'm humbled to be riding through this mountain due to the sweat and blood of their hard labor.

Suddenly, we emerge from the other end of the tunnel, back into the shock of daylight, leaving all those men behind.

EUROPE
Berlin, Germany—1928

I returned to a sadder and darker Berlin in the waning days of summer. Already, I felt a shift in the air as I rode from the train station to the hotel in a taxi the studio had waiting for me. The late-afternoon sky was smoke gray and dingy, threatening rain. It was muggy, but the weather had shifted and would turn cooler in a matter of weeks. Unlike on my last visit four months ago, a touch of melancholy and apprehension hung heavily in the air.

I was awakened from my thoughts when the taxi driver asked, "Is it Madame's first time in Berlin?" I glimpsed his face in the rearview mirror. He was a bearded, middle-aged gentleman who spoke fluent English.

"No," I answered. "I came here in April for two months' work."

"You are the actress," he said, "from America?"

"Yes," I answered, unexpectedly delighted that he didn't say "Chinese actress," or "from China."

"Welcome back," he said. "It is your photo everywhere at the tram stops, then. I thought it might be you. I look forward to seeing your movie."

"Thank you." I smiled. "You speak English very well."

He nodded happily. "I spent some time in America, studying in New York and Boston."

"What did you study?"

"Philosophy." He laughed. "And now, I drive a taxi." He glanced into the mirror, smiling at me.

"Don't Berlin and philosophers go hand in hand?" I asked, hoping Walter Benjamin was in town.

"Ah, unfortunately, we're too many here. No one cares for wasted words when they need to put food on the table."

Before leaving London, I'd heard a news program on the BBC

explaining that, a decade after the war, Germany was at a crossroads. The Weimar Republic faced a young Nazi organization that engaged growing numbers of alienated and bitter German citizens barely scraping by, while their country was taken over by wealthy bankers and "deviants," whom they saw as obscene. It made no sense then, but as I gazed out the taxi window now, I could see downtrodden Berliners walking among the well dressed, beggars on each street corner, and tired workers riding home in the overcrowded trams. An edge of darkness invaded the afternoon light, sending a chill through me.

When we arrived at the Hotel Esplanade, the driver insisted on carrying my bags to the front desk.

I gave him a large tip, and told him, "Just remember, no words are ever wasted."

WHEN SONG PREMIERED AT the Alhambra Theater, I was greeted with adoration by Germans who flocked to the theaters on a daily basis. Nevertheless, as wonderful as my leading role in *Song* was, I still died at the end of the movie. The film received mixed reviews around the world; it was beloved by the Germans and French, while American critics neglected the film itself but were more incensed that the Europeans saw me as Chinese, rather than Chinese American. Given the way I'd been treated by Hollywood, and to a larger degree, by America, I was perfectly happy to be seen as Chinese. It was increasingly obvious that the negative portrayal of Chinese in films created more misconceptions as to who we really were. At least in Europe, I felt recognized and appreciated.

Since *Song* was a hit in Germany, I stayed on in Berlin enjoying the fruits of its success.

JOSEPHINE BAKER BROUGHT HER revue back to Berlin in early September and I was more than delighted to see her again. We had a wonderful dinner together, and the following evening, I sat in the front row of the Berlin Theater on opening night as Josephine shimmied and danced bare breasted across the stage. At the end of her show, the audience stood and clapped for so long, I simply sat back down again.

After the show, I was invited to Josephine's opening night party at a popular cabaret. The El Dorado was well known for its transsexual performers, whose stunning performances were the talk of the town. It also had the largest dance floor in Berlin. On any given night, it was packed with people from all walks of life and brought out everyone's natural preferences and proclivities. Every person there was beautifully dressed and made up; it was the one place I didn't stand out.

When I entered the cabaret looking for Josephine's table, I could barely squeeze through the crowd. The air was hot and smoky, edged with a sickly sweet scent of perfume and sweat. I never liked being caught in the midst of so many people; it always reminded me of the elementary school where Lulu and I were surrounded by those terrible boys, pushed, slapped, and taunted for being Chinese. Ever since, I had suffered from mild claustrophobia in similar, confined situations.

Someone yelled out, "It's Anna May Wong!"

I was instantly recognized by the people in the crowd, their attention quickly shifting my way. As my skin flushed with heat, I was swept forward by a wave of bodies, pushed toward the dance floor by the swarm, and driven deeper into the room. It grew increasingly hot and suffocating as I was thrust into the dancing crowd. I tried to turn around but couldn't find my way out of the mob. I pushed back in panic.

"Anna May, over here!" I heard a deep, sultry voice rise above the crowd. It didn't belong to Josephine.

Where was here? I turned around to find myself face-to-face with a lovely young man. He must have seen the fear in my eyes as I was pushed and pulled by the throng. He reached out and took my hand, weaving us through the crowd of people blocking our way until he had guided me safely away from the dance floor. Then he leaned close, told me that his name was Jurgen, and that he'd been sent to retrieve me from the frenetic crowd by a woman in his party. Before I could ask who the woman was, he'd led me to a table in the back where actress Marlene Dietrich sat waiting.

RICHARD EICHBERG HAD TOLD me all about Dietrich's quickly rising star. It was already predicted that her upcoming film, *The Blue Angel*, directed by Josef von Sternberg and starring my friend Emil Jannings, would make her an international movie star when it was released. I'd been wondering when our paths would finally cross. Marlene already had a reputation for enjoying the nightlife, and everything that came along with it. She had married young and had a daughter, but she and her husband maintained a very modern, open marriage, going their separate ways. According to Richard, she worked hard and played hard and made apologies to no one. It was the opposite of the world where I'd been brought up in Los Angeles Chinatown. The more I discovered about Berlin, the more I wondered what *baba* would think of its brash and uninhibited lifestyle. It was a large and mysterious city, but the film and artist communities stayed close and intimate. Everyone knew what everyone else was doing.

When our eyes met, I felt a flush heat my body from the way she was looking at me. I'd seen that look before but never so openly from a woman. I was both flattered and surprised, not only by the way she appraised me, but by how my body was responding.

"Anna May Wong, at last we meet," Marlene said, her deep, sultry voice rising above the music. She held a long, black pipe-like cigarette holder between her fingers. "Come, come, sit next to me, and tell me how you're enjoying your time in Berlin."

I took a breath, gathered myself together. It was hard not to be mesmerized by Dietrich's dark and penetrating gaze, her sweet narcissus perfume. She had a hypnotic allure about her. Once you were in her sights, I imagined it was hard to get away. She appeared striking and powerful as she held court, wearing what looked like men's trousers, a white silk shirt, and a black satin jacket. It was widely known that Dietrich seduced both men and women, leaving behind a growing trail of lovers. Her entourage around the table seemed to jostle for her attention. She was obviously used to getting what she wanted.

"At last, we meet," Marlene said again, holding out her hand.

"The pleasure is mine," I said, reaching across to her. "I've heard so much about you."

"Not all bad, I hope."

She had a firm grip and held on to my hand for just a moment too long, her eyes never leaving mine. Self-conscious as I was, I forced myself to match her gaze without turning away. Then I smiled and gently pulled my hand away from her.

"Not bad at all," I said.

As soon as I sat down, the music paused. Marlene leaned toward me. "I know how frightening it is to be suffocated by an adoring crowd," she said, glancing toward the dance floor and then back to me.

"Thank you," I said, "for sending Jurgen to rescue me. I haven't felt so helpless in a long time."

I was still shaken and it startled me.

"It was *my* pleasure," she said, and smiled.

I drank down the glass of champagne that was given to me, then raised it to be filled again. She had enough followers, and I wasn't about to be another. I was determined to be an equal.

"It can be overwhelming at times," I said. I took out my cigarettes, offered her one, and felt calmer as the smoke entered my lungs.

"Adoring fans come with the territory," Marlene said. "It's the price of fame, yes?" She placed the cigarette vertically into the pipe of her holder and lit it.

The price of fame seemed to keep inflating, I thought. Was this the cost of making good films?

"It makes me wonder if it's all worth it."

"Of course it is, darling," Marlene said, exhaling cigarette smoke. "We wouldn't be here if it wasn't." She waved a hand. "We wouldn't have all this, and then where would we be?" Leaning closer, she added, "And we wouldn't have met."

I looked at her and realized it was much like *ma ma*'s version of fate; everything was aligned and destined to happen.

"I have no doubt we would have met at some point during my visit," I said.

"Ah, but now it's sooner rather than later," she said, and smiled.

The band started up again, and there was no point in trying to talk above the music.

"Let's dance," Marlene said, rising and reaching for my hand. "Not to worry," she added. "I'll protect you."

I hesitated for a moment before I stood and let Marlene lead me to the dance floor, where the crowd immediately parted to make room for her while she pulled me along, never letting me out of her sight.

JOSEPHINE NEVER SHOWED UP at the El Dorado that night; she had sent a note of apology, along with a bottle of champagne, which I found waiting for me when I returned to my hotel room. She'd been exhausted, had a terrible headache, and returned to her hotel to rest instead. One week later, she left Berlin for Vienna with her revue. I'd read she'd been stormed by adoring fans there and had to be safely escorted away from the frenzied crowd. I sent her a telegram, hoping that she was okay, and received one back that simply read,

THE SHOW MUST GO ON! Love Josephine

BERLIN NOW BELONGED TO Marlene, who was an ardent and lively new friend. The press and photographers ate us up, following us everywhere, keeping our whereabouts around Berlin in all the latest movie magazines. Dietrich was like no one I'd ever met before, brazen and defiant, and I found spending time with her thrilling and addictive. We were young and beautiful movie stars in Berlin, and the public couldn't get enough of us.

Late autumn in Berlin brought to life an entirely different city. It was as if someone had gradually dimmed the lights, the days seeming to grow measurably shorter and more serious. The winds had also picked up and there was a constant chill in the air. While Berlin continued to be the hub of creative innovation and artistic freedom, conservatives and radical right-wing critics condemned Weimar Germany for contributing to the moral decay of German values. Even as the reverberations of unrest moved through the city, life continued to be celebrated to the fullest. I could have easily gone to two or three parties, nightclubs, and bars of all persuasion each and every night if I wanted. There was a frenzied excess here that was both exhilarating and exhausting.

By November, icy winds whipped through Berlin's dark skies and brought out the thick woolen and cashmere overcoats, fur coats, scarves, and hats, while the poor begged on the streets wrapped in blankets, sleeping underneath newspapers. It was a tale of two cities, as crowds of well-dressed Berliners hurried down the Kurfürstendamm to dinner or to the theater, side-stepping those who had nowhere to go.

MARLENE WAS ALWAYS PLANNING our escapades. She called early one afternoon in November to tell me there was a special place she wanted to take me. "Be dressed and waiting downstairs for my car at 9 p.m., *mein liebling.*"

I was shivering outside Hotel Esplanade when her car finally pulled up.

"You're in for a treat," she said.

"I can't wait," I answered.

Twenty-five minutes later, her chauffeur stopped at the corner of a dark and quiet suburban street, a world away from the bright lights and energy of Berlin's city center. It was the opposite of what I'd expected. She told her driver we'd be a few hours and to be waiting across the road.

"This way, *liebling,*" Marlene said, taking my arm and leading me down a narrow side street.

"Where are we going?" I asked.

"One of my favorite places in the world," she whispered in my ear, kissing me on the cheek.

We walked carefully over the cobblestone sidewalks in our heels, clinging to each other. She stopped at a very plain, nondescript building and knocked on the door twice, paused, and knocked again three times. I wanted to laugh, thinking it was just like a scene in a B movie I might have made.

The door swung open, and a svelte middle-aged woman smiled wide when she saw who it was, quickly ushering us in from the cold.

"Ah, Marlene," she said, kissing her on both cheeks. "You've brought a friend," she said in English.

"A very good friend," Marlene said. She looked over and winked at me. "Anna May, this is Sigrid."

The woman, dressed in a silver-sequin dress and decked out in jewels, smiled, and said, "I'm very pleased to meet you, Anna May. You are even more beautiful in person. Please, come in and join the party."

Sigrid led us through the marble foyer and opened a set of double doors. Voices and laughter rose above the music of Louis Armstrong's "St. Louis Blues." I looked around the large high-ceilinged room hung with chandeliers that illuminated walls draped with gold satin. A shiny mahogany bar ran the length of one side of the room. A dozen gaming tables featured everything from roulette to cards to craps. In the back of the room, a curtain covered a stage. This was a high-end nightclub and casino filled with patrons, all of whom appeared to be women.

"Let's get something to drink," Marlene said, leading me toward the bar.

We passed several tables that were filled with women who sat smoking, drinking, and playing cards, stacks of chips lined up in front of them. "Aha," one woman exclaimed, while another laughed.

I stopped to watch for a moment at another table as a blonde woman pushed three tall stacks of chips forward, betting it all on the hand she held.

Another woman teased her in German.

Marlene turned to watch too. As the cards were dealt, the woman scooped them up one at a time. When the dealer turned over her cards, a large smile spread across the woman's face and she threw down her winning hand. The woman next to her grabbed her for a hug, and only let go after a kiss.

"Attagirl!" Marlene said, and everyone laughed. "Come on then," she said to me, leading me to the bar.

That night was the beginning of our intimate friendship. There was nothing Marlene Dietrich seemed afraid of, or embarrassed about. Life was to be lived and she was living it to the fullest. Young and free as I was, I allowed myself to live in the moment with her. She took me to bed as candidly as she had taken so many others. My previous experience notwithstanding, I was such a novice that I found her touch and the softness of her skin and breasts a complete revelation.

We became a bonanza for reporters and photographers, who seemed to be waiting wherever we went. They couldn't get enough of Marlene Dietrich and Anna May Wong, and the magazines caught fire with a photo taken of us by Alfred Eisenstaedt at the Pierre Ball in December with Leni Riefenstahl. I wore a sleeveless black cocktail dress with a long strand of pearls, while Marlene paired black trousers with a black, slinky one-shoulder top cinched with a black sash. She also wore a black floppy hat with her black pipe-like cigarette holder between her teeth, and looked like a ravishing pirate. Marlene was the perfect example of an independent woman that Berlin loved and embraced. She and I could be whoever we wanted to be, with whomever we wanted to be with.

And right then, Marlena Dietrich wanted to be with me.

WHEN OUR PHOTOS BEGAN to show up in movie magazines back home, Lulu wrote with the question: *How well do you know Marlene Dietrich?* Baba *and* ma ma *aren't happy with the photos of you two . . .*

My parents were alarmed by the growing rumors of a relationship that had reached all the way to Chinatown in Los Angeles. Immediately, I felt the same heaviness in my chest that returned whenever I was disobeying or disappointing my family. I realized I wasn't far enough away, after all. Marlene and I were lovers. But more than that, we were loving friends. What was accepted as friendship here in Berlin was viewed as something sordid and unnatural back home. All of our photos together just added to the speculation. What we did in private was no one's business. At least that's what I'd been telling myself, but we were movie stars, which only made the public want to know more.

I wrote back to Lulu, keeping it light and chatty, reminding her how apparently loose appearances were deceiving in Berlin.

You know how it is here in Berlin, everything is over the top, but it doesn't mean anything. Please tell ma ma *and* baba *there's nothing to worry about, it's just idle gossip and publicity for our upcoming movies.*

Inside, I was a nervous wreck.

THAT EVENING AT HER apartment, crowded with curios, books, and paintings, Marlene lounged on her chaise, propped up by an assortment of silk and velveteen pillows. She laughed when I expressed my concerns. "We are living in the twentieth century, *mein liebling*, not back in the Middle Ages."

"It's more than that," I said, irritated with her easy dismissal. "I've always been a disappointment in my father's eyes. He never wanted me to be an actress. It's a profession not highly regarded in China. These photos and insinuations just add to what he has always believed."

Marlene stood from the chaise. "And what is it he believes?" she asked in a serious, gentle tone.

"That acting is not an honorable profession."

She laughed, low and loud. "And what's more honorable, being a politician?"

I knew then it was something I couldn't explain to her. When Marlene saw me suddenly grow quiet, she crossed the room and hugged me.

"Ah, but you see, *mein liebster*, photos don't insinuate anything, they show each viewer their own truths," she said, matter of factly. "What people see is what they want to see. No need for you to explain it to them," she added, kissing me before she pulled away.

From a silver case on the credenza, she took out a cigarette and held it between her lips to light, then handed it to me.

I smiled and nodded, drew in the smoke, and remained silent. I only wished I could be as imperturbable as she was. Marlene would never condone anyone who didn't think the way she did. She had little patience for bourgeois values of the past, much less for the thousands of years of history that came from China.

DURING THE ENDLESS COLD and gray winter days in Berlin, I spent my time writing articles about Hollywood for European publications, and I found myself increasingly missing both my family and Los Angeles. As much as I was adored and feted in Europe as an "exotic beauty and a wonderful actress" in the movies I'd made, I was still Chinese, which meant I could never have a "happily ever after" finale with my leading man. I was also destined not to have love without dying at the end of the movie. After almost nine months away, I'd also begun to worry that Hollywood had forgotten who I was and had nightmares of returning and having to start all over again.

Fortunately, I had to return to London for the premiere of *Piccadilly*. After four months, I left Berlin in late December of 1928. Marlene and I parted as friends. She was already on to her next muse, and I couldn't help feeling a complex blend of jealousy, relief, and loneliness. It was a different kind of heartbreak, the dull ache of longing for a place already left behind. As exciting and intense as it was to be in Dietrich's inner circle, I was also thankful to be going back to work in London.

On the train to Calais, where I would cross the English Channel back to London, my emotions were a mix of sadness, fear, and determination to move on to the next phase of my career.

IT WAS A COLD day in January of 1929 when I checked into my lovely rooms at Claridge's Hotel in London and waited anxiously to see how *Piccadilly* would be received.

THE CIRCLE OF CHALK
London, England—1929

Even before its premiere, *Piccadilly* was being highly promoted around the world, and became one of the most talked about silent films produced in London. Posters and billboards emphasized my exotic beauty, and there was even a topless version of me on a huge billboard in Vienna that would have ended my career in America. And although I faced death once again at the end of *Piccadilly*, at least I was allowed to play out my character Shosho's sensuality on the screen, and I relished mixing the Chinese and Western fashions she wore. With my growing popularity and the publicity abroad, even Hollywood took notice, quickly rereleasing some of my old films. After so many years of pushing me aside, American studios woke up to the news I was a highly respected actress in Europe.

Piccadilly's opening was delayed until February. I'd already begun working on my stage debut in Basil Dean's *The Circle of Chalk*. The play was an adaptation of a thirteenth-century classic from the ancient Chinese theater called *A Hundred Pieces*, and I was proud to be asked to perform the role of Hai-Tang, the second wife of Lord Ma, and the mother of his son. But having to act and sing onstage in front of a live audience terrified me. Still, I knew this was an important step not only to stretch myself as an actress but to show the world that I was more than just an "exotic beauty."

When *Piccadilly* finally opened in London theaters, it was already being considered one of the best films of England's silent era. It was a huge personal success for me, and I was proud of my work. But when Shosho's onscreen kiss with the leading man was suddenly cut from the film, I was emotionally bereft. This demonstration that Britain wasn't as open minded and accepting as I had hoped provided even more reason to succeed in *The Circle of Chalk*. I'd been receiving letters from Hollywood friends telling me that the movie industry was at a turning point, and the play was opening at a crucial time when silent films were transitioning to talkies.

The Circle of Chalk opened in March of 1929. Stage acting was so different. While the larger and exaggerated moves and gestures were easily adapted from my silent film acting, projecting my lines out to the audience was another thing. For the first time, they would hear not only my speaking voice but my singing too. I was terrified. In the end I had every right to be.

The play's reviews were not only unkind, they were downright mean. "She all but squeaks on stage," wrote one critic.

Another wrote, *"To behold her is a pleasure, to hear her just a little strain."*

But the most frightening of all was the critic who forecast the end of my career, saying I'd never make the transition from silent movies to talkies. Back in Hollywood, old friends faced the same problem. Frances Marion, who'd just finished the screenplay for *Their Own Desire*, starring Norma Shearer, wrote of whispers that John Gilbert, and even Clara Bow, had voice problems that would likely end their careers.

I quickly went on the offensive and hired a voice coach and a tutor from Cambridge University to help me gain an upper-class English accent to appease the critics, and to also quiet my own fears about the transition to talking films. Despite all the criticism, *The Circle of Chalk* enjoyed a successful run. I was able to charm the reporters in England while making sure the American reporters I knew played up the success of the play, and not the initial problems concerning my voice.

I wrote to Lulu telling her my fears.

What will I do if my voice doesn't pass muster for talking movies? I'm taking voice lessons and can only hope for the best.

Lulu wrote back.

I know that your best will be more than enough.

LONDON
Talking Movies—1929–1930

Beginning in May of 1929, I collaborated on two more movies with Richard Eichberg. The first was the German-British coproduction of the silent movie *Pavement Butterfly,* filmed in Paris and the South of France, which garnered rave reviews in Europe when it was released. I'd become quite fluent in French and German by then, which brought me further into the embrace of both countries. After another five weeks in Berlin staying at the Hotel Esplanade on vacation and visiting friends, I was back in England in October, for a small part in *Elstree Calling* before collaborating on *The Road to Dishonor,* my last picture with Richard Eichberg. It was my most ambitious project yet, my first talkie shot in three different countries, with three different casts, in which I spoke in three different languages: German, French, and English.

This was a busy and magical time, but I was alarmed one day in London when I spoke into the microphone for the first time and heard my pale, scared voice reverberate in the earphone. Surrounded by Richard and the sound technicians, I still felt completely alone, as if I were walking into a dark room and my eyes hadn't adjusted yet. My voice required a similar period of adjustment in order to gain power and confidence with each word I spoke. This was a pivotal moment. If I couldn't cross the bridge from silent films to talking movies, my acting career would be over.

"That was brilliant!" Richard said as I lowered the microphone.

"Are you certain?" It was obvious that I would need more voice lessons to smooth out the hesitations I'd just heard.

"I'm more than certain, Anna May. You're a wonderful actress not only in silent films but in talking movies as well."

I could only hope Richard was right. I was still reeling from the harsh reviews by British critics of my voice and American accent in *The Circle of Chalk*. That public reproach had made me more determined to improve. I was scheduled to film the next phase of Richard's movie in Paris before returning to London to film the final phase. There was a two-week break in between, and I arrived in Paris early that spring and stayed in a beautiful hotel that overlooked the Tuileries Garden and the Place de la Concorde. Crossing the Seine to the Left Bank, I loved to walk the gravel paths of the Luxembourg Garden whenever possible, falling into a brief affair with a French writer who thought he would be the next Balzac. I ate in small, lovely cafés; worked hard on my French lessons; and attended the theater in the evenings with friends. I was enchanted with the French chanteuse Yvonne Printemps and returned to see her as often as possible at the Folies Bergère. I also loved going to the Théâtre Nègre to see Black Flowers and the Jubilee Singers, a choir out of Fisk University in Tennessee, whose spirituals, including "Swing Low, Sweet Chariot," were breathtaking.

More than anything, I wanted to fully immerse myself in the

language, determined to get the vocal tones right now that there was sound in movies. And it wasn't just mastering French and German; I also needed dialect coaching in English to appease the British audiences and get rid of my American twang. Happily, I was doing what I loved in the loveliest of cities. Completely free and in control of my life, I was determined to be the best actress I could be.

BACK IN LONDON IN April of 1930, I was given another opportunity to appear onstage as the Chinese girlfriend of a Chicago gangster in *On the Spot*. I was both nervous and eager for a second chance with a London audience. Unlike the adoring German and French fans, the British appreciation of my work was more reserved and the critics were often vicious. I had to get it right this time with *On the Spot*, or give up acting onstage in this city I'd become so comfortable in.

One evening I was working on my lines when there was a knock on my hotel door. I opened it, surprised to find Essie Goode Robeson waiting there.

"Essie, come in," I said, happy to see her.

We had talked only briefly since my return to London because both Paul and I were busy with new plays, and we hadn't found time to get together.

"I'm sorry to show up here without calling you first, Anna May, but I need your help." She looked worried.

"Don't be silly, you never need to call first. Please, please come in, Essie. Is everything all right?" I asked. "Is it Paul?" I was concerned, knowing that she'd devoted so much of her life to his work. It seemed such a pity, since Essie was so intelligent, not to mention both beautiful and talented. I loved everything about her.

She nodded, thanked me, and stepped in. I had her sit down and poured her a sherry.

She looked wearily at me. "Paul's a mess with *Othello*, can't seem to steady himself, can't seem to see through the darkness to the light. He keeps saying this play will be the end of his career, that he was a fool to take on something so big."

I felt the same anxieties about starring in *On the Spot*, but Paul was tackling Shakespeare in London, an authentic Black actor playing the legendary Black Moor king. I could understand his fear; the critics were prepared to tear him apart, but Paul had to know he was talented enough to fill an entire arena, never mind a London theater. All he had to do was speak for an audience to be hypnotized by his rich booming voice. When he sang, the world stopped, mesmerized.

"But what can I do?" I asked.

"Just talk some calm into him," Essie implored. "He'll listen to you."

I could tell by her fidgeting that something more was bothering her. "What else is wrong, Essie?"

She looked at me, and sighed. "He's started up with Peggy Ashcroft."

"Are you sure?" I asked, surprised. Paul and Essie seemed to have one of the most solid marriages I'd ever seen.

Essie nodded, drank down her sherry. Peggy Ashcroft, a well-known British actress, played Desdemona to his Othello. That she would openly have an affair with a Negro actor, even Paul Robeson, seemed awfully brazen on both their parts. My heart ached for my friend Essie.

"It can't be serious," I said.

"I've known that Paul has taken many lovers over the years," she said, raising her sherry glass, which I quickly filled. "I've always looked the other way, certain that he would come home to me. But I'm not so sure this time."

It was awful to see Essie in so much pain. I loved Paul, but as with so many famous men, he assumed he could have everything and lose nothing. Paul was making a grave mistake if he thought he wouldn't lose Essie.

"You're going to leave him?"

She looked up at me, smiled sadly. "Not until I make sure he's successful in *Othello*. No matter how I feel about him and this young girl, this play is important. Othello is a Black Moor who should be played by a Black actor. I know that Paul will be a superb Othello, but at the moment, he's afraid he'll fail, and I need your help to reassure him. You can tell him that he was meant to play the part, just as you found the strength to play Shosho in *Piccadilly*." She looked up at me with tears in her eyes. "He'll listen to you, Anna May."

I didn't know what to say at first. Marriage seemed more complicated in Europe. Many married couples masqueraded happiness while really seeking it with others. Although I obviously was in no position to judge anyone, occasionally, I encountered two people who seemed completely right for each other like, Sessue and Tsuru, and Paul and Essie. But I was the last one to know what true love was all about. I'd made so many of my own mistakes.

"Of course," I said. "I'll do it for you, Essie."

PAUL PACED BACK AND forth in his dressing room, his athletic frame arrayed in a long, flowing robe. He already looked the part. Flowers filled the large dressing room, sent to wish him good luck on his opening night. The theater was sold out, an eager audience anxious for the curtain to rise. Paul had been a big success in *Show Boat* onstage in 1928, but Shakespeare's Moor was on a different level and we all knew it. He had little trust in his producers, and the press was already hostile to a Negro man playing the romantic interest of a Caucasian woman onstage. What would result from this scandal? Had the producers known he was entangled in a relationship with Peggy Ashcroft, the show would be shut down. As it was, Paul was on the verge of running out of the theater himself.

"King Othello, you can't be nervous," I said, standing at the doorway of his dressing room. "The great Paul Robeson will not allow a measly role to get the best of him."

Paul laughed, deep and loud. Too loud. He was a mess.

"I'm afraid I am," he said, striding forward to give me a big hug. "But you look beautiful, Anna May."

I smiled. I had purposely dressed in my finest Chinese *cheongsam*, with a long, flowing, intricately embroidered coat in honor of his big evening. "I plan to be back here at every intermission to tell you what you're doing wrong," I teased.

Paul laughed. "I look forward to it," he said.

"Look," I said, pointing to the large mirror in his dressing room. "I've never seen anyone more perfect for the role of Othello than you. Just look at yourself."

Paul turned and gazed at his own reflection, just as I had done from the time I was a young girl dreaming of being an actress. By staring into a mirror, I transformed myself into the character I'd just seen at the movies and I wouldn't settle for less.

"Who do you see?" I asked.

He stood silent for the longest time, then straightened to his full height, looking deep into his own eyes.

"I see King Othello," he said at last.

ESSIE AND I SAT in the front row as Paul made history playing Othello. A thunderous applause erupted after the final scene, followed by ten standing ovations. His face shone with sweat under the lights as he took bow after bow, grasping Peggy Ashcroft's hand, while I reached for Essie's.

Whatever the critics might say about his performance, Essie's wish had come true. Paul was an international star. She looked after his career just as always, but I knew by her distant stare at Paul onstage that night, everything else in their lives had already changed.

LONDON
The Dream—1930

I'm standing under a willow tree with my New York friend, writer, and translator Grace Wilcox, telling her my Chinese name means "Willow Frost." I gesture up to the large willow tree looming over us like an umbrella just as it begins to rain. And suddenly, it isn't rain that's falling but our tears. We both stand crying beneath the willow tree. Neither of us says a word. I don't need words to know that something dreadful has happened back home. Even if I can't see a face, I feel the heavy ache of loss that runs through my body settling like a weight. I look up, now dry eyed, to see blotches of gray sky through the branches, and when the wind blows, leaves from the willow fall like tears.

I WOKE UP FRANTIC, anxious with fear. Even after the dream had faded to a memory, the alarm and distress stayed with me all morning. I worked myself into a frenzy, convinced that the dream foreshadowed some tragedy back home. So ingrained were the superstitions of my childhood, I believed right away that my Chinese name, Willow, kept recurring in the dream as a sign that someone in my family was in danger.

I immediately wired Lulu to see if everyone was all right at home, and then waited, knowing she couldn't respond for hours due to the time difference. Was this dream simply my own subconscious guilt emerging? It had been such a long time since I'd seen my parents, my brothers, and dear Mary who, at almost twenty, still hoped to follow my footsteps into acting. In my head, I conjured up tragic scenarios, though I knew without a doubt that Lulu would have contacted me right away if something bad had happened. Worried, I waited all day at the hotel, unable to concentrate on anything until Lulu wired back to say that everyone at home was healthy and fine.

That evening, I packed in preparation to leave London for Paris again, still unable to shake the feeling of desolation the dream had left with me.

EUROPE
Homeward Bound—1930

In Paris, where I was filming *Hai-Tang*, I was approached by the Viennese director Jakob Feldhammer and his associate, Otto Preminger. They hoped to book me in a performance at Vienna's Volksoper/Neues Wiener Schauspielhaus Theater, which was fighting for survival. So many Viennese were struggling financially that Jakob and Otto were finding it difficult to fill the grand playhouse. They wanted to bring in a short-run theatrical performance with me in the lead role, anticipating that a famous Hollywood movie star, who was also Chinese, would attract more of an audience. When an unexpected script arrived from William Cliffords, my old friend in Hollywood, written for me and titled *Tschun Tschi*, I agreed to a guest engagement in Vienna in the fall performing in German, if I could bring the play with me and have it translated. The plot was similar to *The Toll of the Sea*, only this time I was a Chinese temple dancer who saves an American millionaire and falls in love with him, only to have him leave her for a Caucasian movie actress. I couldn't help but laugh at the same old plotline, but it was a role I'd played many times before, and I had high hopes of making my character more complex while remaining entertaining for a Viennese audience.

Fully occupied though I was, the dream haunted me. I wired home twice a week just to make sure everyone remained well. Lulu continued to answer that everyone was fine, and for me not to worry. On the train from Paris to Vienna, I decided not to take on any new projects after my performances at the Volksoper/Neues Wiener

Schauspielhaus Theater. I needed to follow my instincts, finish my other commitments in Europe, and return home. I missed my family and felt a growing pull to return to the States.

I ARRIVED IN VIENNA in mid-July of 1930, warmly welcomed at dinners and cocktail parties in my honor. I couldn't leave my suite at the Hotel Hübner without being mobbed by Viennese fans. The show was now billed as an "opera" and the title was changed to *The Chinese Dancer*, in which I would be singing songs in Chinese. Through my American and European journalist contacts, I made sure newspapers in the US, China, and Japan were aware of my latest endeavor.

Throughout rehearsals I was nervous, my stomach roiling. I was smoking and drinking more than I was eating. I worried about having to sing so much. On opening night, the theater was sold out, and Jakob and Otto were ecstatic.

"Anna May, you will dazzle all of Vienna," Jakob said. He knew how anxious I was about my singing, and he did everything he could to put me at ease.

"I'm not so sure," I said.

"You only need to be yourself," Otto echoed. "The audience will love you."

But I was a wreck, pacing back and forth in my dressing room like a caged animal, remembering Paul's anxiety before his *Othello* debut. If only he or Essie could be here to calm my nerves. I also thought of Lulu, wishing that she had stayed with me. Having never sung in front of such a large audience, I felt shaky and terribly insecure about my voice. I looked into the mirror and wasn't sure who I saw.

IT TURNED OUT I was right to be concerned. The press had a heyday picking apart my performance. The critic for the daily paper was vicious, writing, "She had no voice at all; at least not a voice suitable for the giant hall . . . she often sings painfully out of tune—we would almost like to say she meows like a cat you place onstage."

I was devastated by the bad reviews and had to be talked out of ending my opera debut by Jakob and Otto. But I was ultimately saved by the adoring Viennese audiences. At each performance they sat quietly listening as my voice filled the theater. You could hear a pin drop as my song wafted through the air, my passable singing voice more heartfelt in the quiet. Thunderous applause followed each song and at the end of every show. The critics must have been dumbfounded by the audience's reaction. I stood onstage, embarrassed by the adulation, but happy, so happy to have proven those critics wrong. I could usually charm most reporters and reviewers simply with a quick retort, or by singing them a Chinese folk song, but the Viennese press had been out for blood.

After twenty-five performances, I was exhausted from the strain of having to sing each night. The opera was a success and I was expected to tour with it to Berlin, and then return to Paris and London. But I'd begun to worry more, not just about my family but about my movie career back in the United States. I was twenty-five and my film career in Europe, while artistically fulfilling, was languishing without the money and power of the big Hollywood movie studios and their publicity machines. Even with all the acclaim and prestige I had achieved in Europe, many of the art films I'd made would never be seen by American audiences.

Still, in almost three years traveling across Europe, I had gained more than I could have ever hoped for. I played leading roles in important films and theatrical productions, crossed over from silent films to sound, learned to speak German and French, made new and lasting friendships, and acquired a huge European following. During the last year, Hollywood also had finally taken notice, becoming more interested in me as my popularity grew in Europe. It was time to go back home to benefit from all my hard work.

What's more, I was homesick. I hadn't seen my family in so long and had never felt completely at ease after the dream. While I relished my independence in Europe, I missed the many intimacies of growing up in a large Chinese community. I missed the traditional celebrations we observed as a family, the dinners, the red packages of lucky money on Chinese New Year's, the Moon Festival cakes made of lard with an egg yolk in the middle. As kids, we divided each round cake into eight sections so everyone could get a piece of the moon. Being so far away for so long, I came to realize how much I missed them all, and how much of what my father had taught me about family and culture now rang true.

I was ready to go home.

From Vienna, I returned to Paris and completed *L'Amour Maître des Choses*. Still nervous, fearful that something bad might happen,

I was relieved to board the RMS *Majestic* sailing from Southampton back to New York in October of 1930.

EVEN BEFORE THE SHIP docked, I had a new job starring again in *On the Spot* on Broadway. The producer of the show had come over to see me while I was in London, and had the contract ready for me to sign as soon as I disembarked from the ship. It couldn't have worked out better.

I was thrilled to be back in New York, seeing Grace and Hazel, and especially Essie, who had escaped the lovebirds in London as soon as she knew *Othello* was a certified hit for Paul. I couldn't explain the immediate comfort I felt being back in the United States. Despite all the disappointments and rejections that shaded my career, I was back on American soil and it felt good to be home.

Only days after I arrived, I was delighted to see writer and photographer Carl Van Vechten, known as Carlo or Carlos to his friends—and his charming Russian Jewish wife, actress Fania Marinoff. Our friendship had begun instantly when we were introduced by colleagues and he offered to photograph me. After writing a double handful of books, Carl had turned to photography and was deeply involved in the Harlem Renaissance. Fania was a dancer and a Broadway actress. A smart, middle-aged couple well known to everyone, Carl and Fania welcomed me to their circle of New York friends. And much like my friends in Europe, they had wonderful dinners and held the same kind of liberal salons I had attended in London, Paris, and Berlin, joined by actors, artists, and writers. I met publisher Blanche Knopf; writers Sinclair Lewis, Langston Hughes, and Zora Neale Hurston; actor Fredric March; and the great Ethel Waters, who dropped by one evening. I loved how everyone I met was on equal footing; no racial barriers divided us as we dined and drank and enjoyed each others' company. It gave me hope that things might have changed in the States since I'd been away, even if I was living in a very small bubble.

At a dinner in early November, I met Eric Maschwitz, a writer and composer from London, where he was also a producer for the BBC. We hit it off immediately. He was quite the talent, smart and charming, tall and lean with dark hair and a mustache, and lovely long fingers that danced effortlessly across the piano keys.

By the end of the evening, he said, "I'm going to write a song for you."

"Really," I said. "I look forward to hearing it." He was married to actress Hermione Gingold, but rumor had it they were on shaky ground.

Eric leaned closer and whispered, "You'll be the very first."

I smiled as he helped me with my coat. He wasn't the only man to make promises to me that were never kept. It came with the territory. I knew that Eric would be returning to London soon, but there was always time for a new friend. What I'd learned from my liaison with Dietrich was that attraction could strike anytime, anywhere, and with anyone.

I WOULD NEED MY friends, new and old, when the dream that had haunted me for the past four months in Europe finally came true.

A telegram from Lulu arrived at the hotel on November 11, 1930.

MA MA IN TERRIBLE ACCIDENT. DIED AT HOSPITAL.
COME HOME AS SOON AS POSSIBLE.

NEW YORK
Decisions—1930

The shock of my mother's death intensified the following morning as I watched the gray light slowly creep into the hotel room. I lay in bed unable to move, only certain of one thing. I couldn't go home. Instead of returning to Los Angeles for the funeral, as my father, Lulu, and the rest of my family expected, I needed to stay in New York with the play. After a sleepless night and a pot of coffee, I sat anxiously by the phone while the hotel switchboard put my call through to the telephone I had installed at our family house after Lulu returned. When the operator rang me back with the connection, my hands were shaking so much I could hardly grasp the receiver. It was one of the most difficult decisions I'd ever made. I specifically asked to speak to Lulu instead of my father, hoping she would understand.

The line crackled with static. "Hello, hello, Anna?"

Just hearing Lulu's voice, so faint and faraway, made the tears fill my eyes. I could see her standing in the hallway, absentmindedly straightening whatever had been left on the hall table.

I cleared my throat. "Yes, Lulu, it's me."

"I'm glad you called," she said, relief and sadness in her voice. "When will you be home, I need to make arrangements. . . ."

"I can't come home just yet," I said, interrupting her.

"What?" Lulu asked, surprised. "Why?" I could see her stopping whatever she was doing, gripping the receiver tighter, wondering if she had heard me correctly.

My heart raced. "I can't leave now," I repeated. "I have an obligation to finish the play here. A lot of money has been put into the production."

A crackling sound filled the void between us. I heard faint voices in the background. Was it *baba*? The boys?

There was a quick intake of breath, followed by Lulu's firm voice. "Don't you have an obligation to *ma ma*? To your family? How will it look if you don't return for her funeral?" she asked.

Lulu kept her voice calm and steady, but it held an accusing tone. I saw her moving farther down the hall and away from the kitchen. I knew she wouldn't want to draw *baba*'s attention if he were nearby. She knew it would only lead to a heated long-distance argument. As always, Lulu continued to protect me after all these years.

"I can't right now . . . I'm sorry."

"They'll allow you to take a short break, especially when you tell them your mother was killed in a car accident," she said, authoritatively.

"It's not so simple," I said.

"It couldn't be simpler."

"It's a business."

The line went underwater silent.

"I can't," I said again, which sounded both weak and pathetic.

"You won't," she said.

I didn't say anything more, because she was right.

"Lulu, I . . ."

I heard a click. Lulu had ended our call.

THAT EVENING I SAT down and wrote:

> *My mother, Lee Gon Toy, died on November 11, 1930. She suffered*
> *a fractured skull and internal injuries when she was hit by a car*
> *while crossing the street in front of our home. She was forty-three*
> *years old. I'll never see her again.*
> *I can't breathe.*
> *I can't breathe.*

LULU HAD ARRANGED FOR a family grave site for burying *ma ma*
and reinterring the remains of our baby sister, Marietta. I should
have handled things differently. I should have told Lulu the truth,
but I wasn't certain she'd understand. I wasn't sure I did. I only knew
I would have drowned in my own despair at being back in Los Angeles.
Ma ma was already gone, and I needed to stay with the play. I needed
to work, to have something to hold on to, or else I'd surely fall into
another bout of darkness. My work was the balm I needed to soothe
the pain of her death. I had to believe *ma ma* would have understood.
My father and the rest of my family didn't.

Baba was furious with me for not returning, but as with all of
our fights, I expected it would blow over, reverting to the constant
irritation that had always festered between us. I hoped for the same
with my brothers, who were busy with their own lives and would

eventually forgive me, as would Mary, but not Lulu. Not Lulu. I was afraid we would never be close again.

Though I continued to write and call home, Lulu remained distant, quickly handing the phone to *baba* or Mary. I had no idea what to expect when I finally saw my family again. I arrived back in Los Angeles in June of 1931, seven months after my mother's death. The sky was blue, the day warm, and the mountains in the distance looked close enough to reach out and touch. It provided the perfect Hollywood movie backdrop.

Lulu was in the kitchen preparing dinner when I arrived home, the rest of the family remaining at the laundry. For a moment, my heart raced because she looked just like *ma ma* from behind, cutting meat and vegetables with a solid thud of the cleaver, the comforting smell of peanut oil heating in the wok, and the low hum of the radio filling the kitchen.

"Lulu, I'm home," I said, just loud enough not to startle her.

The cleaver paused midair. Lulu didn't turn around. Her voice was steady and distant when she said, "Dinner's almost ready," before bringing the cleaver down again, hard and final.

I had returned home prepared for heartbreak, but it stung to realize that I had lost so much more than just *ma ma*.

LOS ANGELES
Hollywood—1930–1931

On the Spot had finished a successful run on Broadway followed by regional performances scheduled across the United States. Throughout my stay in New York, I was nurtured by my friends, especially Carl and Fania, during those difficult months after my mother's death. Their friendship had been invaluable. Without their care, I would have fallen apart from the guilt I felt not returning home. But I hadn't been wrong; the moment I stepped onstage, I became another person whose mother hadn't just died.

Once back in Los Angeles, and quietly reunited with my family, I visited old friends in Chinatown, terribly happy to be back among them. My career was definitely on the upswing. Since I'd been away, actors and actresses were acquiring talent agents, men who had already been working within the industry and knew the business of landing roles and negotiating salaries for the clients they represented. I felt such relief of finally being looked after when I signed with Alan Hayes of the Berg-Allenberg Agency, who was in his mid-thirties, optimistic, and boyishly charming, a welcome change in a cutthroat business. Paramount Pictures had been following my European success and contacted Alan to offer me a new contract but wouldn't commit to giving me a lead role. I was disgruntled and ended a letter to Carlo and Fania with my irritation:

I'm frustrated to find Hollywood hasn't changed. It appears I'll never be given a leading lady role. I'm tired of playing the cruel, murderous villain or the helpless damsel in distress. As I said in an interview, the Chinese culture has thousands of years of history and philosophy behind it, so why would Chinese people only be portrayed as simple, or evil and coldhearted? It's all so maddening.

What Paramount did offer me was a strong role in *Daughter of the Dragon*, and a chance to work with Warner Oland and Sessue Hayakawa again. It was a big budget film, and I was thrilled to share the billing with my old friends. I was also paid a higher salary after returning from Europe, and I was delighted to know that my younger sister, Mary, would make her screen debut in the movie. At twenty-one, she had never wavered in her desire to be an actress. I was the one concerned about the wisdom of her decision, always hoping she might become enamored with another, more sympathetic profession.

The glamour and fascination of Hollywood was only a thin veneer covering up the lies and hypocrisy just underneath. I'd seen firsthand the difficulties and ugliness it held for a woman, especially a Chinese woman who had little choice in the roles she could play. I was much tougher and more headstrong than Mary, and I feared it was a quest that could bleed her dry and toss her aside. I didn't want any of it for Mary but knew she deserved a chance to prove me wrong.

Later, our roles were reversed when I found her sitting in front of the mirror in our old room.

"Who do you see?" I asked, standing in the doorway.

Mary turned to me with a big smile. "Anna, did you hear?"

"I did. Congratulations," I said. Her happiness was contagious, and I hurried over to give her a big hug.

"It's a start," she said. "And I'm happy it's in a film with you."

"It's a very good start! Do you remember, I carried a lantern in my first film, stuck in a crowd of a hundred other lantern carriers?"

"But you stood out, you've always stood out," Mary said. She looked at me in the mirror as I stood behind her. She was so fresh faced and innocent, so filled with joy.

"And you will too," I said, but couldn't help but add, "Mary, don't be discouraged if the roles are few and far between. Acting isn't an easy profession. There are so few roles for Chinese actresses."

Mary nodded. "I just want to be like you, even if it's in a small way," she said.

I smiled and wrapped my arms around her. "You've always been better than me, don't ever forget that."

ONLY WHEN WE BEGAN shooting did I realize how much the studio was putting into this film. Its publicity machine was running at full speed, touting *Daughter of the Dragon* as the first movie that starred two major Oriental stars who had returned to Hollywood. Sessue had come back from Japan, and I had been away in Europe for three years, a fact that was played up in the movie magazines, though they never addressed why we both had to decamp to other countries in order to be appreciated.

When I first returned from Europe, I was told by studio heads and others that I didn't look Chinese anymore, just because I'd been abroad for so long and enunciated my words clearly after being tutored in the King's English. It was all quite absurd, though I had to admit to changing on the inside. I couldn't have experienced other cultures and languages deeply without being transformed in some way. I simply told anyone who commented, "My face has changed because my mind has changed."

Paramount tried hard to bring back *Orientalism*, headlining new cosmetics and fashion. Elizabeth Arden and Helena Rubinstein announced new makeup that inspired the "real Chinese look" with dark eyeliner and bright red Chinese lipstick. The mystery of the Orient was all the rage again. And the fashion I'd been wearing since the beginning of my career, a mix of Chinese silk jackets and *cheongsams* paired with Western clothing, was now back in style, joined by bright and colorful silks and cottons from India, Arabia, and Turkey.

In the movie, I wore a big Peking Opera headdress and danced with my legs bare and on full display, my Eastern and Western sensibilities once again at odds. Fortunately, the movie was a success and I garnered good reviews. And I was more than relieved that my voice was readily accepted in my first Hollywood talkie. Sadly, however, some things hadn't changed during my time in Europe; interracial love affairs in American movies still could only end in death for both Sessue and me.

SHANGHAI EXPRESS
Los Angeles—1931–1933

By September of 1931, I was ready to return to Europe. Once again, Hollywood had been a disappointment, and I hadn't been offered any leading lady roles. While Paramount went all out publicizing *Daughter of the Dragon*, nothing else changed. In Hollywood, being Chinese still determined I was never to be a leading lady, destined never to live happily ever after. Running in a vicious circle, I was getting nowhere. But if the film studios and stage producers in Hollywood and New York wouldn't provide me with the roles I wanted to play, perhaps my connections in Europe could.

Much as I'd tried to avoid worrying about money, I fell into another dark mood as the Depression deepened. Despite all the instability in the world, movies were still being made as if nothing was wrong. They just weren't being made with me. Already despondent, when I heard about the invasion of Manchuria by the Japanese, I grew further depressed. I was living at the Beverly Wilshire Apartments, and even my family knew to stay away from me until this dark cloud passed.

Then, quite unexpectedly, the film I'd been waiting for landed right on my doorstep. The role of Hui Fei gave me third billing in a major new movie, *Shanghai Express*, directed by German director Josef von Sternberg. Starring my old friend Marlene Dietrich, along with Clive Brook and Warner Oland, it was set in China on a train traveling from Peking to Shanghai during the 1925 Civil War. Angered by the Japanese invasion, I had just written my first political piece, called "Manchuria" for the *Beverly Hills Script Magazine* run by my old childhood friend, Rob Wagner, so this film couldn't have been timelier for me. I was excited on all fronts; I would not only be working with Marlene and a first-rate producer and director, but my character, Hui Fei, although a prostitute again, didn't die at the end of the movie. On the contrary—her heroic actions saved the lives of the passengers. Hollywood was abuzz; *Shanghai Express* was already being touted as the next big film, which meant Paramount would set the publicity department running full tilt. I knew the role might provoke more anger from China, but it was worth the risk. For the first time in a long time, I had high hopes this movie would turn my career around.

"DARLING," MARLENE SAID, low and throaty, walking toward me.

It was our first day on the set, a reconstructed train station with three stationary train cars. Dressed in a silk blouse and slacks with a fur draped across her shoulders, she held her favorite black cigarette holder between her fingers. Dietrich looked every bit the big movie star she'd become after playing Lola Lola in *The Blue Angel*. We'd lost touch after I left Europe, though her success made her well known all over the world. I knew that Hollywood studios were vying for her. Now, Paramount had high hopes they had their major star to rival MGM's Greta Garbo.

"Marlene," I said, genuinely happy to see her again.

Dietrich was a hot spark, independent and confident. Standing next to her, you were dazzled by the heat, but it wouldn't last for long because she would soon be gone, and you would be left in the cold. Once you accepted the arrangement, Marlene was more than fun and generous.

She kissed me on both cheeks, and whispered seductively in my ear, "It's so good to see you again, darling." I'd forgotten how intoxicating her sweet narcissus perfume was.

"You too," I whispered, edging a step back.

We weren't in Berlin anymore where anything goes, and usually does, but back in Hollywood where everything could be used as malicious gossip to ruin a career. Columnists Louella Parsons and Hedda Hopper had spies everywhere. Berlin had none of these constraints. The first time I met Marlene at the El Dorado cabaret, she told me she loved whomever she was attracted to and lived life for pleasure. While she certainly changed the way I looked at love and attraction, it was a different world here in America.

"I'm so happy we have this movie together, *mein liebling*," she said, slipping back into German with a wink. "We're just a couple of hardworking, fun-loving prostitutes causing havoc on the *Shanghai Express*."

I laughed. "I know the role well, but will I live to fight another day?"

"Good God, are you still being killed off in every film?"

I was surprised Marlene remembered. She was a woman with many *friends*. I told her it was one of the reasons I left Hollywood for Berlin. "Until now," I said. "In this movie, I actually get to live."

Marlene lit a cigarette. "And live you will!" she said, and laughed. "Come then, darling, tell me all about what you've been up to." She hooked her arm through mine, guiding me to her dressing room.

FROM THE MOMENT I read the script, I knew my role as Hui Fei was special. As with all my roles, I thought a great deal about her and who she was. As I prepared for my scenes, I realized I'd have to play her as understated, slightly acerbic, and quietly intelligent against Dietrich's larger-than-life Shanghai Lil, who easily filled the screen with her beauty and presence. I also thought about Hui Fei's clothes, and what sort of hairstyle would match her smart, ironic character, though I knew von Sternberg didn't want me wearing anything that would outshine Dietrich. Still, I felt nothing but joy to finally have a character with such subtle depth. It was important that I made the most of it.

Between takes, Marlene and I had a good time together, taking cigarette breaks and gabbing away like schoolgirls. Our chats also gave me a chance to practice my German when we poked fun at others. It was evident from the first day on the set that Marlene would rather spend time with me than with any of the other actors. But unlike in Berlin, we had to restrain our affection to stay clear of the Hollywood gossip machines. The movie was generating a great deal of publicity not just in American magazines but also in European publications that gave me a fair share of coverage for my role as Hui Fei, as well as my friendship with Dietrich.

AS EXPECTED, *SHANGHAI EXPRESS* was a huge success when it opened in February of 1932. Parties and more parties! All Hollywood, Europe, and Asia were raving about the movie. The reviews were excellent, with many saying it was von Sternberg's best film. For a change, it felt good to be in a big Hollywood movie that was gaining worldwide attention and accolades.

The other shoe dropped when I wasn't looking. The following week, *baba* came home one evening while I was visiting, and threw down a copy of a Chinese newspaper on the kitchen table when he saw me. The Chinese embassy and the Nationalist government found lines in *Shanghai Express*'s script, as well as my role, offensive and insulting.

"Again!" he shouted before storming upstairs to his room.

"*Baba*," I called up to him, but his only response was slamming his bedroom door.

"What are they saying now?" I asked Lulu. She was the only one of us who could read Chinese with fluency.

"It's all here in black and white," she said, leaning over the table to read the newspaper. I couldn't tell if I saw a small smirk cross her lips. Did she think I was finally getting what I deserved for missing *ma ma*'s funeral?

She held the newspaper up. The headline of the *Pei-Yang Pictorial News* of Tianjin read "Paramount Uses Anna May Wong to Embarrass China Again."

As I expected, China found my portrayal of a prostitute degrading. A Shanghai tabloid called me "the female traitor to China." It also didn't sit well with Chiang Kai-shek's Nationalist government that the movie had two prostitutes in the leading roles while mocking the revolutionary forces. *Shanghai Express* was banned in China, and my father refused to talk to me for a few weeks after the movie came out.

But then, a surprising and completely unexpected honor came from China. Peking University, the most famous and prestigious university in China, had awarded me an honorary doctorate. I was recognized for honoring my ancestral country and having served the arts. It was a relief to know that a faction of Chinese liberal intellectuals appreciated me as an actress and an artist who took pride in her Chinese culture. This honor could prove to my father that I wasn't a complete disgrace. That he always believed so strongly in education, while I had never finished high school, had always grated on him. Even after all the turmoil the movie had caused, this was one of the best days of my life.

I brought the letter to my father at the laundry and watched him read it. He finally looked at me, and said, "Good, Anna, your *ma ma* would be very proud," before handing the letter back to me.

He said nothing more, but that evening, *baba* took the entire family out to dinner in Chinatown.

SHANGHAI EXPRESS WENT ON to play in theaters around the world. Dietrich's star soared, and she was anointed a member of Hollywood royalty just as Paramount had hoped. While she stayed on in Hollywood to reap the benefits, I had no choice but to leave again. All the accolades I received for my performance as Hui Fei seemed to dissipate like mist. My success didn't carry over to other movie roles of depth as I had hoped. I sat down and poured my frustrations into a letter to Carl and Fania, who had become my closest confidantes. Fania was an actress, so she was well aware of how cutthroat the business was, while Carl was a writer and photographer whose portraits of his famous friends covered the current art, literary, and movie professions. They both had intimate knowledge of how difficult a life in the arts could be.

July 7, 1933

Dear Carlo and Fania,

Thank you for the card and flowers you sent for the premiere of Shanghai Express. *I'm sorry I haven't written sooner, but there was so much going on at the time, I barely caught my breath. I consider the character of Hui Fei, courageous and complicated, my strongest yet and I'm so happy you felt the same. I wished and prayed she would be followed by other roles as noble as hers.*

Unfortunately, I'm afraid it hasn't happened and most likely won't. It appears that Hollywood studios still prefer to use yellowface actresses in lead roles when a Chinese character is needed, telling me I'm "too Chinese to play a Chinese character!" It doesn't even make sense. The old prejudices haven't gone away as I had hoped, and once again, I'm left with the taste of bitter fruit on my tongue. I know I'm being dramatic, but it's exhausting to keep running but get nowhere. America and Hollywood aren't ready for a Chinese leading lady, or mixed-race love, or happy endings for the likes of me. So I'm feeling bruised and battered and left at the curb, right where I began. Even if I have no choice but to swallow the bitterness, I refuse to step backwards. I'll be arriving in New York in a few weeks, staying at the Algonquin. I'll send the details shortly. Right now, I could use a few good friends to pull me out of this funk.

Get the cocktails ready, I'll be there at five! Love to you both.

Yours always,

Anna May

Carl wrote back immediately.

July 15, 1933

Dear Anna May,

We stand ready to do whatever is needed to make you smile again. We'll go to all your favorite haunts, see a couple of Broadway plays, something excruciatingly happy like Fantasia, or the H.M.S. Pinafore. I also think a set of new studio photos is called for, so come prepared for a day or two where I'll be in charge for a change. Between you and Fania, I have little chance of getting a word in edgewise. We'll take some beautiful photos of you for all the best magazines, which those cigar-chomping, studio idiots will choke on! Fania will send her own letter, but let me tell you she's so excited you're coming, and is already planning a cocktail party in your honor.

Be happy, dear Anna May. Don't forget that art, like love, comes in all different forms. When the words ran dry for me, I found photography. The camera became my new paramour, and *we've lived happily for the past years. Although some are blind to it, talent doesn't go away. It may change and grow into something completely surprising, but it's always there waiting to make its next grand entrance.*

See you soon.

Love, Carlo

WHEN I ARRIVED IN New York, depressed and dejected, Carl and Fania were the perfect remedy: a delicious dose of humor, intelligence, and talent. I was more than grateful for their support and generosity. And their parties were legendary. Actors, writers, and artists flocked to their apartment. In the midst of the Depression, they provided a haven where friends could forget that the banks had failed us and the world was going to ruin. Some of my happiest hours were spent sitting for studio photos by Carl. He always knew how to bring out the best in me, and his dramatic images were quickly becoming a large part of my portfolio.

"When you stopped writing," I reminded him, "that's when I began."

And I did.

My first article had been "The True Life Story of a Chinese Girl" for *Pictures* magazine back in 1926. I found when I was feeling bothered, putting my thoughts down on paper helped to ground me. I wasn't just going to sit idly by. After that I wrote the piece about the atrocious Japanese invasion of Manchuria, and another article titled "The Orient, Love, and Marriage" on interracial marriage for the French magazine *Revue Mondiale*. I was determined to be more than just a movie prop. The more I was held back, the more I propelled myself forward. I learned a long time ago I'd never get anywhere otherwise.

Carl laughed. "And now you can't stop taking photos," he reminded me.

After inspiring me to write, Carl had given me a Leica camera and taught me how to use it. Once he put that camera in my hands, I was hooked. I couldn't resist photographing the life around me.

"You know me so well. What's next?" I asked.

"*Chef de cuisine,*" he said.

I laughed. "Hosting dinner parties doesn't make me a chef," I said.

"Your culinary skills are steps beyond dinner party fare," Carl said. "I've had the pleasure of feasting on your Chinese dishes while I was in Los Angeles last year. Your delicacies were far beyond that of American chop suey!"

I shook my head. "You're being silly."

Carl put down his camera and turned back with a serious look on his face. "I wonder if you'd do one small favor for me."

"Of course, what is it?"

"Have dinner with Fania this evening."

He glanced away, which was always his tell. I knew he was seeing someone new. Carl never saw his affairs with other men having anything to do with his marriage to Fania. He loved her, and I loved them both. I would do anything to help either one of them, and I suppose that was what he was asking me to do.

"Of course," I said.

He looked at me again. "And don't be late," he added.

It was the one big issue between us, my penchant for being late. How a cocktail or two makes time fly. I was never one to turn down a drink, even if I had appointments or rehearsals the next day. But once on set, I was always professional, always knew my lines, and was always ready to shoot the scene.

"I'll have cocktails with Fania," I said. "Then we can be late for our dinner reservations together."

"Thank you," Carl said. "I mean it, Anna May, thank you."

I knew Carl wouldn't stop having his trysts, and I just didn't want Fania to get hurt.

FANIA AND I TALKED about the movie business all evening, not one word mentioned as to Carl's whereabouts. I had a feeling she knew all about his affairs and knew that I did too. What else was there to say about them? They loved each other and neither of them was about to leave the special relationship they'd built over the years. Whatever Carl did with others, he would always stay married to Fania. From my own heartbreaks and betrayals, I'd learned that life and love was always a balance of acceptance or letting go. Their marriage made perfect sense to me.

So, over cocktails with Fania, I aired my grievances.

"Paramount never had any intention of turning me into another Dietrich, as Alan had hoped. Despite the good reviews—one even said I'd stolen the show—it seems they were only using me because of all my popularity in Europe," I said, running my finger around the edge of my glass.

"They're a room full of bastards," Fania said. She sipped the last of her martini, and asked the waiter for an extra olive with our next round. "You were brilliant in *Shanghai Express*. As far as I'm concerned, Dietrich had to run to keep up with your performance. For Hollywood to treat you with such disrespect is unconscionable."

"Unless I stop being Chinese, I'll never get a leading role in Hollywood."

Fania laughed, and so did I.

"If it wasn't so ridiculous, I'd cry," she said. "Do they really have no idea how ghastly those yellowface actors and actresses look?"

"You don't need to tell me. Monsters!" I said.

Fania nodded. "Life is filled with monsters of all kinds."

I lit a cigarette and blew the smoke upwards. I always liked the bar at the Carlyle. The waiter returned with our second round of drinks. I smiled when he set down a plate with three olives on it before walking away.

"Ah, a man who listens for a change," Fania exclaimed, dropping two of them into her martini.

"Who would have thought," I said, absently, my smile disappearing.

"It'll get better," Fania said, sensing my change in tone.

"I'm just so tired of it all," I said.

Fania reached for my hand. "I can only imagine. It makes sense that you'd return here, and to Europe where you're appreciated," she said.

"And who's to know what I'll find there?" I asked. A glimmer of light was the thought of seeing Eric, the writer and composer I'd met the last time I was in New York.

"The success you deserve," she answered, sipping her martini.

"But first, you have to let us show you how much we appreciate you here. You're one of the loveliest and most talented friends we have, Anna. God knows life doesn't always play fair, but we know how talented you are."

I forced a smile. It was obvious Hollywood wouldn't give me the roles I wanted and deserved, so I'd have to look elsewhere.

"How many times can a person be fooled?" I asked. "Or be a fool?"

Fania sat quiet for a moment. Only then did I realize the question could be construed in so many different ways for each of us.

"I've lost count," she finally said.

INTERMISSION
Travels—1933–1935

Traveling back and forth became a way of life for me from 1933 to 1935. During the three years after making *Shanghai Express*, I was constantly boarding trains and ocean liners, traveling from Los Angeles to New York to Europe and back again. I will admit I was never one to travel cheaply. Sailing first class and staying at the best hotels not only provided me with comfort, but in the movie business, appearance meant everything.

I was excited to see new places and revisit old haunts. Still, I felt a shift in the air as I walked down the same streets I'd strolled through just a year or two before in Europe. The mood felt bleaker, tense with angst and change not only for me but for Europe at large. Friends in London and Paris told me that Berlin wasn't the same since the rise of Adolph Hitler, and I wouldn't be at ease anymore. Everyone there was looking over their shoulders, keeping a low profile. Regretfully, I skipped Berlin this trip.

Moving from London to Paris to London again, I had little time to think about Hollywood while I saw friends, attended parties, and went to the theater. Eric Maschwitz was now a very close friend. After our first inspired meeting in New York, he sailed back to London, and while aboard ship, had penned the lyrics to a song about me. During my visit, he performed "These Foolish Things" for me.

> A cigarette that bears a lipstick's traces
> An airline ticket to romantic places
> And still my heart has wings
> These foolish things remind me of you.

Whether it was truly about me, I'd never know, but he certainly knew the way to a girl's heart.

All the while, the papers and magazines kept me in the news through interviews by following my whereabouts and writing about my latest appearances and upcoming projects. I often escaped to the British Museum in London, or to the Louvre or the Musée des Arts Décoratifs in Paris, spending quiet hours lost in the art and history. It was the same sustenance I'd gained from books ever since I was young, slipping away from my family and Chinatown, and into other cultures and lifestyles.

I kept busy. I saw Josephine Baker again in France at the Casino de Paris and made three films in England. My European agent booked a tour of my new stage show called *Tuneful Songs and Intriguing Cos-*

tumes, which I brought to Dublin, Leeds, and Scotland, followed by shows during the winter of 1933 in Rome, Naples, Florence, and Venice. It incorporated a bit of everything I loved as a performer, singing and dancing, ending with the monologue I had written about the character Hui Fei, who continued to intrigue me long after I made *Shanghai Express*.

Hui Fei remained alive in my heart and mind. As an actress, it was my job to inhabit a character. I always believed Hui Fei's story was cut short, that she had far more to offer than what was shown in the movie. Her dialogue was spare and limited, and though I played her as scripted, I also wanted to give her the unspoken depth of an intelligent woman who was wise and weary of the world. I felt a close connection to her and thought a great deal about the choices she had to make in order to survive, and the fate that had been unfairly dealt to her.

It was during one of my many train rides across the country from Los Angeles to New York that I'd written a monologue about Hui Fei. I'd recited it in numerous languages in the countries where I performed my shows. When I was onstage, I ended each performance with her soliloquy, knowing that we shared so many of the same betrayals as we fought for love and life. It was obviously a reflection of my own bitterness, but I was fortunate enough to expel a fair share of it with each performance.

> . . . Long ago, I loved deeply with all my heart.
> He loved me.
> It was passionate love! We weren't going to leave
>   one another ever, ever

One night, he sold me for two bills, less.
Love is such a beautiful thing? Oh, how
    unthinking we are when we're in love.
But some day, by chance, I'll meet my lover!
How sweet vengeance is! How I am waiting
    for that moment!
I'll smile at him, I'll flirt with him. I'll be very sweet
When he's in my arms, I'll draw him close to me:
"How beautiful life is! What happiness, my love!"
Die, you wretch! Oh, yes, everyone gets his turn . . .

It was a self-indulgent performance piece, a way for me to air my own grievances through art. It was also a perfect expression of the weariness I felt toward Hollywood and all the weak-kneed lovers I'd left behind.

I WAS AWAY FROM Hollywood for over fifteen months, and it'd been almost three years since the filming of *Shanghai Express*. It was a lifetime away in the movie world. When I returned to Los Angeles in the summer of 1934, Alan had landed me a role in *Limehouse Blues*, a new Paramount Picture starring George Raft and Jean Parker. I was already well prepared, having explored the Limehouse District in London with Lulu while filming *Piccadilly*. It was another major Hollywood film, the money was good, and I was looking forward to being home in Los Angeles. I stayed at the Beverly Wilshire Apartments and was happily in the midst of my family again.

Halfway through the filming of *Limehouse Blues*, my father decided to return to China to his ancestral village of Chang On in Guangdong Province. Lulu, Mary, and my two younger brothers, Frank and Richard, were going with him. It shouldn't have been a surprise. While I was in Europe, Lulu had written that *baba* was considering a return to China now that he'd retired, but I never realized it would be so soon. I reread part of the letter Lulu had written to me.

Ma ma is gone, and baba *doesn't know what to do now that his laundry and the entire neighborhood have been torn down to make way for the construction of the new Union train station. Frank and Richard will continue their schooling in Taishan, and Mary wants to see if it's easier breaking into the movies there. I'll go to help them get settled, and who knows, maybe there'll be a movie role for me there too! At least we'll all get to see the homeland that* baba *has always talked about.*

So, while it wasn't a complete surprise, I was shaken that most of my family would depart less than two weeks after my return. For the first time, I was the one waving goodbye to them as they left Los Angeles's harbor in August of 1934 aboard the S.S. *President Wilson*, with a promise I would visit them the following year.

After I finished filming *Limehouse Blues*, I felt too restless to wait around for my next role. Instead, I returned to New York to see Carl and Fania before sailing once again to Europe. I also learned that I was voted the "world's best-dressed woman" in 1934 by the Mayfair Mannequin Society of New York and was delighted to know my fashion sense was appreciated. But again, my good news was followed by more bad. After *Limehouse Blues* was released, it didn't take long for the Chinese press to criticize the film for disgracing China with the portrayal of George Raft in yellowface while accusing me once again of being nothing more than a puppet.

If they really knew me, they'd know I was no one's puppet.

I RETURNED TO NEW YORK again in the winter of 1934 to an unexpected thrill. Carl's dear friends Gertrude Stein and Alice B. Toklas were also staying at the Algonquin. Carl had spoken of Gertrude often, how as a young man in Paris, he attended her literary salons, and she became his mentor and close friend. Carlo and Fania had always played such a role for me, hosting gatherings in their New York apartment and offering me sage advice when I needed it. With their kindness over the years, New York had become a second home to me.

Carl proudly told me that they were in New York from Paris on a lecture tour for a book, *The Autobiography of Alice B. Toklas*, written by Gertrude in the voice of Alice about their literary and art-filled life and friendships in Paris. It was a bestseller that made Gertrude widely known in the United States. Before then, she was already famous in Paris and Europe for her literary salons and her vast art collection. She had embraced young artists and writers, Picasso and Hemingway to name a few, and nurtured their talents. I could easily imagine how Carl, as a young writer, must have loved and revered her. He told me he recognized her brilliance from the first moment he met her, and there was no one I trusted more than Carl and Fania when it came to friendships. They had talked about Gertrude and Alice all through the years I'd known them, and I was eager to finally meet them.

My excitement turned to nervousness on the evening we were all to meet in the lobby of the Algonquin. I went down early and glimpsed Gertrude Stein already sitting in a high-back chair in the lobby. She wore a dark dress with a lovely light gray silk vest accented by a silver brooch, her hair cropped as short as a boy's, staring reflectively at her hands folded in her lap. I was hesitant to approach her. She looked every bit as intelligent and commanding as in the photos Carl had taken of her. Carl and Fania hadn't arrived yet, and all I could think of was how devastated I'd be if Gertrude Stein didn't like me, if she saw me as nothing more than a silly actress who knew nothing about art or writing. It wasn't like me to be so insecure about new acquaintances, but I imagined she inspired a certain amount of fear in everyone meeting her for the first time.

I was walking toward Gertrude when, just out of the corner of my eye, I saw Alice Toklas enter the room from the bar carrying a glass of red wine that she handed to Gertrude. Alice was just as Carl had described her, dark haired, thin, and birdlike, with a hooked nose and thick eyebrows, and like Gertrude, she wore a dark dress and dark stockings. They both appeared as if they lived in another time and place. I watched them for a moment, wishing I had poured myself a stiff drink before coming downstairs to meet them.

When I finally gathered the courage to approach them, Gertrude looked up at me and smiled. In a rich, velvety voice that startled me, she said, "Ah, Anna May, we've heard all about you from Carl."

I answered, "Carl loves you both so much."

That brought a smile to Alice's face. "Then we are already in good company."

"Yes," Gertrude said. "Friends. Where would we be without friends?"

"Quite lost," I said.

She looked at me with interest. "Yes," she said. "And now you are found."

It was the beginning of an evening I would never forget.

DURING THE FIRST FEW months of 1935, I toured with my stage show all over Europe, where I always felt accepted and respected, despite few Chinese living in most of the cities I visited. I was always happiest and most comfortable when I returned to London. It wasn't just the familiar language; I felt less lonely there. Fania came over to visit in the spring, and there was Paul Robeson, and of course, Eric. It seemed inevitable that our friendship would grow closer and more intimate. In May, London was abuzz and adorned in splendor for the Silver Jubilee celebrations for King George V. There were parties and dinners nightly. While I met the Prince of Wales at a reception, the highlight was sitting next to writer W. Somerset Maugham at a dinner at the Dorchester. He had a direct and piercing gaze with dark hair and a mustache, looking more like a businessman than a famous writer. I was thrilled to meet him, having read all his novels, and I was excited to tell him how one of his books in particular had influenced my own writing.

After being introduced and seated, he asked, "Has the Silver Jubilee brought you to London, Miss Wong?"

Suddenly, all the other hum of voices faded away. "No, it's a lovely addition, but I'm here for work and to see friends," I said.

He smiled. "Though I live very happily in France, I find myself constantly returning to London for work and friends too," he said.

His candor put me at ease. "I've read all your books and want to thank you," I said. "It's because of your novel *The Moon and Sixpence* that I was inspired to write an article a few years ago for the French magazine *Revue Mondiale* on interracial marriage."

His story was about Gauguin who, trapped in an unhappy and loveless marriage, defies conformity and sails to the South Seas where he finds the freedom and love of a native woman.

Maugham put down his wine glass, "An actress and a writer, how wonderful!"

"I agree to being an actress," I said. "Writing provides me with an outlet to express myself. I'm not sure my talent goes much further."

"And yet you're published. Tell me, what are your thoughts on interracial marriage?" Maugham asked, with real interest.

I sipped my wine and felt the heat rise to my face. "The article begins with my questioning Kipling's line 'East is East, and West is West, and never the twain shall meet.' I go on to explain I'm a perfect example of both East and West, and live my life a mix of each. All I wish for is the freedom to love, marry, and live a life with anyone I want. I believe that there's a bridge between East and West, and a mixed marriage can work if differences are accepted, and if a couple's lives are built around their marriage without the loss of one's identity."

"Well done!" Maugham said loudly, attracting the stares of the other guests at the table. "And have you crossed that bridge, Miss Wong?"

I laughed. "Not yet, I'm afraid I'm married to my career just now," I answered.

"Well, I'm intrigued. I'll look for a copy of your article," he said, raising his glass of wine. "Then we shall meet again for a lively discussion."

"I'd like that very much," I said, touching my glass against his.

Two more of my favorite new friends were Wellington Koo, the Chinese ambassador to England, and his wife. Through them, I was invited to a reception at the embassy, where I met the lead Peking Opera star, Mei Lanfang, and Hu Die, who was China's leading movie actress. Yet, even with such thrilling new friendships and a successful stage show that paid the bills, I felt a constant ache of loneliness, reminding me of how much I missed my home and my family, who were now both in Los Angeles and scattered throughout China.

Hollywood was also pulling me back to Los Angeles from Europe. In June, I returned to Los Angeles with another goal in mind. MGM was preparing to film Pearl S. Buck's Pulitzer Prize–winning novel, *The Good Earth*. Published in 1931, it was set to be the biggest ever film production about China. As soon as I'd read the book, I dreamed of playing the lead role of O-Lan. At thirty, I was the perfect age to play the Chinese farmer's long-suffering wife, and I had the necessary credentials and acting experience for the role. I was also a Chinese actress with a vast global fan base.

I returned to Los Angeles excited, not only to see my brothers James and Roger but also Frank and Mary, who had both returned from China. Most of all, I was filled with high hopes that a favorable depiction of China would finally star actual Chinese actors and actresses.

THE GOOD EARTH
Los Angeles—1935–1936

"Darling, there you are!"

Hollywood columnist Louella Parsons was waiting for me in a back booth of the Cellar restaurant when I arrived at the new Café Trocadero on Sunset Strip. While the Trocadero was a nightclub upstairs, the Cellar was cozy and clubby and away from the studios. Still wearing her sable fur coat and hat, she was already nursing a gin and tonic. I was early for a change, but she was earlier, always getting the upper hand.

"Louella, you're looking very fashionable." I stroked her fur coat as I kissed her on the cheek, then slid into the booth across from her.

Louella was the most influential woman in Hollywood. Her syndicated gossip column appeared in over four hundred newspapers, and she'd just begun a new radio show called *Hollywood Hotel*, interviewing actors and actresses about their latest films. She had millions of readers and commanded the power to make or break movie stars and moguls alike. Her motto put the fear into Hollywood: "You tell it to Louella first!"

I'd always maintained a good relationship with Louella and knew never to mention her nemesis, Hedda Hopper, when we were meeting. While Hedda, who had once wanted to be an actress, was known for her fashionable style and flamboyant hats, Louella was everyone's sharp-tongued, somewhat matronly mother.

"This old thing, a hand-me-down fur," Louella said, and laughed. "I see you are dressed as beautifully as ever."

The cashmere sweater and skirt I wore were actually rather casual. But now that I had arrived, she slipped off her fur coat.

"But we're not here to talk about fashion, are we?" Louella said.

"No, no we aren't."

I flagged down the waiter and ordered the same as Louella. I had to be careful and keep my wits about me when talking to her. The slightest slip could turn into Louella's next big headline.

"You've been away for a while?"

"I've been in New York and Europe pursuing other projects," I said.

"Such as?"

"A few movies in London, and touring my theater show throughout Europe," I answered, not missing a beat.

I had spent the evening before trying to prepare for any question she might shoot my way. When the waiter returned with my gin and tonic, Louella raised her glass.

"And now, here's to capturing the starring role in *The Good Earth*," Louella said, smiling. "It's about damn time!" she added.

I sipped my drink. "It hasn't happened yet."

"Oh, but it will. The newspapers have been pulling for you as the lead since last year. How do you like that? And you weren't even here." She stopped to sip her drink. "Now, tell me, I've heard you've done a few screen tests, true?"

I pulled out a cigarette. "True."

"And?"

I laughed and decided to say what was on my mind. "I don't plan on doing any more screen tests for the role," I said. "Everyone can see that I'm Chinese, and so is the main character of O-Lan. They know I can act. I've won accolades for playing Hui Fei in *Shanghai Express*, so I don't feel there's anything left to prove. Even Pearl Buck has tried to convince MGM to use Chinese actors and actresses."

As usual, Louella had also come prepared. "I hear there's been an issue with the Chinese Nationalist government concerning the logistics of hiring Chinese-American actors and actresses to work in China before returning to the States."

"There are always issues when making a big movie," I said. "This movie could help foster a positive relationship between China and the United States. Now it's up to MGM."

I lit a cigarette and tried to appear as if I was in control. In actuality, I was nervous about the screen tests I'd done. And I knew the Chinese Nationalist government wasn't a big fan of the roles I'd played. As *baba* always threatened, the past was returning to haunt me now. MGM had also given the casting decisions to Irving Thalberg's assistant, Albert Lewin, who appeared to have his own agenda from the very beginning. He'd set up screen tests with numerous Chinese actors and actresses, including my sister Mary. When I finished mine, he remained serious and grim, saying how beautiful I was but not much more. I walked away from both screen tests feeling nervous and uncomfortable, uncertain of what this dark-eyed, silent man had in mind.

"They'd be fools not to give you the role," Louella said.

I smiled, and the waiter returned to take our order. All I could do once again was anxiously wait for the studio to decide in what direction my career would go.

THE MORNING ALAN CALLED to tell me Paul Muni was cast in the lead role of the farmer, Wang Lung in *The Good Earth*, I felt as if I'd been stabbed in the heart. I slammed down the phone, breathless and doubled over, searching for air. My dreams of playing O-Lan had vanished. Once a Caucasian actor was tapped to play the leading man, there was no chance they'd give a Chinese actress the role of the leading lady. The Hays Code and anti-miscegenation laws prevented me from playing the wife of a Caucasian actor, even if he was impersonating a Chinese. It was infuriating to know that MGM had taken the easy way out by using actors in yellowface. Rumors were also floating around that Albert Lewin never had any intention of casting Chinese actors and actresses for any of the major roles. I wanted to strangle him. I picked up one of the cloisonné vases I'd collected and threw it against the wall with all my strength. When I caught my breath, I tiptoed around the shards on the floor, grabbed a bottle of vodka, and crawled into bed. A silly rhyme rattled around and around in my head.

One drink, two drinks, three drinks, four.
There's nothing left to worry about anymore.

BY THE TIME I AWOKE, the sun had set and the vodka bottle was almost empty. The room was hot and stuffy as I slowly focused. It didn't take long for my fury toward Lewin and MGM to reignite. "Bastards!" I muttered, tasting only sourness.

Beyond my bedroom door came the incessant ringing of the doorbell, followed by an endless knocking that coincided with the pounding of my head. I was relieved when the noise stopped, hoping whoever it was had left. The next thing I knew, Mary had found my spare key and announced she was standing outside my locked bedroom with my brother Frank. Try as she might, I had no intention of opening the door.

"Anna, please let us in," Mary said, now knocking frantically.

"I'm fine," I said, quietly. "Just go."

"Anna, open the door!" Frank demanded.

I drained what was left in the vodka bottle.

"Go away, go away! Just go away!" I began to scream, until my voice became a hoarse whisper. And still, I croaked, "I don't want you here, I don't need you here!"

By the time I stopped ranting, it was quiet.

THE PHONE KEPT RINGING for the next handful of days, but I didn't move to answer it. I fluctuated between tears, anger, and complete exhaustion. I lost track of time and completely depleted my stash of vodka. I just wanted to be left alone.

O-Lan would have been my golden ring. She was the only character since Hui Fei that portrayed a strong Chinese woman with courage and depth, a role that would have given me greater reach as an actress. Why couldn't they have given me the chance? O-Lan was the once-in-a-lifetime role that would have changed the direction of my career. Now, she was lost to me. I needed O-Lan to die, if only in my own heart and mind. And I needed time to grieve her death. It was the only way I could find the strength to get up and push forward yet again.

FOUR DAYS LATER, when I was finally sober enough to face the world, I found several notes from Mary left on the dining room table pleading for me to call her. I knew I had frightened her badly when I refused to open the bedroom door, screaming for her to just leave me alone. I was so pathetic it was embarrassing. If Lulu had been home from China, she would have found her way into the bedroom and given me a good scolding for acting like a spoiled child.

I called Mary and apologized for scaring her. "I'm so sorry . . ." I said as soon as she picked up. "I'm just terribly sorry."

Then I bathed and drank a pot of coffee.

A week later, I began to feel steadier. Alan told me what had been going on behind the scenes at MGM all along, and all I could do was fume. I sat down to write to Carl and Fania, who knew how much I had coveted the role of O-Lan. I'd received a telegram from them days ago, slipped under the door, but hadn't bothered to read it. They must have heard that the part went to Luise Rainer. What could they say? The role of O-Lan should have gone to you. But it didn't. It was something I would have to accept, but in all honesty, I wasn't quite ready yet.

December 15, 1935
Dear Carlo and Fania,

My hopes of playing O-Lan in The Good Earth *is dead in the water. And I just threw the role of Lotus, the mistress and* most horrid character in the cast, back in Irving Thalberg's face. According to my agent, that bastard Lewin, who was in charge of casting, didn't think genuine Chinese actors and actresses fit his conception of what Chinese should look like. It's absolutely insane! After my second screen test, he apparently said I was too beautiful for the role, which made me want to wring his neck. He ended up suggesting to MGM studio heads that Chinese actors and actresses should be primarily used as "background," while all the Caucasian actors and actresses should play the main roles in yellowface. And they listened! They even refused to hire James Wong Howe, who is such a brilliant cinematographer, to work on the film. But some "atmosphere" will at least be provided by my sister Mary who, I'm happy to write, did get the part of "Little Bride" after struggling to get any roles for the past year, as did Keye Luke, and a handful of other "real" Chinese. Instead, there will be what I call "MGM Chinese," with Paul Muni as Wang Lung in the lead role, and Luise Rainer, a German actress, cast as O-Lan. Will she be a Chinese with a German accent? Why not? At least I hear she can act.

What upsets me most is the lost opportunity of bringing American and European audiences closer to the struggles of China, and to understanding the Chinese culture! Was it too much to ask? Now, underneath all that makeup are simply more imposters.

I spent several days unable to get out of bed. I'm not proud of myself, but I had to shake off the darkness my own way. What irony my life has become. Except for Mary, Frank, and Roger, the rest of my family are working and living in China. Will I always feel like this, neither Chinese nor American enough to belong in either world? I might as well be a ghost slowly fading away.

Thank you for your concern and your unfailing friendship.

Love to you both.

Eternally yours, Anna May

Again, Carl wrote back right away.

December 22, 1935
Dear Anna May,

Come to New York. Fania and I would love your company. You can't go on like this and a change of scenery will do you good. Let me thank you in person for taking such good care of Fania when she visited you in London. If you hadn't secured her a room at Claridges's after so many sleepless nights at her hotel under construction, she would have gone mad. Not to mention taking her on trips to Brighton and Eton to lift her spirits after her rift with Robeson. Those two would disagree about the weather! In return, I'll take you to the new Frick museum. The stately mansion is just the right size to hold the "old boys": Bellini, Goya, Rembrandt, Turner, Velázquez, and Vermeer. I promise we'll be done by cocktail hour. Please, consider coming. It's time to look forward to the next project. You are one of the most gifted people I know, and I don't say this lightly. I hate the movie business, I hate all the vampires who run the studios and suck the life out of creative people, leaving them feeling depleted and worthless. It isn't right. You can use this experience, Anna May, to become stronger, or you can allow it to break you. You've never run from a fight, don't run now.

Dear Carlo, I thought to myself, *I don't know what I would do without you and Fania.* I read his letter again and again and then stepped out onto the balcony and into the warm sunlight for the first time in a week.

ALREADY SLATED TO BE a huge success, *The Good Earth* had transfixed the town. I tried my best to ignore all the Hollywood magazines that wrote incessantly about the making of the movie. Rejected by MGM, I needed to get my life back on track and began to think about traveling again. I'd devoted the past three years to racing back and forth to Europe. But this setback made me realize how much I missed my family, who'd spent almost two years living in China. *Baba* was still in his ancestral village of Chang On with my youngest brother, Richard. James was now teaching in Shanghai, and Lulu was working in Hong Kong. Perhaps it was time I followed their lead and pursued a new direction. It made sense, as I approached my thirty-first birthday, that I should finally fulfill a lifelong dream of going to China. I couldn't think of a better time to join them for a reunion. My brothers Roger and Frank, who remained in Los Angeles, could look after Mary while she worked on *The Good Earth.*

It was just the change I needed. My excitement grew as the possibilities of new projects came to mind. I'd always been enamored of the Peking Opera, and my admiration had only intensified after meeting its most famous actor, Mei Lanfang, in London last year. I wanted to study with him and to learn more about the old Chinese plays so that I might tour with them back here, or even start my own theater company over there. I felt invigorated by all the possibilities, along with the prospect of discovering more about my culture, and finally seeing China for the first time.

I quickly wrote back to Carl and Fania so they wouldn't worry.

January 7, 1936

Dear Carlo and Fania,

Thank you for your kind letter and the beautiful flowers for my birthday. After so many weeks of feeling sorry for myself, I have bounced back from losing the role of O-Lan. I hope you both know how much your support has meant to me over the years. Taking Carlo's words to heart, I've gathered my strength, and I intend to finally visit the motherland. In preparation for a trip to China, I'm reading Lin Yutang's famous book, My Country and My People, *an important work on Chinese customs and beliefs, and I've just this morning signed a contract to write several articles for the* New York Herald Tribune. *Best of all, I've arranged with the Hearst corporation to have my friend, H. S. "Newsreel" Wong, who is already in China, travel with me to chronicle the trip. I also have this idea of making my own home movie of the visit. I want to use my personal journey as a way to show American audiences what the real China and Chinese people are like.* The Good Earth *will be nothing compared to my China story! But beyond everything, I miss my family. I haven't seen my father, brothers, and Lulu in two years. I need all of this right now, to be with my family and to visit the land of my ancestors. Tell me I'm not crazy for wanting to do this. Love to you both.*

Yours always,

Anna May

It was Fania who wrote a quick note back this time.

January 14, 1936
Dearest Anna,

    Carl and I think it's wonderful that you're going to China.
What better way to forget the ugliness and unfairness of life in
Hollywood than to leave it behind! You'll be able to see your family,
as well as discover an unknown part of yourself by seeing your
ancestral homeland. I envy you, as I know what it's like to be born
of a rich culture that flows through your blood, yet remains so far
away. When I first arrived in New York, I missed the trees of my
Russian homeland and found myself walking through Central Park
each day with tears in my eyes.

    Go, Anna May. We wish you safe travels and await your
letters telling us all about your new discoveries. We're always
here for you, pulling for you, knowing that the time will come
when Hollywood looks back to see all the terrible mistakes it's
made.

    And, before I forget, Carlo has your photos taken outside the
Algonquin during your last visit ready to send out. He'll get them
to you before you leave.

    Love to you,
    Fania

MY DECISION TO GO to China lifted me out of my depression.
After I confirmed all my travel plans and blazed through a string of
farewell parties with my nearest and dearest friends, I packed my box

movie camera, along with the Leica camera Carl had given me, and was more than ready to escape Hollywood.

I left Los Angeles for San Francisco, sailing from there on January 26, 1936, aboard the SS *President Hoover* to Shanghai, with stops in Honolulu and Yokohama. Being at sea was just the tonic that I needed. The first week aboard ship, I began filming my home movie, and I slept off all those farewell parties while we sailed to Hawaii. In Honolulu, I swam in the Pacific Ocean at Waikiki Beach, as beautiful and perfect as the snows of the Swiss Alps.

"Honolulu! I'm beyond happy here," I wrote to Carl and Fania. "The clean, white sands of Waikiki Beach beckon."

For the short time that we were docked there, I saw as much of the island as I could and swam in the ocean, the water so warm and caressing, I wanted to stay forever. Each day I returned to the ship exhausted with my hair dripping, and I slept better those two nights than I had in years.

When we left port in Yokohama, I resumed filming my home movie on the ship. I expected to capture my own excitement at glimpsing the first dark shapes of China's landmass when we finally approached the coast on February 16, 1936. Instead, the closer we came, the more nervous I felt about what lay ahead for me. I knew I wouldn't be welcomed by everyone. Many Chinese magazines were questioning whether I should be welcomed at all after shaming and humiliating China with the movie roles I'd chosen to play. Worse, I'd also broken a cardinal rule of the motherland: at thirty-one, I was unmarried with no children.

Though I was no longer a wide-eyed, young optimist, I knew that

I was never going to be Chinese enough for the Chinese in China; nevertheless, I was determined to find out where I did fit in.

IOWA
1960

The second notebook comes to an end. I close my eyes and feel weightless again, remembering how good it felt to be swimming at Waikiki Beach, so light and insignificant in the vast ocean, as if all time had stopped. But the sudden screech of metal against the track makes me bolt right up, reminding me there's no ocean remotely in sight. I'm moving through the middle of America. When I look out the train window, all I see are flat fields of corn as we make our way across Iowa. It couldn't be more different from Hawaii, or the busy and vibrant cities I experienced while traveling in China. I put away my notebook as my journey to the motherland is about to begin, filled with so many bright and dark memories.

FAMISHED AND FATIGUED FROM sitting, I stand and stretch. My body could use some exercise as well as a change of scenery. Hunger pushes me to leave my cabin for the dining car. In the corridor I run into Joseph.

"Can I get you anything, Miz Wong?" he says.

I smile. "I'll be eating in the dining car this evening, Joseph," I answer. "About time I get some exercise."

Yesterday, I'd taken both my lunch and dinner in my cabin. Every time Joseph delivered my meals, there was a rose on the tray. He likes to linger a few minutes and talk about *Shanghai Express* with me.

"What do you think happened to Miz Hui Fei?" he asked. He removed the cover over my chicken and dumplings from my dinner yesterday.

"I think she was a survivor who definitely landed on her feet," I answered, thinking how lovely it was to have someone who cared about her so much.

Joseph smiled widely. "That's good, that's real good," he said, "because I'd like to see her have a happy ending. She suffered enough."

I wanted to hug this man. "Yes," I said. "I think she suffered enough too." I couldn't go so far as to say she had a happy ending, but like Joseph, I wanted to hope so.

He's a charming man and I'm fortunate to have him looking after me.

"Well, I'll recommend the roast beef then," he says now. "Need anything else, you just let me know."

"Thank you, Joseph," I say, grateful for his kindness and his company.

I MOVE THROUGH TWO train cars before I reach the dining carriage, which is already abuzz with people. Fortunately, I'm able to secure a small table to the side, where I proceed to order the evening's special, roast beef with potatoes and carrots. There's a family sitting across the aisle from me, mother, father, and a daughter who appears around four or five, who stares at me wide eyed.

"Mama, look!" she says, pointing in my direction.

Her mother glances over. "Baby, don't stare," she tells her daughter, and quickly looks away.

In that moment, I'm struck by the realization that the little girl has never seen a Chinese person before. I wonder if she views me the way I saw my first yellowface? Scared and alarmed. I want to tell her there's nothing to be afraid of, but she seems to be watching me more out of curiosity and fascination than fear. I look up and smile, wink at her, and the little girl smiles back.

I've learned a long time ago to face things head-on.

Sipping a glass of red wine, I glance at a young couple a few tables down from me, lost in each other; an older man even farther down the car eating alone; and two middle-aged women, perhaps sisters, dining across from him. But it's the clink of the silverware against plates, the soft murmur of voices, and the rattling of the dessert cart just behind me that bring me an unexpected comfort as we speed through Iowa toward Chicago.

I'm here and I'm happy.

PART THREE

Success is not a jewel that you can purchase and keep for your entire life. On the contrary, the brightest star can fall down at any time for short-lived reasons and can miserably fade away into the dust.

—Anna May Wong

MOTHERLAND
1936–1937

ARRIVAL
Shanghai, China—February 1936

When the SS *President Hoover* finally docked in Shanghai on February 16, I was apprehensive stepping off the ship after receiving a wire from my brother James. Rumors had circulated that many of the Chinese film critics and members of the Nationalist government weren't happy about my impending visit. They viewed me as an opportunist, an actress who had only brought *shame* to the motherland. That word had been a thorn in my side since I was young. Certainly, I would have never brought *shame* to the homeland if I were a man.

For days prior to my arrival, I'd been nervous about my reception. Now I was careful to dress respectfully in a conservative dark dress, fur coat, and black wool hat. Steady goes it, I told myself as I left my stateroom, eyes downcast. My heart pounded as I reached the top of the gangplank, preparing myself for the worst.

A hum in the icy air grew steadily louder before it erupted into cheering voices. Surprised, I saw a sea of faces below. At the very bottom of the gangplank stood Lulu, James, Ambassador Wellington Koo and Madame Koo, along with actor Mei Lanfang. Beyond them appeared to be a thousand exuberant fans waiting to greet me. It was astounding, only made better by having newspaperman H. S. "Newsreel" Wong there to record my arrival for the Hearst newspapers back home. I smiled and waved, overjoyed to see the turnout.

Cameras flashed in bright bursts. Voices yelled out to me. It was like walking down the red carpet in Hollywood. Above the clamor, I heard a slew of reporters' questions as I was being ushered through the crowd by my family and friends.

"Miss Wong, what brings you to China?"

"I've come to see my family, and learn about my motherland," I answered. "I want to study the language, and absorb the rich culture that has made this such a great nation."

"Do you have anything to say to those who think you've disgraced our country?"

I paused, searching the inquisitive crowd of reporters for which one had asked the question.

"I've had no choice but to take the roles I was offered in Hollywood. If I hadn't, they would have been played by Caucasian actresses in yellowface, and I would have never been able to show Americans what a *real* Chinese looked like."

"Do you think that you've portrayed Chinese women in a favorable way?"

I looked out at the crowd of reporters and found the correspondent easily this time, a slight, older man who wore an overcoat that looked too big for him.

"I believe that any portrayal of a Chinese woman, played by a *real* Chinese actress, is an important start," I answered. "We shouldn't remain invisible in the movies, or be represented by ugly caricatures in yellowface. There have been so few roles for Oriental actors and actresses. If I hadn't accepted the roles that were offered to me, true Chinese representation would have remained relegated to the background in most movies. That said, I've made very few movies in the past three years, having spent my time doing theater in Europe. And now, let me just say that I'm so happy to be here," I seamlessly changed the subject, "back to the motherland, and into the arms of my family once again."

"How long will you be staying in China?"

"For as long as I can," I said, waving to the crowd.

My brother James took hold of my arm and led me away.

SHANGHAI WAS THE LARGE, cosmopolitan city I'd read about, filled with grand hotels, bustling restaurants, cinemas, and department stores. Its fashion magazines featured the latest styles from around the world, and much like Berlin and Paris, it pulsed and partied into the early hours of the morning. I fell into its *joie de vivre* with complete ease, staying at the Park Hotel, with its high ceilings and chandeliers, polished marble floors that led to a grand staircase, and bellhops dressed in smart gray uniforms. My room overlooked the Bund, the waterfront esplanade that ran along the western bank of the *Huangpu* River, and though it was noisier than a room in the back, I relished its view of the Mother River of Shanghai.

On my first day, I was excited to see Shanghai. Outside the hotel reporters were waiting, snapping photos, and asking questions, but I simply smiled and waved, strolling down the Bund wearing a traditional *qipao*, the high-necked, close-fitting dress with a slit partway up the side of the skirt, also known as a *cheongsam* in Cantonese.

With Carl's Leica camera, I snapped photos of the grand buildings that lined the Bund, known for their various architectural styles, Gothic, baroque, Renaissance, and neoclassical. They housed the Hong Kong and Shanghai Banking Corporation, the Custom House with its Big Ben clock tower, the Sassoon House, the Cathay Hotel, and the famous Jardine Matheson & Co. trading house. Well-dressed men and women, both Chinese and foreign, sauntered down the esplanade or sat at the many cafés lining the river, deep in conversation. I had a coffee at an outdoor bistro, and watched the sampans and boats on the river before walking to the Garden Bridge, which crossed the Suzhou Creek. By the time I returned to the hotel, I'd walked the mile-length of the Bund and back, and bought postcards to write Mary, and Carl and Fania, before I took a short rest. That evening, I would be feted by Ambassador Wellington Koo and his wife, the first of many receptions and dinner invitations I'd received.

February 17, 1936
Dear Mary,

I'm in beautiful Shanghai with Lulu and James. I'll see baba in the weeks ahead. I think of you often, hoping that your work on The Good Earth *has been a wonderful experience. No matter how badly I was treated, I'm so happy and proud that you were cast in the movie. I know it will lead to bigger roles for you, so don't give up. I'll write again soon.*

Love,
Anna May

I wrote two more postcards in quick succession.

February 17, 1936
Dear Carlo and Fania,

A note to tell you I've arrived in Shanghai, but I'm unable to describe the happiness I feel standing on Chinese soil. My family and fans were waiting for me when the ship docked, instead of my dreaded critics. I'll write more soon, but wanted to let you know that I made the right decision. China is where I need to be at this moment. Thank you for always listening. Love to both of you.

> *Yours,*
> *Anna May*

February 17, 1936
Dear Carlo and Fania,

Another postcard before I've even mailed the first one! I was walking down the Bund this morning, dressed in a long qipao, thinking I might pass as a local, however, the stares I received prove that I'm anything but! I'm a bit dazzled by everything here. Will I always stand out like an alien?? Carl, I can't stop taking photos with the Leica. You would both love it here and should consider visiting.

> *Love,*
> *Anna May*

THAT EVENING, AMBASSADOR WELLINGTON KOO hosted a dinner in my honor. The fifteen-course banquet that kept us at the table for almost three hours was like nothing I'd ever experienced. Not only was the food delicate and exquisite, but the execution was almost like a dance. Sublimely timed, each dish was perfectly presented. I was mesmerized by the pageantry, by the beautiful red, blue, and gold cloisonné dishes, the delicately carved ivory chopsticks, the crystal wine glasses. The menu included a delicious cold plate of abalone and octopus, chicken and pork blood soup, steamed hairy crab, smoked chicken, Peking duck, and braised pork and mustard greens. It ended with a dessert that brought laughter—a wedge of apple pie with vanilla ice cream in honor of his American guests. Ambassador Koo had gone out of his way to show me friendship and respect, for which I was greatly touched and honored.

The following day I called on Bernadine Fritz, whom I met two years earlier in London. The Gertrude Stein of Shanghai, Bernadine held salons for foreign writers, artists, actors, and musicians, and welcomed me to join them any time. No matter the country, I sought out such sanctuaries to feel that I belonged somewhere even briefly. Bernadine was lovely and helpful in every way, and I was happy to have found a friend so far away from home.

That evening, I met writer Lin Yutang and his wife at another reception. He was well known in China for his satirical essays, and I was a great admirer of his successful book *My Country and My People*, the English-language account of Chinese culture and people that I'd read before I came. He appeared exactly as I envisioned him, a thin man with a high forehead, wire-rimmed spectacles, and the deep gaze of an intellectual. When we were introduced, he warmly grasped my hand in both of his.

"Ah, Anna May Wong, I'm delighted to meet you," he said, bowing slightly.

Blushing, I bowed in return. I felt such admiration for Lin Yutang, who was witty, intelligent, and courageous. He used his popular humor magazines to poke fun at the Nationalist government without ever crossing the line. I couldn't imagine what he must think about me and my movies after all the negative articles written in Chinese newspapers and magazines over the years.

"It's such an honor to meet you," I said. "I can't tell you how much I loved *My Country and My People*."

"And I am a big fan of your work, beginning with *The Toll of the Sea*," he said, catching me off guard.

"You've seen the movie?"

"Yes, of course," he said, and peered at me with smiling eyes. "You were so young, just a teenager, and yet you conveyed her struggles with such heartbreaking accuracy. I knew you would become a big star."

I was so surprised I was at a loss for words.

"Thank you," I finally said. "It feels like a lifetime ago."

"When a work is good, it lasts," he said. "Once a work is in the world, it remains."

"Oh dear, does that mean the bad work remains too?" I asked, and laughed.

"Yes," he said, "but then you must hope it's short lived!"

All my shyness slipped away. We hit it off immediately. Life was filled with introductions, but only the significant ones remained. I knew it was the beginning of a friendship that would continue to thrive when Lin Yutang expressed his wishes of coming to America.

ALTHOUGH SHANGHAI'S LEFT-LEANING LIBERALS were accepting of me, many others despised everything I represented—a spoiled Chinese-American actress who brought nothing but embarrassment to her homeland. A stream of negative Chinese and English-language magazine and newspaper articles began to skewer my presence, refusing to leave me in peace. I had begun studying Chinese again before I arrived, which helped me to pick up most of what was said about me. I made Lulu translate the rest.

"Instead of staying at an offered guesthouse, Anna May Wong prefers to stay in the finest international hotels and wears expensive *qipaos* as she leaves each day for dinners and parties with the wealthy and elite. How is that getting to know the Chinese people?" Or, "Anna May Wong is certainly an accomplished actress as she struts through Shanghai 'acting' as if she's Chinese."

While I carried on with a brave face, the constant personal attacks were taking their toll. Was I really that awful? Was there no other news in China than that of my daily schedule? Each morning as I sat down to breakfast and read the papers, I found it more and more difficult not to rehash all the cruel and spiteful words written about me.

"At over thirty years old, Anna May Wong remains without a husband, or even a boyfriend. One can only wonder if there's something wrong with her."

"No more!" Lulu finally said, removing every single magazine and newspaper from my hotel room. "Don't let them turn your visit into something ugly."

"There's some truth to what they're saying," I said, hoarsely.

"There are two sides to everything," Lulu said. "It's up to you to prove them wrong."

She scooped scrambled eggs onto my plate, buttered a piece of toast, adding a generous dollop of marmalade on top, and poured me more coffee.

"Now eat your breakfast," Lulu ordered.

I had to smile. How endearing it was that she'd picked up all the traits of *ma ma*, who used food as a form of love and comfort. Lulu forbade me from reading any more newspaper and magazine articles while we were in Shanghai. But perhaps she was right, it was up to me to prove them wrong, instead of wallowing in self-pity.

Until this trip, Lulu and I had not been alone together for ages. Ever since *ma ma* died, things between us were never quite the same. We talked and visited, even had our family meals together, but I could always see in Lulu's eyes that nothing would ever forgive my not returning home after *ma ma*'s death. For the past six years, we'd remained at a distance, but this morning I felt we had bridged the gap. Lulu was my older sister again, taking good care of me. One day, I hoped to explain to her why I hadn't returned so that she might understand how fragile I really was. What Lulu had never understood was just how much stronger she was than me. It was time to test my resolve.

I SPENT SIX SUMPTUOUS weeks in Shanghai. And it was time to see the "real" China. I only had to walk a few blocks to experience a very different world. Away from the stately buildings and grand hotels, the Shanghainese people lived their lives separate from the westernized Bund. Walking along the crowded street stalls, I listened to the high-pitched, singsong Mandarin coursing through the air as customers and merchants bargained. The makeshift stalls sold everything from sewing needles and makeup to handbags and bicycle tires. Tantalizing aromas came from food stands that sold noodles and dumplings with chili paste, green onion pancakes, and dried salted fish over rice porridge. Dogs and cats roamed the streets in search of food. In an alleyway, near a small, dark hovel, a family sat eating noodles around a table made of wooden crates while a small child defecated nearby. Farther down the street stood blocks and blocks of crowded apartment buildings; bamboo poles suspended from their windows were hung with drying laundry, fluttering like flags. Shanghai was a study in contrasts. I thought of all the misleading articles written about me and flushed with embarrassment.

I was learning.

ARRIVAL
Hong Kong—March 1936

The voyage to Hong Kong was rougher than expected. I woke up with a splitting headache and an upset stomach, closing my eyes against the throbbing pain. The ship was scheduled to dock in a few hours and I prayed to feel better by then. I was looking forward to my stay with Lulu. She'd left Shanghai the week before and returned to Hong Kong, where she now lived and worked, to prepare for my visit.

Upon arrival, I was scheduled to meet a delegation from the Association of Fellow Provincials of Taishan, the largest city near *baba*'s ancestral village of Chang On. Along with the managers from the Duguan Film Company, they all planned a celebratory welcome to Hong Kong before my pending visit to Chang On. Unfortunately, I didn't feel like celebrating.

Stepping onto the gangplank, I felt nauseous and warm with fever. Rain and humidity made the ramp slippery and difficult to descend. By the time I made it to solid ground, exhausted, I was mobbed by members of the delegation, along with reporters and fans. A bouquet of flowers was thrust into my arms as the crowd pressed forward, hoping for a glimpse of me. I'd encountered this kind of frenzy before and always managed to keep my composure, but today, it felt like I was being attacked instead of adored. Without thinking, I reacted with fear by stepping back and away from the crowd as it pushed toward me.

"Please, stay back," I said, the bouquet of flowers slipping from my hands. My head pounded as I raised my voice louder. "Stay back!"

The crowd pressed forward, especially one heavyset middle-aged man dressed in a brown suit, who waved another bouquet of flowers at me. He seemed to be driven forward by the momentum of the pushing crowd.

I tugged at my collar, hot and sweaty. "Stay away!" I yelled. "Leave me alone! Just leave me alone!"

I was fighting for my life. Instinctively, I stepped forward and shoved the man in the brown suit away from me. He stumbled back against the crowd. A look of astonishment swept across his face as he dropped the flowers he carried. He stopped and held his ground, raising his arms wide to hold back the people behind him.

"Stop!" he yelled, waving his arms over his head. "Stop! It appears Miss Wong doesn't want us here."

Amid the confusion, he repeated his command for the crowd to stop, "Miss Wong doesn't want us here!" It took a while for his words to work their way to the back of the crowd. And slowly, the pushing stopped. I heard a scattering of boos, which quickly grew to shouts of anger.

"Then we don't want her here. Don't let her go any further!" someone shouted.

"Go back to America!"

"You have brought China nothing but shame," another voice shouted.

"Go home, Wong Liu-Tsong! Go home, Wong Liu-Tsong!" they chanted with increasing vehemence.

"You don't belong here!"

I swayed with dizziness, tearful and feverish; my head pounded, my heart raced. How did everything get out of control so quickly? I feared their anger, and the hatred that suddenly filled the air. Just as I tried to return to the ship, Lulu broke through the swarm with several dignitaries, who surrounded me. The crowd continued yelling for me to leave, trampling the row of flower baskets that awaited me by a makeshift stage. I began to cry as I was rushed through the mob, and I didn't dare look up until I was in the safety in the building, going through immigration.

FOR THE NEXT TWO DAYS, I hid from sight in Lulu's apartment until I felt better. I'd always made sure to be grateful and available to my fans and couldn't explain what had come over me. Ashamed and embarrassed by the melee, Newsreel Wong buried the story for me, and a statement was released to the press explaining it was all a misunderstanding. I hadn't felt well, and the charging crowd had frightened me. But every time I ventured from the apartment, reporters and angry crowds were waiting outside with signs reading, "Go home, Wong Liu-Tsong!"

This time, I vowed not to give in to my despair. In order to turn the situation around, I apologized multiple times and acknowledged that I hadn't felt well. But I refrained from saying that everything escalated when the man in the brown suit rushed at me. I'd since learned he was a council member from Taishan. Not long after, *baba* received an angry letter from leaders of the Taishan delegation, telling him to advise me not to visit Chang On.

Baba sent a telegram telling me to stay in Hong Kong or to do some traveling elsewhere. "Give them time for their anger to die down. I'll continue to explain. It won't be too long," he said.

To get away from Hong Kong, I planned a quick trip to the Philippines with Lulu, where we were warmly welcomed. It was a relief not to be shouted at by angry crowds. When I returned to Hong Kong four days later, tensions remained high in Taishan, so we headed for Macao, where I was also relieved to be enthusiastically received by both reporters and fans.

By the time I returned to Hong Kong during the second week of April, it was time to prove my loyalty, and to see my father and our ancestral village, the home of *baba*'s stories and memories. More importantly, this was the rural China I'd been longing to see. I called Newsreel Wong and hired a car to drive us to Taishan in Guangdong Province, a little more than three miles from the village.

We arrived in Chang On the following day.

THE ANCESTRAL VILLAGE
Chang On—April 1936

Newsreel Wong snapped photos while I kept my movie camera rolling as I exited the car to a crowd of smiling and welcoming Chang On villagers who surrounded my father and my youngest brother, Richard. I'd remained cautious since a small incident had occurred several miles back as we were driving up the dirt road to the village. Newsreel, Lulu, and I were talking in the backseat, planning how to film my arrival when a hard, loud thud hit the door on my side of the car. It was followed by another solid blow to the back of the car, and yet another that splattered against the back window. I flinched, and leaned away from the door and closer to Lulu. My heart pounded as the driver looked back and began swearing in Cantonese.

"What's happening?" I asked.

Lulu squeezed my hand.

Newsreel turned to look at the streaked back window. "Let me see what's going on," he said, then rolled down his window and stuck his head out.

"Don't!" Lulu said.

"It's okay," he said, calmly.

As a photojournalist, Newsreel had worked all over China and knew the country well. He'd found himself in several precarious situations over the years, from irate farmers protesting a water shortage in Yunnan Province, to running from marauding gangs in the Gobi Desert. He was well trained for unexpected situations.

"Can't see anyone," he said. "They must have run off."

The driver pulled to the side of the road. Before I could gather my wits, he and Newsreel had both jumped out of the car to look for the culprits.

"Be careful," I called after them.

Lulu and I turned around to watch them through the cloudy window that dripped with pulp and seeds. It wasn't long before they headed back to the car. While the driver cleaned off the rear window, Newsreel opened the door and slipped into his seat.

"Did you see anyone?" I asked.

Newsreel shook his head. "They're gone. Looks like they were throwing rotten fruit at the car," he said. "Makes a bigger mess."

I stayed quiet in thought, worried that I'd come to Chang On too soon. Obviously, some villagers here were still angry with me.

"Throwing at the car?" I asked. "Or do you mean at me?"

"Anna," Lulu said softly.

Newsreel leaned closer. "I wouldn't worry, Anna May. They threw fruit. If they were really angry, they would have thrown rocks," he said, and smiled kindly.

I nodded, shaken. Newsreel was a good friend, and I was extremely thankful to have him with us on this visit to China. Before I could tell him, the driver swung open his door and climbed in. Although he smelled faintly of overripe fruit, he appeared relieved that there was no real damage to his car and drove the rest of the way to the village without uttering a word.

FROM THE START, Newsreel and I were putting together two very different interpretations of my trip—the news footage he compiled for the Hearst newspapers was a travelogue of places and events, while my own film was a personal journey back to my father's ancestral village. Gone would be the flashy footage Newsreel shot of me in Shanghai doing press interviews, or buying flowers and gifts from street vendors, or having *qipao* fittings. Instead, I cradled my box movie camera and looked forward to filming Chang On, my father, and the villagers, eager to capture the real essence of Chinese life in the countryside. One day, I hoped those narrow-minded Hollywood moguls would see my film and realize how ridiculous it was to have Caucasian actors and actresses pretending to be Chinese.

BABA LOOKED RELAXED AND happy to see me as Newsreel and I walked up the dirt path and through the village gate followed by Lulu and Richard. I'd been waiting for this moment since childhood. After all the struggles that preceded my visit, I was thrilled that the villagers were welcoming, and I had made sure to bring along enough candy and coins in red envelopes to appease both the children and the adults.

A hillside village with a high stone wall surrounding it, Chang On was only accessible through a gate and gun tower, built in the ancient days when bandits roamed the countryside attacking villages. The houses were constructed of brown brick and stonework, connected by walkways that led to each front door. Many of the houses had small ponds and gardens in their front courtyards, which I found quite beautiful. But what I loved most were the narrow alleyways that snaked between the houses like a secret maze running throughout the village.

ON THE NIGHT OF our arrival, the village council hosted a welcome dinner at the community hall for us. It was attended by their families and local representatives from the surrounding villages. Much to my relief, no officials from Taishan were there. I couldn't imagine they would ever forgive me. After taking photos of my arrival and at the dinner, Newsreel and the driver stayed the night. They would return to Canton the following day and pick us up in two weeks.

My father sat next to me at the head of a long table. In Chang On, he was a well-respected and admired elder who was successful in America and sent money back to the village through the years. My half-brother Huang Dounan, his wife, and his mother (my father's first wife) sat to his right, while Lulu and Richard sat to my left, along with Newsreel and the driver. I'd never seen *baba* so openly joyous. For the very first time, he seemed completely at ease with himself and with those around him. At home in Los Angeles, he was always reserved and guarded.

Watching him now, so happily interacting with his long-time friends, I understood how much Chang On and China meant to him.

Before we ate, the leaders of the community made welcoming speeches followed by a series of toasts in my honor. I was happy to be served plum wine and plenty of whiskey with dishes that were rustic and tasty. Newsreel photographed it all. After we'd eaten, there was entertainment, showcasing some of the talents of the villagers—a poet, magician, dancers, and an acrobat. It was a lovely gesture, and I made sure to show my appreciation. As a final act, a young girl was ushered up to the makeshift stage. She couldn't have been more than thirteen, wearing a white cotton top and black pants, her hair in pigtails. The girl stood on the stage looking terrified until a woman, who must have been her mother, smiled reassuringly at her.

Only then did she straighten and begin to sing, accompanied by a woman playing an old upright piano.

Immediately, the buzz of voices in the room quieted. The girl's voice was crystalline, so beautiful everyone was immediately drawn to it. She seemed to gain more confidence as she sang. Her captivating voice had the powerful pull of a mythical Greek siren that swayed sailors and their ships to their doom. When her song was over, there was a moment of stillness before the room erupted in applause. She blushed and shyly took a bow. As the evening came to an end, I wanted to thank the young girl and praise her singing, but was told that she and her mother had left soon after she finished her song.

LATER THAT EVENING, after opening the gifts I brought them—a padded silk jacket for my father and a leather jacket for my younger brother—Richard went to bed, leaving *baba* and me alone in his tiny kitchen for the first time since my arrival. My father's house in Chang On was too small to accommodate all of us comfortably, so while I could sleep in his extra room, Lulu went to stay with relatives in the nearby village of Wing On, where our Wong clan originated. I planned to spend a few nights there with Lulu before we left.

Happy and relaxed after the welcoming dinner, my father set a pot of water on the fire for tea. We talked about my brothers and sister in Los Angeles, and his life in Chang On. "I'm a wealthy man here," he said. "I'm rich in time and in friends."

I was touched to see him so lighthearted, and knew better than to disrupt our tranquility, but I wanted him to know how grateful I was for his support.

"I'm sorry, *baba*, for all the trouble I've caused you by coming to Chang On."

He put down the teapot and turned to face me. "When have you ever been easy, Anna?" he said, without malice. He smiled. "The most important thing is that you're here now. Everything else will settle down in its own time."

He seemed so tranquil; it was hard to believe this was the same man who had fought me nonstop growing up. "Chang On is everything I imagined it would be from your stories," I said.

"I'm glad you were able to visit," he said, "to see the home of our ancestors."

"I am too," I said. "Thank you, *baba*, for everything."

He looked at me for a moment. "It's important to know your history so it isn't lost."

"I promise, it won't be," I said, feeling his urgency for the first time. When his generation was gone, it would be up to us to carry it on.

He placed two cups of tea on the table and gestured for me to sit. Had we reached a new plateau? I was honestly happy to be here with my father in our ancestral village, no longer arguing, and finally finding a comfortable peace between us. Only time would tell if it would last.

Chang On was a step back in time. Despite its lack of modern conveniences, I loved everything and filmed it all. I cherished the small house, the old charcoal stove that warmed the rooms, the plain brick walls tinted by smoke, and my small bare room where I slept on a thin mattress atop a twin bed.

I quickly fell into a routine. Each morning I made breakfast for *baba* and Richard before he went off to school. The last time I'd seen my brother was almost three years before, when he boarded the ship at the Los Angeles harbor. Richard was fourteen now, and we were almost strangers. After being apart for so long, I wanted to get to know him better. *Ma ma* had died when he was only eight years old. I couldn't imagine how hard it was on him being raised by *baba*, who was old enough to be his grandfather. My brother Roger, who was the closest to him in age, was seven years older. The rest of us were already grown, with everyone except me studying or working in Los Angeles, while I'd been away in Europe making movies. It was left to Lulu to be our youngest brother's primary mother figure, but I wanted him to know that he had another older sister he could count on.

My first night in Chang On, Richard was shy and quiet, but he slowly warmed up, becoming more comfortable and talkative with each day. I asked him to give me a tour of Chang On, and made him promise to show me what he did to occupy his time when he wasn't at school. He smiled wide and nodded. Even as a boy, I saw traits of both of my parents in him; he had my father's fortitude and my mother's sense of duty.

"DID YOU ALWAYS WANT to be a movie actress?" Richard asked.

He'd returned from school while *baba* was out playing cards with his friends, leaving us time for a walk. In the almost three years, he'd grown so much taller, but I was still surprised to hear his voice two octaves lower than when I'd last seen him. I followed Richard out the front gate and onto the dirt road we'd driven up the week before.

"Since I was a girl," I answered. "I used to skip Chinese school and sneak off to the movies all the time."

"I bet *baba* wasn't happy."

"Not happy at all," I said, and laughed. "I think he's not entirely happy I'm an actress."

"But you're famous. What's it like to be famous?"

I smiled at his inquisitiveness. Richard was a good kid who hardly complained about having left his life in Los Angeles to follow his elderly father back to a small rural village in China. Not that he'd had a choice, but he seemed to have weathered the move and was taking good care of *baba*.

"It's both good and bad. It's hard to be an actress in Hollywood, even harder if you're a Chinese actress," I answered.

"But you did it," he said, proudly.

I followed Richard as he turned onto a narrow dirt path hidden between some trees and foliage. Thankfully, I was wearing sensible flat shoes as I hurried after him.

"Acting has been an uphill climb," I said, when I caught up to where he was waiting for me.

"But you reached the top."

"For a moment, I did," I said. "Then I began sliding backwards."

Richard paused in thought. "Doesn't matter," he said. "What's important is that you reached the top." He shrugged and continued down the path.

I liked this younger brother of mine.

"Where are we going?" I asked.

"You wanted me to show you something I liked to do when I'm not in school. Come this way and you'll see," he answered.

I followed him down the path until we emerged from the trees into a large open meadow. In the near distance stood the shell of a brick building no larger than *baba*'s house, with the roof and two walls missing.

"How ever did you discover this ruin?" I asked.

"By chance," Richard answered, smiling. "I was out walking, noticed the path and followed it to see if it led anywhere. It led me here, to what I think was once a temple. There's an altar in there. You should have seen it when I first found it, there was only part of one wall still standing. I've been working on it ever since."

"You've been rebuilding it?" I asked, astonished.

Richard nodded.

It looked old, but there was no way to tell how long it had stood in the meadow. It appeared to be the only structure within miles. "What's it doing here in the middle of nowhere?"

"No idea," my brother said. "I imagine a village must have once been closer, and the villagers came here to pray. I've been slowly restoring it whenever I can find bricks and materials from Chang On and other nearby villages. I use an old wheelbarrow to cart the bricks and mortar in. Hopefully I'll have it rebuilt before I have to leave."

"When did you become so skillful?"

"Comes naturally," he answered, pleased.

I laughed and listened as he explained to me what he'd already completed. Even without training, I could see my teenage brother was already talented as a builder.

"You've done all this by yourself?"

"It keeps me busy," Richard said. "I had to find something to do."

It was the first time I had a real sense of what Richard was feeling. "How are you doing here?" I asked.

"It was hard in the beginning, but it's better now," he said.

"It's good of you to stay with *baba*. I know it must have been difficult leaving LA and all your friends there."

"It's better now," he repeated. "I have a few friends from school. Anyway, *baba* needs me to help with everything. It won't be forever."

"No, it won't," I said, surprised at his maturity.

Baba hadn't said a word about returning to Los Angeles. This was a reminder to talk to my siblings about Richard's future, to make sure he was taken care of when he returned home, with or without my father.

"Does *baba* know what you've been doing here?" I asked. I inspected his handiwork, impressed with the wall he'd managed to rebuild to match the one still standing. There was a stone altar inside, and remnants of wooden pews, and a wood floor eaten away over time. Even so, I could envision what it must have looked like so long ago.

Richard shook his head. "Nah, this is just a hobby, something to do with my free time. I thought you might like to see it."

"It's beautiful," I said, delighted he would share his project with me. "Thank you for showing it to me. I'd like to return again with my movie camera so I can film you and your temple before I leave," I added.

Richard smiled broadly.

I WALKED EACH DAY for exercise, surprised to find the walled village much larger than I expected. I especially liked wandering down the narrow, cool alleyways between the houses, curious as to where they led. Wearing trousers and a cotton blouse with no makeup, I roamed freely with no reporters or cameras waiting for me, only the Leica in my hands. This morning was no different, until I heard the unmistakable singing of the young girl from my welcome dinner. I followed the voice to a small house tucked away at the end of an alley. The front door was open, a stale coolness emanating from the dark interior. The singing came from the back of the house.

"Hello," I said in Taishanese, and then again, louder.

The singing stopped.

I heard a rustling from within the house and the young girl's mother, dressed in a white cotton tunic and pants, appeared. She stared wide eyed when she recognized me standing in her doorway.

"I'm sorry to bother you," I said, "but I wanted to thank your daughter for singing at the dinner last week. Her voice is beautiful."

She smiled and relaxed. "I'm Mei. Please," she said, stepping back and motioning for me to come in.

I followed Mei through the cool, sparsely furnished house and out another doorway that led to a bright courtyard in back. Her daughter had begun to sing again, sitting at a wooden table beneath the shade of a large banyan tree where she was wrapping dumplings. I was glad I had the camera with me. Carl would adore the photos.

"Would it be all right if I take a few photos?" I asked.

Mei nodded. I snapped several shots as the young girl scooped a spoonful of minced meat and cabbage filling into the middle of a circular wrap, folded it, and pinched the edges together into a half-moon. She added it to a bamboo tray already laden with dumplings.

"Your daughter is a lovely girl," I said.

Mei smiled. "She is my youngest, Liling," she said.

"She has a beautiful voice."

"You are very kind."

I stood by the entryway to the courtyard, listening to her voice in awe while her mother disappeared back into the house. With the right training, Liling could one day be accepted into the Peking Opera. I couldn't wait to tell Mei Lanfang and Hu Die when I returned to Shanghai. At that very moment, Liling turned and abruptly stopped singing, embarrassed to see me watching her.

I stepped closer. "I wanted to thank you for singing the other evening. You have a beautiful voice."

The girl looked down bashfully. It was a rare pleasure to see someone with such natural talent so modest and unaware. Hollywood was filled with so many talentless actors and actresses who never hesitated to flaunt their gifts.

"I like to sing when I'm working," Liling said, pointing to the dumplings.

"You have a lovely talent. Is singing something you might like to continue doing professionally?" I asked. I could certainly help to get her started, invest in her talent.

She looked at me, puzzled. "I don't understand," she said.

"To have a career entertaining others with your singing and, perhaps, one day become very famous."

Liling looked at me with curiosity. "I like to sing for myself, not for others," she said. "Unless it's for an honored guest like you," she quickly added.

"I believe I'm the one who came all the way to China to hear you sing," I said.

"Do you like living in America?" she asked.

"Yes, I do. Most of the time," I answered.

"What don't you like about it?"

"There are laws against being Chinese in America, rules we always have to follow."

"Why?" Liling asked.

"Not everyone wants us in America, so they make it difficult for us," I said. "When you're older, you'll understand that life is complicated."

"I have all that I want here in Chang On," Liling said, earnestly. "I don't need to be anywhere else, especially somewhere that makes life difficult for Chinese."

"Then you are truly blessed," I said, marveling at her words. Could life be so easy? I asked myself, already knowing that it would never be for me.

Mei returned to the courtyard carrying two bowls of soup noodles and dumplings.

"Please, sit and join us for lunch," she said, gesturing for me to take a seat at the table across from Liling. "We sell our dumplings here and to the surrounding villages." She placed a bowl of soup noodles, a plate of dumplings, and a mixture of soy sauce and vinegar in front of me.

That bowl of hand-pulled noodles and dumplings was one of the best meals I'd ever eaten. Even the fifteen-course banquet in Shanghai, though exquisite, couldn't compare to the humble goodness of this lunch. This was a taste of Liling's life, food made of joy and fulfillment, along with the freedom to sing whenever and wherever she wanted, without judgment from others.

In America, I couldn't take a step without being judged. Here in Chang On, the heaviness was lifted from my shoulders. Liling and her mother sent me back to my father's house with a basket full of dumplings, which Richard happily devoured when he returned from school.

ANOTHER HIGHLIGHT WAS MY visit with Lulu in the village of Wing On, where we stayed with *baba*'s cousins, Auntie Chen and Auntie Yee. Both widows, they were strong and robust and quite the businesswomen. They owned an old stone farmhouse and raised a passel of squealing pigs. Each year, several of their pigs were chosen to be slaughtered on Chinese New Year for the surrounding villages, while the others were either sold or kept to breed.

Both women fussed over me, telling me I was much too skinny

and needed to eat more. "A good husband wants a wife with some meat on her bones," Auntie Chen said. Lulu stifled a laugh, while I followed their orders to sit and eat, and Auntie Yee scooped more food into my bowl every time I blinked.

"The aunts think you'll show them around Hollywood," Lulu whispered, as she poured me some tea.

I leaned closer to her. "I bet they could run Hollywood."

"With ease and efficiency," she said.

"Maybe I should take them back with me."

"God help us all," Lulu said, and laughed.

THE REST OF MY days in Chang On went by quickly. I was sad to leave my father, and especially my brother Richard, whom I was just getting to know. I was due back in Shanghai for interviews, and the possibility of a new movie project. I took Chang On's beautiful, uncomplicated lifestyle with me, along with the image of Liling sitting under the banyan tree, singing while she wrapped dumplings, clearly happy where she was.

MY CHINA STORY
Peking—May 1936

When I returned to Shanghai, I was accosted by reporters as soon as I arrived at the hotel. Along with Newsreel Wong reporting for Hearst, I was kept in the headlines by doing nonstop interviews with

Chinese newspapers and magazines, reiterating my reasons for taking the movie roles I did, once again defending my career as a Chinese woman struggling in the movie business. It was the only way I could reach a wider audience. I was determined to make the people understand that Hollywood was a world in which I had little say if I wanted to act. Often, it felt like I was chiseling through stone.

Fortunately, visiting my family's ancestral village in Chang On was seen as a step in the right direction. My photos continued to be featured in all the Chinese magazines. And in articles, I was portrayed as not only an actress but also a fashion icon. Back in the United States, footage of my trip in China sent back to Hearst was constantly included in the opening newsreels shown in the theaters before major movies. Ironically, I was getting more press in the States now than when I was actually there.

IN MID-MAY, NEWSREEL AND I arrived in Peking by car after making stops in Nanjing (the capital of the Kuomintang party) and the port city of Tianjin. Once again, I was immediately chastised by the newspapers for staying at the grand Peking Hotel instead of a private guesthouse, while the press continued to focus on what dinners and events I attended, and with whom I was spending my time. They also homed in on how many silk *qipaos* I had ordered to take back to America, and seemed particularly interested in my changing hairstyles, which alternated between my trademark bangs with a bun, to letting my hair hang down loosely over my shoulders. They called me a tourist, which I was and never denied. All the while, Newsreel filmed me visiting monuments, and riding streetcars, rickshaws, and sedan chairs, to send back to Hearst.

At the same time, I was a serious student who desperately wanted to learn more about my homeland. I relished the beauty of the Summer Palace and was astounded to see the man-made Great Wall, which stretched over twenty-five hundred miles and was built over centuries by emperors to keep out invaders. Peking was everything I had hoped for, a formidable city steeped in the traditions of old China. I was proud of the countless accomplishments that came from such an ancient civilization and finally understood why my mother and father had drilled all the principles and values of being Chinese into us children growing up. It was a culture ingrained in us and would always define how we lived our lives, no matter how far away we were from the land of our ancestors.

BY JUNE, I HAD rented a small house within a residential compound, where I kept up with my Chinese lessons and began speaking much more Mandarin during my interviews. I continued to explain the Hollywood studio system and the career choices I had to make in order to keep working. Gradually, the Chinese media's attacks lessened. It also helped to be photographed often with Mei Lanfang and Hu Die, who were both popular Chinese stars and remained good friends. During the four months I spent in Peking, I met John Leighton Stuart, the founding president of Yenching University, an early supporter of the Kuomintang party and a close advisor to Chiang Kai-shek; many leading artists and intellectuals; and the first lady of Peking, Tan Jun Wu. One evening after I came back from a particularly inspiring dinner party hosted by her, I couldn't wait to write Carl.

August 8, 1936
Dear Carlo,

Thank you for your last letter. I so hoped that you and Fania could have come to visit, but I do know how important your work is. A photo opportunity with Georgia O'Keeffe can't be missed! We have both been spending time with great ladies! I've just returned from a dinner hosted by the first lady of Peking, Tan Jun Wu, and her brother, where I met many of Peking's leading artists and thinkers. How wonderful it is to feel included in every way, at one with the whole. Tonight, I realized how much I've missed this simple sense of inclusion, like being wrapped in a warm blanket and not left out in the cold. It's meant everything to me being with other successful Chinese, and feeling as if I belong. Even if I only experienced this one evening of being culturally and professionally accepted by my peers, I'd consider this trip to China a huge success. It was an awakening in so many ways. I needed to feel this harmony, to know it exists. Now, I can return to the US, and to the ongoing fight for acceptance in the country where I was born and raised. I'm sad to think my trip is coming to an end, but it has been quite a year. I'm returning home to Los Angeles for a quick visit before I'm back to London for a new film. I hope for a stay in New York on my way back from London. I look forward to seeing you and Fania in person. I'm most eager to see your new portraits of Willa Cather and Bessie Smith, and to hear all about Fania's upcoming role as

Charmian in Antony and Cleopatra. *She must be so excited. I can't wait! Love to you both.*

>*Yours always,*
>*Anna May*

FROM THE OLD WORLD of Peking, I returned to the bustling world of Shanghai to sail back to America on October 23. I arrived back in San Francisco at the end of November, returning with a new resolve to show Americans the beauty and resilience of the Chinese people. I was also thrilled to finally offer audiences a glimpse of what the real China was like through my own home movies. I wanted to improve their national image, and to show Hollywood that the Chinese were so much more than the caricatures portrayed in the movies. Most importantly, I returned to the United States reenergized. I held a new outlook and knowledge of what it meant to be both Chinese and American, and how important it was to bring them together for the world to see.

CHICAGO
1960

I have a three-hour layover at Union Station in Chicago, not enough time to venture into the city but just enough for the studio to have set up my first interview for *Portrait in Black*. After visiting New York and the Northeast, I'll be returning to attend the Chicago opening. For now, a reporter is scheduled to meet me at the Union Café in the

station in fifteen minutes. I suddenly feel nervous and crave a cigarette or a drink, but when I think of Dr. Bloom, I refrain from either.

I pull my hair back, dress in a silk blouse and skirt, and step off the
train into the humid stagnant air. The station is crowded as I ease my
way around passengers on the platform and into the main building.
The Union Café is at the far corner of the large, cavernous building,
and by the time I arrive and ask for Ellis Drucker, I'm ten minutes
late (even without stopping for a drink). It's the middle of the afternoon, and the café's almost empty compared to the crowds hurrying
to catch their train just steps away. I'm shown to a table in the back
near a tall window, where a heavyset gray-haired older man sits waiting, staring out to the street. I'm surprised to see he's my age, perhaps
older, expecting to meet a cub reporter just starting out, but this man
appears seasoned and well traveled, and I can't help but wonder what
he has done to draw the short straw of having to interview an older,
Chinese actress trying to make a comeback. I don't know who I feel
sadder for, him or me.

"Mr. Drucker, I'm sorry to be late," I say.

He looks up, quickly stands. His wrinkled shirt and slacks make
me want to laugh. I can see *baba* shaking his head. My father prided
himself on his ironing, every shirt washed and pressed and packaged
for delivery.

"Miss Wong, I'm very pleased to meet you."

We shake hands, and I take the seat across from him. He's definitely older than I am, sixty, if not more, with a graying beard and
intense dark eyes that slightly bulge. "Thank you for coming to the
station," I say, and smile. I glance down at my watch to remind him I
don't have a lot of time.

"Of course, it's my pleasure. Would you like a coffee?"

"Tea. Thank you."

He raises his arm, flags down a waiter, and orders a tea for me.

"I hope you've been having a good trip so far," he says, settling back into his seat.

"Yes, I've always enjoyed taking the train. It's much more relaxing, and there's room to move around."

"And to sleep," he adds, with a grin. "I can't tell you how often I've had to sleep in my car while chasing a story."

The waiter returns with my tea.

I imagine he has spent many a night chasing down real stories, so why is he here?

"I don't mean to be rude, but I don't seem like your typical story," I say, already finding this interview more interesting than I expected.

He looks at me, sips his coffee, and says, "Actually, when I found out you were coming to town, I asked for the assignment."

I look up from my tea, and ask, "Why?"

"I'm a big fan," he says, and chuckles.

I smile. He's the last person I would think of as a fan of mine. For one, he looks like a hardcore newspaperman. And he doesn't look the type who takes the time to go to the movies. Before I have the chance to say anything, Ellis Drucker, like any good reporter, has sized me up.

He rubs his beard, and nods. "Let me explain myself. I do have an ulterior motive being here for this interview. I'm familiar with all the basic facts, Miss Wong; I can easily write an article about you from what I already know, including everything needed to promote your latest film." He leans back in his chair. "I'm here for other reasons."

"And they are?"

Ellis Drucker shifts in his seat. "What I want to know is, how does it feel being a Chinese woman who has survived Hollywood? I bet it wasn't easy. How have you dealt with it all? Hollywood, the anti-miscegenation laws, the roles you should have gotten but never did because of Hollywood's bigoted belief that Caucasian actresses in yellowface would make stories about China look just as real." He laughs out loud.

I need something stronger to drink. "Who said I survived?"

"You've just completed a major movie with Lana Turner and Anthony Quinn. I'd say you survived," he says, adding, "even if it's been a long time coming and you were never given a fair shake."

I size him up, and say, "It hasn't been easy."

"I didn't think so. The moment I saw you in *The Thief of Bagdad*, I knew you ran circles around all those other actresses."

"*The Thief of Bagdad*! I was a child back then."

"I've seen almost every movie you've made since," he says, proudly.

"Well, you are a surprising man."

I sit back, astonished. After all these years, a journalist is finally openly addressing my plight. If only that was what the article was about. I look at this disheveled reporter and smile.

"I never thought anyone cared," I finally say.

"We aren't all bigoted jackasses."

I laugh. "Would you mind if I ordered something a bit stronger?" I ask.

He smiles. "Not at all, I'll join you."

Again, he flags down the waiter.

Not long after, I sip my gin and tonic and relax. "Let me tell you a story that I believe sums up what it's like to be Chinese in America, whether you're an actress or a teacher or a secretary. I spent a year in China visiting my family in 1936, and when I returned to San Francisco and disembarked from the ship, I was rudely reminded that I still had to report to the Immigration and Naturalization Service to receive my certificate of identity. I was the only Chinese-American actress who was well known worldwide at the time, and I still had to prove to them who I was. And, it wasn't only my whereabouts I had to let them know about, I had to report where everyone in my family was living, and what they were doing at the time. I had just returned as an honored guest in China, only to be treated like a criminal in America. I suppose that's what I've felt all my life, that being born in America doesn't mean you're American in the minds of others. Just because I don't fit the criteria, I've had to fight to prove that I belong here from the time I was a young girl. The irony is that I'm a third-generation American."

Ellis shakes his head and sips his beer. "I'm a third-generation American myself, and Jewish to boot. So, what made you keep running against the wind?" he asks.

"I would have had to live in another country to feel the freedom that was my birthright. I'm also very stubborn. I refused to let them win; I was just as American as they were." I stop to sip my drink. "Besides, Hollywood is in Los Angeles, where I was born and raised. My family's there."

Ellis raises his glass of beer, and says, "Here's to Anna May Wong, who refused to be anyone other than a Chinese American!"

I raise my glass against his.

"But you have spent quite a bit of time in Europe?"

"Where I am more readily accepted, much like Josephine Baker."

Ellis Drucker shakes his head. "Dumbass Americans."

I like the man.

ELATED, I RETURN TO the train with just minutes until departure. I have never spoken so freely about my feelings to anyone other than my family, or Carl and Fania. I should be worried telling a reporter my simple truths, but instead, I feel pleased and content, I feel lighter. I trust Ellis Drucker to write the right story, and hope to see him again upon my return to Chicago for the premiere here. Maybe I'll tell him part two of my sad saga.

The train shivers and rumbles as it moves slowly out of the station. I sit down, rifle through my bag, and retrieve the last notebook to read during the remainder of my trip to New York.

LOS ANGELES
A New Outlook—1937

After returning from China, I refused to fall back into my old pattern of accepting any movie role that I was offered. I was especially determined not to dishonor China or the Chinese people and, most importantly, not to take on roles that were personally demeaning. Visiting China had illuminated my life as a Chinese American who admired the long history and accomplishments of my ancestors. Understanding the importance of where I came from gave me a greater sense of pride and worth.

Nevertheless, I knew Hollywood hadn't changed. It was run by a handful of men who ignored the world beyond the hallowed walls of their movie studios. Within a few days of being back in Hollywood, I was already losing Oriental roles to Caucasian actresses, but I was determined to fight harder for upcoming parts. My goal was simple: to make films in a permanent relationship with a major studio again.

I returned to my Beverly Wilshire apartment, happy to see old friends and to have dinner with Frank, Roger, and Mary at our new family home on North Fifty-Fifth Street. As much as I'd loved China, I was delighted to be back. My brothers had gone on with their lives and seemed happy enough. My sister Mary was still seeking movie roles, anxious about her career, and lamenting that she was rarely called back for a second audition, even after her appearance in *The Good Earth*. Meanwhile, she was working part time as a stenographer.

"The day will come when it's easier," I said, trying to soothe her anxiety one evening after dinner at the family house together. We sat at the kitchen table after cleaning up.

Mary had always been the most vulnerable of all us Wong children. Lulu and I worried about the difficulties she still faced in the fiercely competitive, soul-stealing movie business.

"It doesn't feel that way. I don't understand why I'm not getting at least second call backs," she said, staring at the floor.

"Look at me." I waited for her to raise her eyes. When she did, I said, "From the time you were a little girl, you knew how simple expressions could express big emotions. You were wonderful as Little Bride in *The Good Earth*. Don't worry, I'm determined to help change the way they treat us in the movies. You'll see, pretty soon Chinese actors and actresses will win more roles."

Mary remained somber for a moment. "I know that some girls will do anything to be cast. But I can't. I just can't," she whispered. "Is that why I'm not being called back?"

I reached for her hand, remembering how difficult it was to avoid those producers who grabbed and pawed at me. "You're doing exactly the right thing," I said. "Don't worry. I'll see what I can do."

When Mary finally smiled, I saw a hint of the young girl I'd always known and loved. Since my return from China, she seemed changed, easily distracted, with moments when she drifted away and I wasn't sure where she'd gone.

"You promise?"

I could only try to reassure her. "I'll do the best I can," I said.

That brought another smile. "Thank you," Mary said.

She stood from her chair and gave me a big hug. As I felt her body relax against mine, I wished I had the power to make everything easier for her.

In the ensuing weeks, I tried to help Mary get auditions, but there were few roles for Chinese actresses other than bit parts or crowd scenes. I talked to my brothers, asking them to watch over her.

IN FEBRUARY, TWO MONTHS after I returned from China, I was thrilled when Alan negotiated a new contract for me with Paramount Studio, which gave me hope that I could help Mary find film work along the way. Working with a big Hollywood studio again was wonderful, especially one that had a successful publicity department operating within it. I looked forward to collaborating with Edith Head on costume designs in her famously cramped studio office. She had a large closet full of dressmaker mannequins shaped to the exact measurements of all the stars she dressed. (Mae West's having the "largest melons," she once told me.)

Edith remained one of my dearest friends, even adopting my virgin-child haircut for herself after we met; she wore it ever since. We gabbed endlessly about fashion and she always welcomed my input and encouraged me to wear some of the beautiful silk *qipaos* I'd had made in Shanghai in my upcoming movies. Now that everything was finally falling into place, I hoped that Paramount would finally see me as an asset to have under contract, a Chinese actress who had firsthand knowledge of China.

As much as I hated to admit it, the success of the movie *The Good Earth* had increased the rise in America's sympathy for China and the Chinese. Americans also appeared to support Nationalist leader Chiang Kai-shek and his beautiful wife, Soong Mei-ling. She was charming, smart, and a graduate of Wellesley College. Together they were showcased in international newsreels and magazines, a striking couple who comfortably addressed China's war with Japan to growing audiences around the world. While China had once been disdained as a faraway, barbaric country, it was now seen with more tolerance and acceptance.

I'd only been home for only a few months when the Japanese began to escalate their advances in China, and soon news reports indicated that they had Shanghai in their sights.

I kept in close touch with Lulu, now living and working in Shanghai, and James, who was teaching at a Shanghai business college. I wrote often to my siblings and made them promise to return home at the first signs of Japanese movement toward Shanghai. I'd also begun volunteering for the United China Relief, the main organization for American citizens to provide aid. I had a personal connection to China now, and I was determined to help in any way that I could.

IT WASN'T LONG BEFORE I returned to my old traveling habits, rushing from Los Angeles to New York to London and back again.

In London, I saw my old friends and savored an ecstatic reunion with Eric Maschwitz. Everything was going well for him. Our previously carefree yet blissful relationship when meeting in London or New York seemed suddenly charged. This time, for whatever reason, when we traveled to Paris together, our connection assumed a more serious tone of love and commitment.

He'd been offered a six-figure contract for his hit London play, *Balalaika*, to open in New York. I persuaded him to take a leave from his job at the BBC, go to New York for contract talks, and then come to California to work in Hollywood. Being together for an extended period of time would allow us to see if what we had was something more than simply the romantic whirlwind of seeing each other several times a year.

"Please come," I'd said to him. It was our last night in Paris before I had to return to Los Angeles for discussions about a new movie with Paramount.

"What will I do with all that sun?" he asked.

I laughed. "You might enjoy it," I said.

"I'll think about it," he said.

This was just what we'd been waiting for. His play was a big success and everyone wanted it. Hollywood was exactly where he needed to be. Eric's marriage was something rarely discussed, and I'd convinced myself he and his wife remained together more out of convenience than love. I knew his love for me was strong enough to have inspired one of his most popular songs. It was enough for now.

When he finally agreed, I returned to Los Angeles to await his arrival. At thirty-two, this was what I hoped for, finally feeling a sense of permanence and devotion grounding my life for the first time. Eric was still married, but his coming to California was a conscious step for a stronger commitment.

BACK IN LOS ANGELES in March, while I waited for Eric and for news from Lulu in Shanghai, I spent time with Mary, who thankfully appeared happier. I felt clearheaded and blissful, until the afternoon a letter arrived in my mailbox. It was nondescript in a plain white envelope with my name and address typed in capital letters but no return address. I almost discarded it but opened it anyway, then wished I hadn't. My heart raced as I read and reread the lines.

IF YOU DON'T PAY ME $20,000 TOWARD MY MOVIE PRODUCTION, I WON'T HESITATE TO THROW ACID AT THAT PRETTY FACE OF YOURS. AND JUST SO YOU KNOW HOW SERIOUS I AM, I'LL DISFIGURE YOUR FATHER AS WELL . . .

He wanted the money deposited in a bank account he supplied. If I did as I was told, no one would be hurt. I felt sick to my stomach. I was being threatened, blackmailed by some faceless extortionist who used words to frighten and wound. Thankfully, *baba* was in Chang On, but I was alarmed that whoever it was knew about my family and where I lived. While I hadn't made a movie for a few years, I remained on prominent display in all the newsreels and movie magazines showcasing my trip to China. I had inadvertently turned myself into a prime candidate to be blackmailed with all the publicity I'd generated. I immediately called the police, who appeared nonplussed about my situation, simply telling me not to pay the ransom while they investigated. Meanwhile, I should stay alert to my surroundings.

"And then what?" I asked, feeling hot and sweaty. "How am I supposed to stop someone who lies in wait to attack me?"

The middle-aged policeman looked at me as if I were the one who needed to be subdued. "Miss Wong, most of these people are just looking for a little attention. Nine out of ten times they get off on frightening people, not really harming them."

"And what if I'm that tenth person?"

He shook his head. "Let us do our job, Miss Wong. We'll let you know as soon as we have any new information."

And with that he was gone. The following weeks, I was terrified to leave my apartment alone. I never felt at ease and was always looking over my shoulder, hating the hold this person had on me.

Over the years, I'd heard so many stories about fanatic fans and wannabe actors and actresses who would go to any lengths to be in a movie, or to be near a movie star. One young woman had actually broken into a house that she thought belonged to Clark Gable, had made dinner, and sat in the candlelit dining room waiting for him. When the real owners returned, she berated them for trespassing and threatened to call the police. There were more horrific stories, one about a young man who was so enamored with an actress that, when he was spurned by her, he waited outside her house. When she returned, he attacked and killed her with a knife. He later told the police that he had no recollection of what he'd done.

Other fears kept circling my thoughts. I couldn't sleep. Every sound and shadow set me on alert, thinking it could potentially be the blackmailer. When I needed to attend big events, I hired a bodyguard and stayed at the family house most nights. It wasn't until the wife of producer David O. Selznick was similarly threatened and blackmailed a few weeks later that the police took my case more seriously. I tried not to think that it had to do with my being Chinese. A few names surfaced, though they were soon deemed delusional and released. Soon, the FBI became involved, and after being interviewed by the authorities yet again, I let them know I wasn't about to just sit quietly by waiting for them to finally do something. I was tired of living in fear.

I left Los Angeles in late May for the East Coast, doing cabaret shows in Washington D.C., much like the ones I'd done in Europe, followed by a week at the Loew's State Theater in New York. I felt in control again being onstage dressed in a black *qipao*, singing Chinese folk songs, and doing dramatic sketches while staying at my beloved Algonquin Hotel.

BY JUNE OF 1937, the news from China became more serious. I received increasingly urgent letters from Lulu as China braced for war with Japan. When I had left Shanghai seven months earlier, I had no idea the Japanese government would be gathering its armies to continue its sadistic, imperialist rage to defeat China, which began with the invasion of Manchuria in 1931. Every day the news reported rumblings that Japan was rallying an all-out assault across China, setting its sights on taking Shanghai first, quickly followed by invading the Chinese Nationalist capital of Nanjing. I wired Lulu. *You and James must leave Shanghai as soon as possible. I'll wire you the money to return to LA.* Thankfully, *baba* and Richard were still safe in Chang On. Guangdong Province remained far away from any fighting at the moment. I also knew my father would never leave his ancestral village until he was left with no other choice.

With tensions escalating in China, I felt guilty enjoying myself in New York and was soon filled with dread for Lulu and James, still in Shanghai with the Japanese bearing down on them. I returned to Los Angeles to be with my family, despite having heard not a word about the blackmailer. The case was labeled ongoing. But I had more pressing matters now; my main concern was to do everything in my power to bring Lulu and James home safely.

LETTERS FROM CHINA
Lulu—Summer of 1937

June 24, 1937

Dear Anna,

Things are changing fast here. Shanghai is on high alert. The Japanese have been moving closer this week, aiming for swift takeover on their way to claim their real prize, the capital of Nanjing. Working in the customs office, I hear bits and pieces, and it doesn't sound good. Talk and speculation only adds to our growing fear. At my boarding house tonight, the remaining foreign boarders were sitting around the dinner table making plans to leave Shanghai for other parts of China, or to leave China altogether. I couldn't help but think about all my Chinese colleagues with nowhere to go. I could barely finish my dinner before escaping to my room.

You asked what it was like here in your last letter. Walking home from work this evening, I noticed how everyone seems to be on edge, walking too fast to get somewhere, or too slow to avoid arriving. At the central market, people's voices lack the camaraderie of everyday life like when you were here. Now, it's a lot of arguing, frantic bursts over nothing, quarrels about the quality of the bok choy or the cost of pork. One woman slapped another woman over a bunch of green onions. When they broke into tears, I could only imagine their fear. Everyone's waiting for the other shoe to drop.

The streets are a miserable sight since many of the poorer Chinese, who already have so little, have also lost their hope. They try to go about their daily business as if this war wasn't whispering in their ear. Everyone knows the Japanese are coming, but they have nowhere to go, and their despair feels heavier every day. Only the powerful and wealthy can leave Shanghai for other cities or for the countryside. It's hard to fathom these rich Shanghainese ladies walking down dirt roads or tilling the fields without their servants and amahs. What would they wear?

By day, Shanghai is bustling as always but when the sun goes down, you can feel the low hum of panic. We are lucky to be able to leave as soon as our papers are approved. I've already packed, ready at a moment's notice.

> *Love,*
> *Lulu*

I smiled at Lulu's quip even amid her fear. *What would they wear?* If the Japanese had set their sights on seizing Nanjing, the heart of the Nationalist government of China, then capturing Shanghai, with all its wealth and power, was akin to severing China's right arm.

July 17, 1937

Dear Lulu,

I'm so thankful you received the funds I wired to you and James. I want you both to leave Shanghai as soon as your papers are approved. The news reports here describe Japanese aggressions that are cruel and barbaric, their indiscriminate bombing of civilians in apartment buildings, hospitals, and schools. It isn't safe there anymore, even if you are American citizens. Perhaps you should go to baba and Richard in Chang On first. It's just a matter of time now before the Japanese reach Shanghai and then you'll be trapped, and there's no telling if you'll be able to get out.

I know you hate to leave all your friends, but you'll see them again when this horrid war is over and China stands tall again. We Chinese Americans will help them to rebuild. But to do that, you must stay safe. I await when you'll return.

Write or telegraph me at the Westchester Theatre in Elmsford, New York. I'm here rehearsing for Turandot, *which opens in August for a week. Then I leave for the Westport Playhouse in Connecticut for another week. I can't wait to hear that you're both safe and sound. Take care and leave as soon as possible.*

Love,

Anna

I SENT A FLURRY of telegrams to *baba*, asking him to come home with Richard. As expected, he refused to leave Chang On.

He responded: *We are home.*

I insisted: *Think of Richard! Please come home.*

He responded: *Do you think I would endanger your brother's life?*

I wrote: *Of course not. I just want you both home and safe.*

To which he replied: *We will return when we absolutely have to.*

August 15, 1937

Dear Anna,

We heard the roar of the planes overhead first—so many, they looked like a flock of birds in the sky. When the bombing started, we took cover in designated bomb shelters with other Americans and Europeans trying to leave. I'm so glad that America isn't involved in this war. The Japanese are relentless. You can't imagine the death and destruction. Entire buildings collapsing, countless people killed in a matter of minutes. I'll never forget what I've seen. Are lives worth so little? Running to the bomb shelter, I hadn't time—or breath—enough to cry for all those poor souls.

I know you want to scold us for waiting so long to leave. But by the time James and I had settled all our affairs and had our travel documents filed and returned, the Japanese started bombing Shanghai. We were transported out with other American citizens and have just arrived in Hong Kong.

Love,

Lulu

WESTCHESTER, NEW YORK
Turandot—Summer Stock–1937

Since I wasn't scheduled by Paramount to begin filming my next movie until autumn, I took the chance to do some summer stock theater for the first time in Westchester County, New York, and Westport, Connecticut. I returned to New York City for a few days in mid-July to stay at the Algonquin and see friends, including Eric, before rehearsals began. He had finally arrived in New York along with his wife, Hermione Gingold, so he and I kept a low profile. I was also looking forward to seeing writer Lin Yutang who, with help from Carl, had immigrated not long after I'd met him in Peking.

More than anything, I was excited to be doing theater again, starring with Vincent Price in *Turandot*, a dramatic adaptation of the Puccini opera, at the Westchester Theatre followed by the Westport Playhouse, where Carl was a board member. Not only would I be donning an elaborate Chinese headdress for the role, I was also wearing some of the *qipaos* I'd bought in China.

I was in good company, wined and dined by some of New York's elite, the Astors and the Knopfs, who were driven out of the city by the incessant heat to their summer homes. Between rehearsals, I enjoyed playing tennis and swimming. And playing the role of the Chinese princess as written was a thrill. This was my chance to show an erudite, well-rounded audience that it did make a big difference not to have an actress in yellowface.

The Westchester Theatre attracted throngs of influential New

Yorkers, as well as movie and stage stars who also had second homes in the area. I was apparently a bigger draw than I had imagined.

"What did I tell you?" Carl reminded me when he told me to break a leg before the performance. "They've been waiting for you to come to their theater."

"Talk to me after the curtain drops," I said, already anxious.

"You're going to be a sensation," he said.

It wasn't until I slipped into my brightly embroidered Chinese silk jacket, and placed the enormous ornate headdress on my head that I looked into the mirror and fell into character. *I am Princess Turandot*, I repeated to myself. Taking the stage, I made it mine. Opening night was a huge success, and Vincent and I were greeted with thunderous applause as we made our bows, returning for three curtain calls. Afterward, I was delighted to greet Tallulah Bankhead, Ethel Barrymore, and my old friend and mentor, Alla Nazimova. They all came backstage to offer their congratulations, along with invitations to lunches and dinners. Their presence at the play guaranteed major write-ups in all the New York City newspapers, as well as in the local press.

After everyone had gone, I sat in my dressing room, gazing into the mirror as I took off my makeup. Looking closely, I saw *ma ma* in the shape of my eyes, the slight curve of my pencil-thin eyebrows. How I wished my family could have seen the performance tonight, which *baba* would have also enjoyed. But despite the evening's success, I couldn't be completely at ease until I knew Lulu and James were safely home.

A knock on the door of my dressing room and here was Carl, holding a bottle of champagne and two glasses.

"You were amazing!" he said, smiling as he stepped in and popped the bottle open.

"Thank you," I said, feeling nothing but relief.

I'd had no idea how the performance would turn out. I could have just as easily been sitting in front of the mirror, miserable. Carl handed me a glass of champagne and poured another for himself.

"To many more successes!" he said, and touched his glass against mine. "I have some terrific photos of you wearing the head-dress. And another good shot with you and Vincent. We'll add them to your portfolio."

"Thank you, Carl. You and Fania are so dear to me." I paused. "Where is Fania?"

"She went on to the party," he said.

I drank down the rest of my champagne. "And we'll be late if we keep toasting," I said, standing up to gather my things.

"So what else is new?" he teased, winking.

It would always be a bone of contention between us, even said in jest. I suppose I wouldn't be irritated by his comment if there wasn't some truth to it.

"Unlike other celebrations, this one is for me," I said. "It's bad form to be late to your own party."

Carl laughed, offered his arm, and escorted me out.

WHAT AN UNFORGETTABLE EVENING! I felt so lucky to be relevant. Although I hadn't made a new movie in a few years, I had managed to appear in the news, and in major fan magazines. Carl's photos from *Turandot* expanded my ongoing allure. The Westchester

Theatre was delighted with my sold-out performances, and there was already talk of bringing me back the following summer.

MY JOY WAS COMPLETE when I finally received a wire from Lulu.

August 16, 1937
> *SAFE IN HONG KONG. STAYING HERE THROUGH AUGUST. SAILING HOME NEXT MONTH. NEVER SO TIRED IN MY LIFE.*
> *LOVE,*
> *LULU*

August 17, 1937
Dear Lulu–

I can finally breathe again knowing you and James have arrived safely in Hong Kong. I can't wait to see you! Baba still refuses to leave Chang On, saying the Japanese aren't anywhere near Guangdong Province. "For now," I tell him. "But you must leave with Richard at the first sign their army is heading south."

The Japanese will stop at nothing to take our homeland. I worry about baba and Richard but trust that elder brother, Huang Dounan, is watching over them and will know when they should leave. Meanwhile, you'll be home soon, Lulu, your nightmares will end. I'm so happy to hear that you're resting in Hong Kong.

I'm off for a quick trip to London but will be home waiting for your return next month. I can't wait to see you both. Take care and rest well after your terrifying ordeal.

Love,

Anna

LOS ANGELES
"These Foolish Things"—1937–1938

Eric finally arrived in Los Angeles at the end of August, leaving his wife in New York discussing future theater projects before she returned to London to star in a new play in the West End. I rushed back to meet him, and we were finally alone. Our first month together was the most carefree and romantic of my life. I showed him all the Hollywood nightspots I frequented, the Cocoanut Grove, Café Trocadero, and the Chateau Marmont. We walked the beaches and ate at all the good restaurants, Perino's and Chasen's, including those in Chinatown where we dined with my family, welcoming Lulu and James back home in September. We threw cocktail parties at my apartment, and I took Eric to lunch at the studio commissary, where he met John Barrymore and Jean Harlow. I laughed at how boyishly starstruck he'd suddenly become at meeting what he called "real movie stars."

"Am I not a real movie star?" I teased.

He looked at me, considering, before he answered, "You, my love, are a queen."

"I thought you left her back in England."

He laughed. "Ah, yes, but she is second only to you."

"Don't you know the right words to say," I said, leaning in for a kiss.

While London was a world away for Eric, he seemed to enjoy rubbing shoulders with Hollywood stars in the easygoing atmosphere of Los Angeles, where cocktails could be ordered by the pool or down by the beach, and the weather was perpetually dry and sunny in early fall. We also spent some time in Palm Springs, where he marveled at the desert sunsets. I had to stop and pinch myself. This was how it felt to have someone walking in the world beside you. It was one of the few times in my life that I was completely at peace and longed for the permanence of marriage.

While Eric was happily writing, entrenched with his transplanted British and Hollywood friends throughout September to keep him busy, I went to work, filming *Daughter of Shanghai*, the first movie under my new contract with Paramount. Since returning to Los Angeles, I'd told Alan I wanted to incorporate my travel experiences into every role I played. While Paramount appeared committed to presenting China, and Chinese actors and actresses, in a better light, they weren't willing to give me a starring role in a big budget movie to help promote my career. Again, I was left with no choice but to accept the role I was given, in a B movie that would accompany a big budget film on a double bill at the theaters. As usual, I had to play second fiddle to Barbara Stanwyck or Katharine Hepburn or Carole Lombard. But I was in no position to push my luck, so determined I was to do the best with what I had.

Still, there was much to be happy about starring in *Daughter of Shanghai*. The story presented a favorable depiction of China, provided sympathetic roles for the two Chinese stars, and included a happily-ever-after ending. The film also starred Philip Ahn, who was a good friend, so it felt like I'd hit a home run. I wore a number of gowns that I'd brought back from Peking and made sure they covered my legs in keeping with China's standards. The only awkward incident came after filming the movie, when Paramount tried to link Philip and me romantically as a way to promote the film.

Before I knew it, reporters were swarming around me wherever I went, asking if it was true that we were getting married.

"I don't discuss my personal life," I answered, thinking of Eric.

"Come on, Miss Wong, just tell us if there's any truth to the rumors."

"Philip Ahn and I are longtime friends," I said. "We're more like brother and sister," I added, refusing to acknowledge anything more.

I heard that Philip was unhappy with my response, wanting to keep the Hollywood hype going, but I knew it would soon blow over. Fortunately, the film received very good reviews from around the world. I even garnered a positive review from a Chinese magazine, leaving me hopeful for a new beginning.

WHILE MY CAREER FLOURISHED with several more movies on the horizon, my personal life, which only those closest to me knew about, had hit a rough patch. Although Eric didn't voice any discontent, I could feel him becoming disenchanted with Los Angeles and pulling away. He became quieter and more introspective as he worked on new scripts and songs. In late October, he began mentioning that he'd have to return to work at the BBC soon, or they would fire him for good. I wondered if he had heard from his wife, but couldn't bring myself to ask. I refused to become one of those jealous girlfriends who whined and nagged.

By mid-November, I tried to remain cheerful, taking Eric back to all the spots he favored, having long romantic dinners, and another weekend getaway to Palm Springs, though I knew it was like trying to hold on to air. I loved his *joie de vivre*, but it seemed after three months, he was losing it a little more each day in "eternally sunny" Los Angeles, as he called it. I was finally ready to settle down and could have cried and screamed for him to stay with me, but that was never our way. It would only make things ugly. At the end of the month, I drove Eric to the airport and he was gone. When I returned home alone, I couldn't stop crying, and I couldn't keep my heart from breaking.

> A cigarette that bears a lipstick's traces
> An airline ticket to romantic places
> And still my heart has wings
> These foolish things remind me of you.

After Eric returned to London, there were many transatlantic phone conversations, but those static, hollow calls were only a reminder of just how far away we were from each other.

December 8, 1937
Dear Carlo,
    Forgive me for not writing sooner. I've been busy, busy.
Lately, I feel like I'm at the studio most of the time, leaving little

occasion for a social life. After Daughter of Shanghai, *I'm set to begin filming* Dangerous to Know. *Afterwards, I have two more films, one I'm so looking forward to called* King of Chinatown. *I'll be working with good friends, Edith Head, Philip Ahn, and Tony Quinn. Best of all, I'm playing a doctor modeled after Dr. Margaret Chung, the brilliant Chinese-American surgeon who is collecting money for China Relief. I usually have just enough energy to brush my teeth and fall into bed, but I'm simply glad to be working. It keeps my thoughts focused with less time to wallow in my sadness over Eric, though he still weighs heavily in my heart and mind.*

On a brighter note, Lulu and James finally returned from Shanghai in September. Lulu was traumatized by the Japanese bombing of Shanghai and the deaths she witnessed before they left. She's much better now, back home with my brothers and my sister Mary. Who would have thought we'd all be so happy to have Lulu telling us what to do again!

Still, the situation in China grows bleaker by the day. The Japanese are ruthless, and I can't convince my father to bring Richard to Los Angeles. He stubbornly refuses, believing Chang On is a safe haven for now. Meanwhile, I'm doing all I can to help the homeland. I've thrown myself headfirst into helping China in any way I can. Right now, it's with cash. Later, I hope to be more hands on in helping the cause.

But how are you? I saw your portrait of Georgia O'Keeffe in Life *magazine. You are such a talent. And how is dear Fania? I miss you both and can't wait to get back to New York in the New*

Year. Or perhaps you might be yearning for some of our California sunshine?

Write when you can. I promise to answer, no matter how busy. Love to you and Fania.

Yours,

Anna May

LOS ANGELES
In Service—1938–1939

My busy schedule continued into the New Year. In March of 1938, *Dangerous to Know* was released, and I graced the cover of the second issue of *Look* magazine, an image that showed me brandishing a bloody dagger along with the caption, "World's Most Beautiful Chinese Girl." However contradictory, I saw it as a major step toward acceptance. Finally, a Chinese actress was on the front cover of an American magazine with a circulation of over two million readers.

On June 25, five years after demolishing Old Chinatown and our childhood neighborhood to make room for the new Union Station, there was the grand opening ceremony for New Chinatown, built by Peter Soo Hoo and a group of businessmen. It was a blend of Chinese and American architecture, featuring the Central Plaza, a large, ornate entry gate, restaurants, and shops to attract more tourists. I happily shoveled dirt for the planting of a ceremonial willow tree and was one of several Chinese actors and actresses, including Keye Luke and Soo Yong, featured at the inaugural day festivities.

It was exciting to see that the Chinese-American community would have a new commercial center for their social and business lives.

AS EVENTFUL AS THE year was, *baba* and Richard's absence weighed heavily on my mind as the Japanese continued to push through China, taking possession of ports and railways. After Lulu and James's return, Nanjing, the Nationalist capital, fell in December of 1937, leaving hundreds of thousands Chinese slaughtered. When the Nationalist capital was moved to Hankou, the Japanese troops followed, toppling cities, including Xuzhou and Wuhan, along the way. As the invaders pushed their way south, *baba* and Richard finally departed Chang On for Hong Kong right before the Japanese land invasion of Canton on October 21, 1938. While it was a relief to know they were on their way home, I was terrified for friends in Peking and Shanghai, and for my elder brother, Huang Dounan. He spoke Japanese, having studied in Japan, so he remained in Chang On to work as an interpreter and to protect the village. I couldn't help fearing for Mei and her daughter Liling, the young girl with the nightingale voice. How would they remain safe? I was more determined than ever to keep China in the news.

WHEN LULU CALLED THE studio where I was filming *King of Chinatown* to tell me *baba* and Richard had arrived home, I wept with relief. Now that my immediate family was back where they belonged, I secretly hoped *baba*'s return might rouse Mary from her unhappiness. When she didn't receive a call back for a small part in

Charlie Chan at Monte Carlo or for my current film, *King of China-town*, she'd become increasingly distant and distracted, leaving Lulu and me worried about what to do.

I hurried home from the studio as soon as we hung up.

"*Baba?*" I called as I stepped inside, eager to see him for the first time in almost two years.

Thin and tired, he sat at the old kitchen table in our new family residence, a two-story house with a large yard and a detached garage. He had spent very little time here before returning to Chang On. In 1933, Old Chinatown, our Figueroa Street neighborhood, along with the laundry and our house behind it, had been torn down to make room for the new railway terminal. That's when my father returned to China, feeling that there was little left for him here. Now, he sat dispirited in a house and a neighborhood he no longer knew.

"Ah, Anna," he said as I sat down next to him.

"*Baba*, how was your trip home? You must be tired."

He looked up at me, his face pale and gaunt. "A sad and long trip," he said.

"I'm so happy you were able to get out in time," I said.

"I was fortunate to have Richard with me. I never thought those Japanese devils would get so far," he said, more to himself than to me.

"The important thing is that you and Richard are home safe."

He looked around the kitchen. "Everything has changed," he said, his fingers unconsciously tapping the kitchen table.

"Not so much," I said, sad to see him so old and forlorn. Where was the man who had lectured and battled me on almost every move I made growing up? "And what has changed is mostly for the better.

You'll see, this weekend I'll take you to see our New Chinatown. Many of your old friends are around. They're looking forward to seeing you," I added.

He smiled faintly, nodded. "I would like that," he said.

I leaned down and gave him a hug, then went off to welcome my brother, Richard, back home.

MY WORK WITH THE China support organization grew with each day. I was sickened by the massacre in Nanjing. As the Japanese continued their brutal advance, I threw myself headfirst into fundraising, even auctioning off many of my gowns collected over the years in Paris, New York, Shanghai, and Hollywood to send medical supplies and money to help aid the resistance. I'd made earlier sales to benefit the Assistance League, and now I was helping out China Relief. After all, how many *qipaos* could one woman wear when her homeland was under siege?

IN THE SPRING OF 1939, I made my last film under contract for Paramount Studios, *Island of Lost Men*. When the film wrapped, I was told by Alan that Paramount had decided not to renew my contract. "I'm sorry, Anna May, I don't know what they're thinking."

"But the movies have done well," I said, unable to hide my surprise. I assumed Paramount would want to retain me. It wasn't as if there were a multitude of Chinese actresses in Hollywood to choose from, especially one who already had a large fan base.

"I told them as much," Alan said, exasperated. "I told them

there's only one Anna May Wong and they're making a big mistake. It's their loss." He added, "We'll find you a new home in no time."

Fists clenched, I was both incensed and dejected, but once again, I put on a brave face and tried not to show how upset I was.

"I know you will," I said, with a certainty I didn't feel.

Despite knowing that no one in the movie business was completely secure, I was staggered. After hearing so many stories of actors and actresses who had fallen on hard times, I couldn't help worrying. Many were now working in downtown department stores, or in restaurants, or had left Hollywood altogether. For the first time in my life, the thought hit me. *Who was I if I wasn't acting?* I'd spent my life focused on one singular goal, to become a movie star.

At thirty-four, that star appeared barely visible now.

FORTUNATELY, I'D GROWN UP watching my mother and father work twelve- to fourteen-hour days, seven days a week, at the laundry. I always knew the importance of putting savings aside for the lean times. Over the years, I'd saved enough money to buy two large lots on the corner of Fourth Street and San Vicente Boulevard in Santa Monica, just a few blocks from the Pacific Ocean. It was one of the loveliest streets in Los Angeles, lined with coral trees in one direction and palm trees in the other. On the corner lot was an apartment house that I converted into four separate units that I named the Moongate Apartments. In front of the apartment I lived in, I installed a small pond and garden surrounded by a wall and moongate, a circular entrance with a round wooden door, just like those in Chang On, offering an auspicious welcome to all that passed through it. Photos of Lulu and me sitting by the pond were circulated around China. I wanted them to see how serious I was about bringing China to America.

Not long after the pond was installed, I dropped white lotus flowers in, beautiful and buoyant on the surface. I closed my eyes, wished for such resiliency, then prayed to any god who would listen. "Let this be home," I whispered, "let me find peace here."

The new apartments were a great distraction, keeping me from slipping into self-pity as I was pushed to learn other skills in life closer to home, decorating and gardening. While my father stayed at the family house with Lulu and Mary, my brother Richard, who just turned sixteen, came to live with me. He'd gone through a great deal of upheaval in the past few years, and I hoped that he would relax and settle back home again. The building skills he'd acquired early on in Chang On made him very handy to have around the apartment. Soon, Richard was always painting or fixing something in one of the four units.

Together, we worked in the garden and began cultivating exotic plants and orchids. "You're good at gardening," Richard said, as he stood and surveyed our work.

"I am?" I said, surprised. I had that "for me?" look like someone had just handed me an unexpected gift.

I enjoyed running my fingers through the soil (I even trimmed my famously long fingernails), planting and watching the flowers bloom. I soon learned what a gift it was. Gardening gave me peace of mind, providing me with a minimal sense of control in an otherwise uncontrollable world.

A few months later, I was delighted when the magazine *Better*

Homes & Gardens caught wind of my new interest through Alan and devoted a full-page layout to my Chinese-influenced interior decoration and flower arrangements at Moongate. At long last, we were making headway.

Without any film roles, I also found solace in my continued work for China Relief. I entertained and cooked for friends near and far, including Victor Sassoon, visiting from China, and Carl and Fania, from New York. We soon began collecting a number of dogs and cats, including two Pekingese pups named Maskee and Dumshaw who, given to me by the Chinese consul of Los Angeles, became part of the family. It hadn't been a transition of choice, but of necessity. I was lucky I was good at it, though my entire body ached to be in front of a camera and living someone else's life again, even if it meant dying at the end.

In between, I made fundraising trips for China's aid, doing whatever I could to help with the war effort.

May 5, 1939
Dear Carlo and Fania,

What better way to raise funds for the China cause than to be in New York with such dear friends. Thanks to you both for hosting such a wonderful party for Lin Yutang and me. And during such a busy time for you, Carlo, photographing the World's Fair! The photos I've seen so far are stupendous. The fair's theme, "Building the World of Tomorrow," seems very appropriate as we all look toward the future. Imagine, Albert Einstein giving a speech about cosmic rays and RCA introducing television to the mass public. I especially love the photo of the television set made with a transparent case so that all its internal tubes and components can be seen. That should tame the skeptics!

With the war preventing any travel to China or Europe, I leave for Melbourne, Australia, in three days for a series of variety shows where I'll sing and dance called Highlights from Hollywood. *I'll also be able to lecture and raise funds for my China aid crusade. I'm so happy working for the war effort and promise to write more from there.*

> *Love to you both,*
> *Anna May*

By September of 1939, after a successful tour in Australia, in which I enjoyed Melbourne and fell in love with Sydney, I returned home, only to be met with the unspeakable.

LOS ANGELES
Mary—July 25, 1940

Mary.

Dear Mary.

My sweet Mary is dead.

My beautiful sister was found hanging in the garage of our family home, dangling from a rafter, one shoe on the ground next to the toppled stool. Hanging limp like a Raggedy Ann doll with no one there to save her.

Where was I? Why didn't I save her?

I want to be an actress like you, she'd said over and over, ever since she was just a young girl.

"You don't want to be like me," I told her.

I should have explained more, been tougher and angrier. Acting is not the life I thought it would be. Hollywood doesn't care if they use real Chinese in their movies. We're expendable to them. Please, Mary, I've had so many disappointments, such heartaches. Find something else, anything else that will make you happy.

I want to be an actress like you.

It isn't a world for goodness and kindness.

I want to be an actress like you.

It will swallow you whole.

I want to be an actress like you.

Run as far away as you can.

Mary's ghostly voice filled every room I walked into. I cried so many tears there weren't any left. I should have paid closer attention when she began slipping away. Selfishly, I hadn't.

For days and then weeks after her death, I woke and slept and woke, watching the sunrise.

I only knew one thing.

Hollywood did this.

LOS ANGELES
Madame Chiang Kai-shek—1941–1947

After Mary's death, I traveled continuously on behalf of China Relief. I couldn't sit still, or I'd be consumed by the guilt and darkness, and was thankful to have the distraction. It became a full-time job since I was selected as head of the motion-picture division of the Rice Bowl fund, providing medical aid to China, and to the China Aid fund. The irony was that Hollywood, which I blamed in part for Mary's death, was financing China Relief. I could live with it for the greater good, I kept telling myself. With the Japanese bombing of Pearl Harbor on December 7, 1941, and the United States entering World War II, my mission to continue helping the war effort felt even more vital.

With no studio contract, I was free to support the Chinese cause against Japan in any way I wanted. After my many fundraising benefits, which ranged from Hollywood luncheons to fashion shows, I spoke on radio shows and starred in *Bombs over Burma*, produced by Poverty Row Producers Releasing Corporation (PRC) in 1942, donating my salary to the fund. I saw it as an effective propaganda film in support of the China cause. During much of the year, I continued with my fundraising efforts working with the Red Cross, USO, and United China Relief.

I also returned to writing when I was asked to pen the preface for a cookbook, *New Chinese Recipes*, authored by Mabel Stegner, a home economics consultant. The sixty recipes were selected by Fred Wing, a young Chinese restaurateur, to help raise money for United China Relief. This was one of the first Chinese cookbooks published in the United States, and writing the preface gave me the unique opportunity of making it more than just a book of recipes. I'd always enjoyed cooking for family and friends, and I wanted to see Chinese food as a new mainstay in our everyday lives. America was finally opening up to Oriental cultures, and Chinese restaurants were suddenly all the rage. I couldn't see why cooking ethnic foods at home shouldn't be included as part of our acceptance. It seemed a natural progression, and I was determined to take full advantage of what many Americans already liked.

Growing up, we were raised on my mother's Chinese cooking—stir-fried chicken or pork with vegetables, braised chicken, slow-cooked soups, and crispy-skin roast duck on holidays or special occasions, while rice remained a main staple. Even now, every time Richard and I returned from a visit to New York, I'd make my special fried rice with eggs, barbeque pork, baby shrimp, and green onions, which had become our version of comfort food as we settled back home again. I found myself experimenting with new Chinese dishes all the time, inviting over guests who enjoyed my cooking as we sat around my round black lacquer dining room table.

In late summer of 1942, though I was as good as retired in Hollywood's eyes, I made my second film for PRC called *The Lady from Chungking*, again donating my salary. While the reviews were lukewarm, I was happy to have played the heroine for a change, a strong Chinese woman who would have formerly been played by a Caucasian actress in yellowface.

In November, I flew from Los Angeles back to New York to be queen of the Rice Bowl Gala at the Waldorf Astoria. I also hosted a fashion show featuring evening gowns inspired by traditional Chinese dress. What I'd worn for decades, a mix of Chinese and American dress, was now at the height of fashion. American audiences loved what they saw, and the fashion show was a big success. I traveled up to Boston on behalf of the Rice Bowl fund and then toured the rest of New England doing fundraising shows and parties.

In mid-December, I took the train back to Los Angeles from New York, not just exhausted but physically unwell. I knew I'd been doing too much, drinking too much, and sleeping badly. By day, I was occupied by one benefit after another, but at night, I was haunted by Mary's death and the quick demise of my career. For the past two years, I'd been running from both, fundraising for China at a breakneck pace. When I stepped off the train in Los Angeles, I was more than thankful that Richard, at twenty, had taken it upon himself to deal with Christmas.

MY LIFE CHANGED AGAIN not long after the holidays. All my hard work for the war effort through United China Relief fell to the wayside when Madame Chiang Kai-shek began her very successful publicity tour through the United States, capturing the world's attention. She was beloved by the Nationalist-supporting Chinese and Americans alike, presenting the perfect example of a well-spoken, educated, and beautiful Chinese woman. Hollywood swung open its door to welcome her in the spring of 1943. Henry R. Luce and David O. Selznick hosted a tea for two hundred Hollywood stars, followed by a dinner that was attended by fifteen hundred celebrities. I was not only lost in the crowd but left out completely when she spoke to an audience of thirty thousand at the Hollywood Bowl in April. Afterward, when she stood onstage, flanked by Hollywood's most famous and glamorous actresses, including Ingrid Bergman, Barbara Stanwyck, Ginger Rogers, and Loretta Young, I was nowhere in sight. I hadn't been invited to participate, though I'd done more fundraising for the cause than all those actresses combined. I wasn't the only one excluded; it appeared most of the Chinese-American movie stars were also left out of the events.

"WHO DOES SHE THINK she is?" Frances Marion roared. "After all you've done to help China in this war! I don't care who Madame Chiang Kai-shek is, she's even more prejudiced than the rest of them."

"It's over," I said. "But the cause isn't."

I'd stopped by France's house to commiserate. She poured us a drink and sat down across from me. "Doesn't matter? Just shows what's really underneath all the smooth talk and her beautiful facade. She's just as bad as the communists—worse, because she comes off as righteous and upstanding, when she's small and petty. And I thought Hollywood was bad!"

I laughed and put up a good front. Inside, I was seething. When I learned from my writer friend Rob Wagner that Madame Chiang Kai-shek had specifically ordered that I not be invited to the Holly-wood Bowl event, I was so angry and hurt I could hardly get out of bed. My past, as *baba* always warned, was catching up with me. I knew the more conservative Nationalist Chinese always thought I'd disgraced China with my movie roles, but I'd mistakenly thought I might be forgiven after all my hard work raising funds for China's war effort. Instead, I was slapped in the face and embarrassed right in my own hometown of Hollywood.

"She hates everything I represent," I finally said. "Let's start with the fact that I'm an American-born Chinese. Did you see any other

Chinese-American actors and actresses up on the stage with her? And even worse, the Chinese living here are mostly from Southern China, and we speak Cantonese, lacking what Madame Chiang Kai-shek believes is the language and culture of the Mandarin-speaking Northern China. Add that to the films I've made, and the characters I've played, and she sees me as the worst kind of Chinese, nothing but shameful and reprehensible. What better way to dishonor me than to leave me out of the festivities?"

"The Chinese are prejudiced against each other?"

"Who would have thought," I said, trying to lighten the mood.

In truth, I'd been too naive. Throughout my career, I'd been left out in the cold by Hollywood, never given the roles I deserved because I was Chinese. While I'd come to expect it from Westerners, it was unconscionable to be treated in the same way by my own countrymen. Was it so hard to understand I had no choice but to take the roles I did? Apparently, I would never be forgiven, so I was left to do what I'd always done, accept my fate and put on a brave face.

"Unbelievable!" Frances said. "Don't worry, Anna May, everyone who counts in Hollywood knows you were shafted by her."

"China's a large country," I added. "One end is so different from the other, even in terms of language and food. Just like everywhere else, there are going to be prejudices."

I found myself defending China, though many of the Chinese critics had done nothing but rage against me over the years. Why was it so important for me to be accepted by a country that wanted nothing to do with me? I looked up to see Frances watching me.

"You've done everything in your power to help China," she said.
"Obviously some would prefer I didn't."

Frances leaned forward and topped off my drink. "What does she know?" she asked. "We'll see who has the last laugh."

I sipped my drink, already knowing it wouldn't be me.

ALTHOUGH COMPLETELY HUMILIATED BY Madame Chiang Kai-shek, I continued working for the China cause. Richard's life had also taken a sudden turn when he answered a casting call for an *Oriental* male for a new movie. The war had increased the need for Chinese actors to portray Japanese characters, and Richard, whose screen name was Kim Wong, was hired and appeared in *The Amazing Mrs. Holliday* with Deanna Durbin. Unfortunately, his acting career was cut short when he was drafted into the army. Thankfully, he went into intelligence work and was based in Europe.

With Richard in the army in August of 1943, I starred in *The Willow Tree* at the Cambridge Summer Theater in Cambridge, Massachusetts, while my Christmas holidays were spent touring military bases in Nebraska. I only had one bad incident when we were passing through a small Kansas town and I went to buy cigarettes during our lunch stop.

"We don't need you Japs in our town!" an older man yelled from the doorway of a storefront I'd just walked pass.

I could see the disgust in his face, which sparked my anger. "I'm Chinese, not Japanese!" I said back at him.

"Can't tell one of you from the other," he said. "Best move on!"

I stood there and simply stared at him until he said, "You probably don't even understand English," before disappearing back into the store.

IN THE SUMMER OF 1944, I went on tour with the USO camp shows organized by the Hollywood Victory Committee, and toured American bases from Edmonton, Canada, to up near the arctic circle. The young soldiers were an appreciative audience stationed so far away from anywhere. Their admiration was uplifting, and it couldn't have come at a better time. I needed to be appreciated and was happy to be there with the soldiers serving our country.

When the war came to an end in 1945, I felt a vague malaise, as if the world had reached the end of an era. And for me, I suppose it had. I'd done all I could for China and the war effort. At the same time, there were no movie roles in sight, leaving me with nothing but time on my hands. Without any new acting jobs, I began to worry more about money. I was fortunate to have invested in real estate and had saved enough to take care of myself and Richard. He had just returned home after completing his military service and was returning to USC to finish his college degree. Still, I felt a growing anxiousness as each week passed without any acting opportunities.

November 5, 1945
Dear Carlo and Fania,

All quiet here. The movies roles have run dry. I talked to Richard and made up my mind to sell the apartments on San Vicente. It's heartbreaking after all the work we've put into Moongate, not to mention our lovely garden and all my beautiful orchids!

Now that the war is over, there has been plenty of interest. Fortunately, or unfortunately, the buyers who've come by to look at the property have been less than eligible candidates. You might laugh, thinking that I feel this way because I don't want to sell, which is true, but it's more than that. I simply don't want to sell a home that I've nurtured and loved for so long to someone who doesn't feel the same.

And just as I was mulling over what to do next, we were besieged by a windstorm yesterday that swept through the area and blew down the "For Sale" sign in front of the apartment building. I immediately saw it as an omen from my mother telling me not to sell just yet. All to say, I've taken the property off the market. We'll see what life brings in the months ahead . . .

Please tell me that all is well with you both. I hope to make it back East in the spring, but would be most happy to see you here too.

Thank you for listening to me yet again. You are both so precious to me.

    Sending love to you both.

    Yours,

    Anna May

THE YEARS AFTER THE war left me virtually absent from the movies. Ingrid Bergman, Gene Tierney, and Katharine Hepburn filled the screens now. Even Frances Marion had retired from the Hollywood rat race to write novels and plays, leaving a larger chasm. I spent my days gardening, cooking, and dressing up for dinner parties with longtime Hollywood friends. I played cards at the Dragon's Den in

Chinatown while reminiscing with childhood friends about the old days. It kept me busy, but deep down, I was unhappy not working. It felt as if all the air was slowly seeping out of my life. I was also drinking and smoking too much. I'd fallen into my role as second mother to Richard as he finished up his studies, and had become what I could only see as a homemaker and hostess.

At forty-one, I longed to travel, to be in New York or Europe again, and I was worried those wonderful days were over. So I jumped at the chance to do an arduous cabaret tour throughout the Northeast in 1947. It allowed me to spend some time in New York with Carl and Fania, Lin Yutang, and Bennett after the tour ended. They were some of the happiest days of my life, being back with people who understood my struggles working in the arts. Fame was fleeting; we were all the rage one day, has-beens the next. I cherished simply being accepted for who I was, a long-treasured friend. The following summer of 1948, I was scheduled to do another tour through the Pocono Mountain resorts in upper New York state that would help to keep me in the limelight. Even if I wasn't on the big screen, it was something.

LOS ANGELES
Moongate—Winter 1948

Back home, Moongate Apartments needed constant maintenance that had to be taken care of immediately, while my rentals and savings were now supporting me and Richard, who had just graduated from USC with his undergraduate degree. He'd been studying nonstop since he returned to college, and I couldn't have been prouder of him. I kept my own busy social calendar, throwing a dinner party for Edith Head when she was nominated for a newly established Academy Award in Best Costume Design for *The Emperor Waltz*. A week later, I was front and center when Tony Quinn was in Santa Monica touring with *A Streetcar Named Desire*, greeting him backstage with flowers from my garden and chocolates from Edelweiss, his favorite chocolatier in Beverly Hills. It was a lovely reminder of all I had gained in Hollywood.

Richard's plans were to continue with his graduate studies in the spring, but before then, he returned to what he enjoyed most, building furniture and photography. He also worked in the garden with me and managed to make most minor repairs in the apartments without calling expensive plumbers and electricians. Just when we thought everything was running smoothly, we were completely caught off guard by a fire that broke out in our apartment.

Fortunately, it occurred during the day, so I smelled the smoke before I saw any flames. As Richard and I rushed to my bedroom, a thick plume of smoke billowed from the fireplace. I'd been using it through the winter to ward off the cold, always careful to make sure the embers had died down before I left the room.

"Call the fire department!" Richard yelled.

While I grabbed the phone, he ran toward the sliding glass door to the courtyard and returned with the hose.

Oh God, I thought. My small study area lay at one side of the bedroom, and I was heartsick to think of losing years of papers and correspondence.

Richard saved them all. By the time the firemen arrived, his quick actions had nearly extinguished the fire. Outside, it was discovered that the fire had originated, and was still smoldering, inside the wall behind the fireplace, also causing substantial damage to the adjacent room. I was grateful that no one was hurt but grew anxious thinking about the costs in repairs and rebuilding the walls.

February 25, 1948
Dear Carlo and Fania,

Thank you for your last letter. And yes, I'm thrilled they've finally overruled the anti-miscegenation law here in California. I may finally get that leading "old" lady role yet! I can only hope it will really make a difference in the movie industry. As you know, my trust is worn thin, and change moves like molasses in Hollywood. I'm afraid my time has passed. Still, it's nice to have some good news after the fire here at Moongate, which left us scrambling. My bedroom wall had to be completely gutted and rebuilt. Thankfully, other than damage to two rooms, the rest of the apartment is fine.

I was hoping to make it to New York again this spring. It's what I miss most not working and having to keep the purse strings tight. Because of the fire, I'm sad to say that travel will have to wait. Still, you can't blame a girl for dreaming. I want nothing more than to meet you both at the Carlyle for cocktails and dinner before heading off to the theater as we've done so many times before. Perhaps you'll come out to Los Angeles, and I'll cook for you. One way or another, we need to see each other soon. Sending love to you both.

Yours,
Anna May

IN DECEMBER, TRAVEL BECKONED and I accompanied my old Chinatown childhood friend to a furniture convention in Chicago. I became terribly ill and collapsed upon my return to Santa Monica. The years of smoking and drinking, along with the stress and disappointments combined with my current money worries, had finally caught up with me. I found myself at the Santa Monica hospital, where I was diagnosed with Laennec's cirrhosis of the liver. The doctors pondered whether I should be operated on, but finally decided to send me home, warning me in no uncertain terms to stop drinking.

I tried.

I lasted just over a week.

LOS ANGELES
Letting Go—1949

After a five-year absence from the screen, I was finally given a small role in *Impact*, a film noir movie starring Brian Donlevy. I had no idea if anyone remembered who I was after so long, or if I was even an occasional mention in any of the movie magazines whose covers I once adorned. Still, I was delighted to be on the big screen, no matter how small the role. I only wanted to leave enough of an impression that a Hollywood studio might come knocking on my door again.

But any thoughts of a revived movie career quickly dissipated when my father, Wong Sam Sing, who had been in declining health for the past year, died of heart failure at the age of eighty-nine. Though he'd been frail, I thought he would live forever. He'd always be both my tormentor and my savior, my compass when I drifted too far. Whether I listened to him or not, he continuously brought me back home. Now he was gone and I was left spinning, not knowing which direction to go.

The 1940s had proven to be a decade of loss. Mary's untimely death was the first unexpected blow, followed by my father's first wife, Lee Shee, in 1942, and that of my elder brother, Huang Dounan, who had died a hero the previous year in 1948, having protected Chang On through the war by being the only Japanese speaker in the region. I wished I had known him better, though he thought I was too independent, too wild for my father or for any traditional Chinese husband to rein in. He had grown up in a small Chinese village where women married young and had children. God forbid they had careers of their own! When Huang Dounan died, he left behind four sons and four daughters, making up for all of the childless Wong children back in America. It wasn't just me; my siblings were all mostly middle aged, and unmarried. The two things my father drilled into his children growing up was to secure a good education and carry on our family name. I'd like to think it wasn't too late for his American-born family, that marriage and children might be on the horizon. At forty-seven, Lulu had been seeing someone lately, and Richard, at twenty-seven, just might be the one to carry on the family name for all of us. I, on the other hand, established my own family legacy through the films I made.

NOW, A YEAR AFTER Dounan's death, *baba* was gone too.

At my father's funeral, his death hit me harder than expected. I couldn't imagine him no longer with us. Growing up, we had more than our share of arguments, at times creating chasms too wide to cross. Still, I always believed we never stopped respecting each other, regardless of our strong wills.

When I visited him two weeks before at the Homestead Lodge, a nursing home that gave him full-time care, I found my father sitting at a table in the sunroom where he spent every afternoon reading his Chinese newspapers. I imagined he was happy no longer seeing my name in any of them.

"*Baba*, how are you feeling?" I asked, walking into the sunroom.

He looked up, and smiled. "Anna," he said.

What I would have done for one of those smiles when I was young and there was so much animosity between us.

"I thought you might like to go out for a walk?"

My father shook his head. "I have my papers to read."

"Anything about me in them?" I asked. I don't know what possessed me to say such a thing, considering most of our past conflicts had stemmed from what the Chinese papers had written about me.

Instead, my father turned the page, and said, "I keep looking, but not a thing."

I smiled. "Those days are over," I said.

Baba looked at me for a long moment. "But we're still here."

I leaned over and put my arm around his shoulder. "Yes, we are."

I'd always hoped that my succeeding in becoming a movie star brought him some gratification, even when he had to defend my film roles when he returned to Chang On. I knew he wanted to return to his ancestral village again, but due to the war, and then his health, it wasn't to be.

THESE THOUGHTS CIRCLED MY mind as I sat between Lulu and Richard at *baba*'s funeral, held at a graveside at Rosedale Cemetery near to where *ma ma*, Mary, and Marietta were buried. The service was conducted by a thin young reverend, who sported a crew cut and had come from the Chinese Presbyterian Church. His words felt distant and empty of spirit to me. Lately, with my ongoing health problems, I felt a real need to find my own form of religion, a welcoming and sacred place that might bring me some peace. Now, all I felt was hot and dizzy, heavy with sadness.

"Are you all right?" Lulu asked.

Always the mother, I thought, feeling irritable. *Baba* was gone, and now she could finally get on with her own life.

"Yes," I whispered.

But I wasn't all right. I felt nauseous and leaned forward.

"Are you okay?" Richard asked.

I wasn't okay.

That was the last thing I remembered.

OVERCOME WITH HEAT AND GRIEF, I'd collapsed and had to be hospitalized for two days at the Queen of Angels Hospital. During my first night there, *baba* came to me in a dream, appearing the way he looked when he ran the laundry and I was the young girl who had skipped Chinese language school to watch movies at the nickelode-ons. He stood tall by my bed. I glanced at his hands to see if he was carrying a bamboo switch, but he wasn't.

Baba, please forgive me, I said.

For what?

For never listening to you.

You were always headstrong, he said. You should have been the son I wanted so badly back then.

It made me angry hearing him say that again.

It was because you always wanted me to be a son that I tried so hard to show you how fortunate you were having a daughter.

And you gave me nothing but trouble. He laughed.

It was nice to hear him laugh, something he rarely did.

I was a handful, I said. I'm sorry for all of our fighting. I was set on finding my own way.

And you did.

Not without grief.

There's no life without happiness and grief.

Is that how you felt?

I've had both. I just wanted my children to do well and be happy, to be Chinese and to be American.

I am. Both.

Then you have nothing to apologize for.

I didn't know what to say, the words caught in my throat. I looked toward the window filled with bright sunlight. Had he for-given me? Why couldn't we have talked like this when my father was alive?

Baba, I said, hoping to ask him. But when I turned back, he was no longer there.

PITTSBURGH, PENNSYLVANIA
1960

The train slows and pulls into the Pittsburgh train station, the only stop before I arrive at New York's Penn Station tomorrow morning. I have the final pages of the last notebook to read. I can take my time, ease into the finish before any decisions about showing them to Bennett need to be made.

The notebooks have reminded me of the expansive life I've led. I was just a child when I began acting, filled with so much hope and certainty. I remember Edith Head, or was it Katherine DeMille, once telling me, "Life gets harder before it gets easier, and then it ends." If so, I'm at a stage in my life where I'm waiting for it to get easier, accepting whatever comes my way. I've had enough grief; now it's time for the happiness *baba* had told me about in my dream. After my father's death, I did turn to religion again, hoping to find some stability. While I was raised Presbyterian and always believed in Confucianism and Taoism, including the writings of Laozi, I hadn't found true contentment. As an adult I first embraced the Christian Science theology but am now attending classes at the Unity School of Christianity, led by Dr. Sue Sikking, the pastor of Unity Church, whose teachings have finally brought me a sense of peace and happiness.

I put down the notebook and stare out the window. All the lingering ghosts from my past have returned, staying with me like a dull ache through the pages. I close my eyes and see Eric, the only man I had hoped to share a life with. There'd been other lovers following the same pattern, Western European males in the movie business, along with an actor here and there, but none was Eric, who had arrived in my life at the perfect time, when I was ready to settle down, longing to. Unfortunately, it wasn't to be; he already had a wife and a country far away from mine. Over the years, it all proved too much for us and we faded in the mist of the war and distance.

I was shaken when I saw a photo of him recently in some theater magazine. He looked older, slightly paunchier, but it was the dull and distant look in his eyes that surprised me. Eric was always so full of life, as jaunty and alive as anyone I've ever known. To see him less so saddens me. But what would he think to see me now, aged and frail from all my chronic health problems, bouts in the hospital, the drinking? Perhaps the dull ache I'm feeling comes from letting go, the realization that some memories should be left as just that, a moment in time when the fruits of life are at their sweetest.

I OPEN MY EYES, pulled from my thoughts by the sudden loud voices outside my compartment, rising and falling like waves, carrying me back to the present.

A HOLLYWOOD STAR
1951-1961

NEW YORK
Television—1951

"Richard! Richard!" I called throughout the house, realizing he must be in the garden.

For years, I'd found solace working in the garden with the beautiful orchids we'd cultivated. They calmed me whenever I became anxious about money and the lack of acting roles. I worried about exhausting my savings with no steady income, even though I knew Richard was completing his graduate studies at UCLA and would be working soon.

Through the glass door, I watched Richard watering the garden wearing a white T-shirt and jeans, looking like a younger version of my father. The way he watched over me, it was easy to forget he was just twenty-eight. I couldn't imagine the past dozen years without him.

I slid the glass door open. "I've been offered my own television show!" I blurted out, happily.

The last movie I made, *Impact*, opened some doors to more work, which included several misfires that didn't pan out and a trip to New York last year for another project that was also dropped. Today, when

Alan called, it wasn't about a film role, but work in the quickly grow-ing world of television, which was considered a "lesser" medium to that of big screen movies. Still, TVs were quickly becoming a staple in many households.

"Anna May, television producers are looking for experienced film stars to add cachet to the new format," Alan said, excitedly. "It's going to open doors for so many more actors and actresses. You've heard all the buzz about the new half-hour comedy series called *I Love Lucy*, starring Lucille Ball, debuting in October."

"I don't think there's anyone in Hollywood who hasn't heard about it," I said.

He laughed. "I rest my case then," he said.

For the past twenty years, dear Alan had tried hard to keep my name relevant in the business. Yet I couldn't help but be skeptical after so many letdowns.

"This project is different, Anna May," he continued. "This series was created and written specifically with you in mind."

Out of the blue, I was being offered my own television show with DuMont Network, which was affiliated with Paramount Studios.

"What's it about?" Richard asked, wary of false promises.

For a good part of his life, Richard had seen what effect the emo-tional and physical perils of the movie business had on me, and to a greater degree, on Mary. He knew all the disappointments I'd re-cently suffered, and learned to take things matter-of-factly and never emotionally when it came to my work.

"It's a Chinese detective series called . . . are you ready for this, *The Gallery of Madame Liu-Tsong*. Not only is it written for me, they're also using my real Chinese name in the title. I play the owner of an art gallery who moonlights as a detective in search of treasured artifacts."

I sounded like a child who had just received the new toy she'd been wishing for.

Richard smiled. He turned off the water and came over to give me a hug, then stepped back and asked, "It's really happening?"

"I begin shooting next week in New York!" I said, unable to contain my excitement thinking of being back in New York with Carl and Fania again.

It wasn't just a small film role; it was my own series of ten half-hour segments that would be shown in every household with a television. While it wasn't the big screen, it would reach a much larger audience. My only wish was that *baba* had lived to see that his daughter was the first Chinese-American actress to have her own television series.

I SPENT LATE SUMMER and the fall of 1951 in New York filming *The Gallery of Madame Liu-Tsong*. When I first arrived, I was given a welcome back cocktail party by Carl and Fania. Through the years, both good and bad, they'd been there urging me on and lifting me up when I no longer had the strength. They were an indispensable part of my life, and it was wonderful to finally see their new, stylish Central Park West apartment.

"So, how does it feel to be a big television star?" Carl asked, taking my wrap.

Carl had just turned seventy-one, almost a good twenty-five years older than I was, but it was the first time that he looked much older to me, his hair white and receding. He must have noticed I had aged too. But he was as gracious and sharp as always.

"Do I hear sarcasm in your question?" I asked happily.

Carl laughed. "I never could pull one over on you," he said. "All sarcasm aside, I'm happy you'll be in town for the next few months so we can catch up. I want to show you my latest group of photos. I think you'll like them."

"I'd love to see them," I said. "You know I think all of your work is genius."

He smiled, and a sweet boyishness returned to his face. Carl was working as much now as he had as a young man, and had all my admiration.

"I bet you say that to all your photographers," he teased.

"You're my only photographer, so I know what I'm talking about."

He laughed and poured me a drink. "Welcome back!"

"I'm so happy to be back," I said.

"Stop hogging the guest of honor," Fania said, coming over to kiss my cheek.

"She's all yours, my dear," Carl said, kissing my other cheek.

"Come then," Fania said. "There's someone I want you to meet."

"There's always someone you want me to meet," I said, and laughed.

Regardless of what would become of the television series, just being in New York with Carlo and Fania again had already made it a wonderful experience.

I wanted them to live forever.

FILMING A TELEVISION SERIES was very different from making movies. Everything moved much faster, and no matter how late I came in the night before, I showed up on the set knowing my lines and prepared to do the scheduled scenes. I fell into the different rhythm and pace of television production and found I liked it. I welcomed the challenge of learning a new format, just as I had enjoyed learning new languages. It was hard work, but there was no time wasted.

When *The Gallery of Madame Liu-Tsong* debuted on August 27, I was thrilled to be appearing on television in households all across America. The show was well received, finding momentum as the weeks progressed, each episode after the first having a clever title like "The Golden Women," "Shadow of the Sun God," and, my personal favorite, "The House of Quiet Dignity."

On my rare days off, I enjoyed dinners with Carl and Fania, Bennett Cerf, Lin Yutang, and his wife. There were also occasional nights at the theater to see *A Tree Grows in Brooklyn*, *Oklahoma*, and *The King and I*. I longed to be on Broadway again but knew not to be greedy. If I couldn't be onstage, I could at least appreciate those who were. I was burning the candle at both ends, but I'd never felt happier.

BY THE TIME I returned to Los Angeles I was exhausted but delighted to celebrate two happy events that I quickly included in my letter of thanks to Carl and Fania.

November 28, 1951

Dear Carlo and Fania,

Thank you for taking such good care of me while I was in New York. I don't know what I've done to deserve you both. I wanted you two to be the first to know I returned home to some very happy news. Lulu is marrying a local businessman, Howard Kwan, and Richard will be graduating from UCLA with his graduate degree at the end of the year. I'm going to throw them a big to-do early next year in celebration and would very much like you both to be there. Consider these my first two invitations. Knowing Lulu, we'll have to adhere to all the old Chinese customs. To make her happy, it'll be a nine-course banquet toasting the couple late into the night!

Lulu is happier than I've ever seen her. As eldest daughter, she has always taken care of all of us. It's her turn to relinquish the "mama bear" title and live her own life. Richard will also be off looking for work after he graduates, so life is changing for the Wong clan in good ways.

As plans come together for the celebration, I'll let you know the date, keeping my fingers crossed you'll be available to fly out. I know it's a lot to ask of you, but you're family and I'd love to have you here. Thank you again for all the laughter and care. Love to you both.

> *Yours always,*
> *Anna May*

A month after my return, following what I thought was a successful first season of *The Gallery of Madame Liu-Tsong*, and with story lines already sketched out for the second season, DuMont un-expectedly canceled the series. Back where I started, I prayed another opportunity would come my way.

LOS ANGELES
A Rough Patch—1952–1955

Since returning from New York, I hadn't been feeling well. Morning after morning, I'd wake up uncertain of how I would feel, both phys-ically and emotionally. A constant surge of heat rushed through my body, making me irritable and out of control, my nightgown and bed-sheet soaked in sweat for the third night in a week. It wasn't just my liver problems that left me nauseous and fatigued; I was also going through menopause, and together, they were giving me a real roll-ercoaster ride. Distracted and unfocused, I found myself doing just what my doctors had advised against, drinking more to anesthetize myself from everything. I knew it was wrong, but I couldn't stop.

For years I'd taken care of Richard; now, he had to take care of me. It wasn't easy for him, with one crisis after another. My liver pain and discomfort, coupled with my changing emotions, made me a beast to live with. He was also working long hours at Douglas Aircraft Company here in Santa Monica. Thankfully, my dear old friends didn't abandon me. Carl and Fania wrote often with words of support, and Bennett sent boxes of books, which proved to be a lifesaver, as reading transported me away from my illnesses. Edith, the Vidors, and the DeMilles called regularly, while my days became routine. I spent time in the garden, took a nap in the afternoon, and never drank in front of Richard who, along with Lulu, banned alcohol from the house. Instead, I took my daily walks with a weekly stop at the market for a bottle, or two, of vodka.

What Richard and Lulu didn't know wouldn't hurt them.

Only me.

MY CONDITION CONTINUED TO worsen, and by early December of 1953, I had abdominal pains so bad I could barely walk. By the time Richard took me to the Santa Monica Medical Center emergency room, it felt as if I was being repeatedly stabbed in the gut. I honestly feared that I could die before we arrived at the hospital. I don't remember much of anything else. When I woke up the next morning to find I'd had surgery to stop the internal hemorrhaging, the doctors looked at me and shook their heads again. They knew that I'd been a bad girl with self-inflicted Laennec's cirrhosis of the liver.

Later in the day, a new younger doctor came in and introduced himself as Dr. Daniel Bloom. His hair was unruly, wild, and windblown, and he gazed at my chart, frowned, and let me know immediately that he wasn't going to put up with my drinking.

"I have two words for you," he said, in a serious, matter-of-fact tone. "If you want to feel better, stop drinking. And I do mean feel better, not get well. You're never going get rid of this disease but you can live with it, or you can dig your own grave."

"You don't mince words," I said.

"That's not my job. My job is to make you feel better."

"What happened to having a good bedside manner?" I asked, egging him on. It was the first time in months that I felt a spark of interest in the world again.

"Coddling you won't help, Miss Wong. You're dealing with a serious disease here, and the only way you're going to feel better is to help yourself."

"How old are you?"

"Old enough to know that it's up to you to help yourself," he repeated.

I looked at him for a long moment, which didn't seem to faze him. I liked him all the more for it.

"Okay," I said.

"Good then," he said.

I detected a slight smile, although he tried to hide it.

NO ONE HAD EVER spoken to me as straightforwardly as young Dr. Bloom. It made me stop and think seriously. If I continued down the path I was walking, I would surely die. Instead, I was transferred to the Sierra Madre Lodge in Pasadena in early 1954, where I would convalescence for the next two months to get my strength back and stay off the booze.

The Sierra Madre Lodge was exactly like it sounded, a very pleasant woodsy place, and not like most convalescent homes. There were only nineteen patients surrounded by mountains and majestic pine trees to soothe the soul. I had my own private room and spent most of my days walking, sitting out in the sun reading, writing letters, and eating like a pig, just as my doctors ordered. Despite worries about the cost, it was a quiet, idyllic place to recuperate and to decide where life would take me next.

January 21, 1954
Dear Carlo and Fania,

Thank you both for the cards and the beautiful chrysanthemums. They were the envy of everyone here. You don't know how they've brightened my days while I've been recuperating. Forgive my long silence. I wasn't feeling up to writing, but I'm feeling better now. I'm fat as a cow and will have to diet to get into my evening clothes once I return home. I don't know if you'd recognize me if you saw me now! It makes me think of how awful I must have looked the last time you did. I believe all the anguish I've held inside for all these years has finally found its way out. It was always easier denying it. Look where that got me! I've done a great deal of thinking while here, and I'm going to overcome my awful habit of worrying about things that are not worth the time and energy.

Dearest Fania, I have yet another favor to ask of you. The cost of the hospital, followed by the two months here at Sierra Madre Lodge won't be cheap. After a great deal of thought, I've decided to put some of my jewelry on consignment here in Los Angeles hoping it will help cover the costs. Could you put the word out in New York to see if anyone might be interested there? Don't worry, I'm not destitute, there's always my property, which every realtor in Santa Monica seems to want. I'm just not ready to go in that direction yet, especially when I have jewelry that I rarely wear anymore that I can sell first.

I know that working right now would be the best medicine, but it doesn't look good. Hollywood has moved on without Anna May Wong. I've always felt like something was missing in me when I wasn't working. I know I sound needy, but I think what saddens me the most was coming so close to being a leading lady but not being able to cross the finish line. I often wonder, had I been born ten or twenty years later, would my career have turned out differently? No use lingering on the "what ifs." Just get well, I tell myself, and see what comes next. I think of you both often. I hope you're both healthy and happy.

All my best love,

Anna May

RELIEVED AFTER PULLING THROUGH another difficult period, I spent ten days in New York in 1954 to see Carl and Fania, Bennett, and a few other close friends. I was invited to lunches and dinners and felt loved and comforted. By the time I returned to Santa Monica, a lot of expensive work needed to be done on Moongate Apartments. Richard was working full time at Douglas Aircraft Company but took care of small fix-it jobs around the apartments. He was also exceptionally creative, still taking photos and designing and building furniture in whatever spare time he had, hoping to one day open his own Chinese arts and crafts shop. With no solid acting jobs on the horizon, I finally came to the conclusion that I would need to sell the other parcel of land I'd wisely bought years ago in order to continue our comfortable lifestyle.

Once it was sold, however, my beautiful view was lost when

developers built eighteen rental units on the land right in front of me. While I was heartbroken, I now had the funds to return to Europe. By the summer of 1955, the hot flashes had calmed to an occasional flare-up, and I felt well enough to travel again. I happily planned to go to London, Paris, and possibly Munich. In early September, I was back in London and had accepted a small role in a British series titled *The Voodoo Factor*. It was the first time I'd acted in any science fiction, and it felt good to not only be back in London but stepping in a different direction with my career. I stayed at the Westbury Hotel near Berkeley Square, and the early fall weather was particularly warm and beautiful. I couldn't have been happier going to the theater and seeing friends, including W. Somerset Maugham, whom I met for lunch at the Dorchester. Smart and wise, we'd kept in touch for the past twenty years. He'd led a complicated life that shaped his many plays, short stories, and novels, all of which I adored. Every time we met, I had lovely conversations with him about life and literature. In the days in between, I walked and walked, gaining back my strength, visiting Covent Garden and Bloomsbury, Kensington, and Whitehall, ending each day in one of the many city parks to sit and enjoy the beauty. It was just the medicine I needed.

When it came time to travel on to Paris and Munich, I looked at my finances and decided against going. I left for home in October, and by the time I arrived, I was exhausted. Fortunately, Richard was waiting at the Los Angeles International Airport to pick me up.

"You won't recognize the place when you see it," he said on the drive back to Santa Monica.

I smiled tiredly, not paying a great deal of attention. But when I arrived home, I was surprised to see that he'd painted the entire apartment, and I was grateful to see how good everything looked. But my old health problems rose up again, a stabbing pain in my stomach, along with swollen ankles that sent me back to the Santa Monica Medical Center to recuperate for two days.

LOS ANGELES
Television—1956–1960

In the spring of 1956, I finally sold Moongate Apartments on San Vicente Boulevard where I had lived for eighteen years. Being a single Chinese-American woman, buying real estate was an almost impossible ordeal in 1938, and owning the property had given me a sense of success and achievement. I still wasn't allowed to buy property in certain areas like Beverly Hills or the Hollywood Hills, where many in the movie community lived. Others might have folded, but they didn't know who they were dealing with. I had survived the Hollywood studio system, proving that a Chinese-American woman could succeed as an actress and performer, and make a decent living at it. I was determined to own my own home back then, and when I finally bought the place on San Vicente, it was my badge of honor.

Real estate agents had been knocking on my door ever since I'd sold off my first parcel of land, hoping that I would sell the rest of my prized corner property. I was truly surprised at the number of people who came to look at Moongate, and I dismissed most of the offers straight away. They just didn't seem like the right fit. Eventually, the right person finally came along and Moongate was sold over the weekend. Even then I was hesitant, but when the prospective buyer told me I could take as many of my rare plants and orchids as I wanted from the garden with me, I knew the deal was sealed.

It was an achingly bittersweet moment for me to have to relinquish Moongate. I suddenly realized this was what it felt like to slowly disappear; first from the movies, now from my longtime home.

WE CONSOLIDATED AND MOVED to a smaller house I bought at 308 Twenty-First Place in Santa Monica. Richard took time off work and handled the move, managing all the small details. He even papered the interior with Japanese grass wallpaper so that it felt more like home. I walked around the living room, everything in place, including most of the antiques I had accumulated over the years—the carved teak coffee table, the cloisonné vases, and the black lacquer screen inlaid with mother-of-pearl swans that gleamed with beauty and poise. They provided me with needed comfort, along with my cats, and so many of my favorite plants to start a new garden, however small the garden would be now. There was no use dwelling on what was gone. The important thing was having the Moongate property to sell in the first place. With the San Vicente sale, I could breathe again. All my financial anxieties of the past few years were finally easing.

THE NEW HOUSE ALSO brought me unexpected luck, what *ma ma* would have deemed a good omen. She would have walked around the house, observing that the living room was open and filled with light and positive energy, the kind of *feng shui* that promised good fortune.

And indeed, a few months after we settled into our new house, director William Wyler hired me for a featured role in his NBC Producers' Showcase version of W. Somerset Maugham's *The Letter* in 1956. My visit last year with Somerset in London had brought me this surprise television project, just another of the many gifts I'd received through the years from old friends who hadn't forgotten me. They still invited me to lunches and dinners, and out to theater openings, and rallied for small parts to be sent my way. Friends like Edith Head, who made sure I heard the latest Hollywood gossip at our monthly luncheon dates, and Tony Quinn, who always tried to slip me into movies he was in. And now, Somerset had also put in a good word for me.

It brought tears to my eyes.

For forty years, I'd had to play "the other woman" who acquiesced to the Caucasian actress at the end of the movie, either through submission or death. With *The Letter*, I altered my role to give my character a sense of power and dignity. In my version of the script, when the Caucasian lead actress needs a letter from my character to implicate her husband at the end, I had her kneel and beg my character for it. To my great delight, William Wyler agreed to conclude the drama with my changes.

I FELT BOTH HUMBLED and relieved to be working again. After another dry spell, it seemed this time television was going to be my saving grace. *The Letter* was followed by other small parts, and by the end of November, I appeared in two highly praised episodes of the *Climax* series on CBS, along with Macdonald Carey, Rita Moreno, and Constance Ford. Encouraged by all the good reviews,

I was hopeful that more work would come my way in the months ahead.

I didn't have to wait long. My next television project brought me full circle. An ABC TV series called *Bold Journey* wanted to use the movie footage from my China trip in 1936, and invited me to New York to introduce and narrate the film, which was called *Native Land*. Little did I know that some twenty years later, my home movie would be used to kick off the new season of *Bold Journey* and would be shown to a larger audience than I could have ever dreamed of!

I met Carl at a diner just down the street from the studio on Sixth Avenue the day after I arrived in New York. He was well into his seventies, his hair white and thin, but when he smiled, Carl was ageless.

"I'm so happy for you," he said.

"Who would have known?"

"I knew Anna May Wong wasn't over yet," he said, taking a bite of his apple pie.

"You were in the minority, then."

"I'm just smarter than most." He laughed.

I sipped my coffee. "Thank you."

"For what?"

"For all the years of friendship," I said. "For never forgetting me."

Carl smiled. "I couldn't forget you even if I tried, Anna May. Whether you believe it or not, you're not someone easy to forget. It's what they look for in Hollywood, only you were born too early," he said. "Instead of following the trail, you had to blaze it."

I didn't know what to say. "You are a kind man," I finally said.

"As you well know, I'm nothing of the sort, just truthful. You'll see," he said, taking another bite of his pie.

"And Fania? She's feeling better again after the operation?"

"Completely," he said. "She'll outlive both of us!

I smiled at the thought. They were both years older than I was, and the thought of losing either one of them filled me with despair.

"I certainly hope so," I said.

I RETURNED TO LOS ANGELES, happy and reenergized. After all Richard had done for me over the years, I decided in the summer of 1958 to help him with his long-hoped-for business venture, a Chinese gift shop. He was so creative and good with his hands, pursuing his photography and a new side business of silk-screening coolie coats with butterfly designs while working long hours for Douglas Aircraft Company. Now he had a place to display and sell his wares.

One hot afternoon as he was busy painting the small shop and readying it for its August opening, he stopped and turned to me. "I don't know how to thank you," he said.

At thirty-six, Richard was a fine blend of both of our parents, but he had *baba*'s dark gaze and a full head of hair.

"We both need a change," I said. "Besides, it's time you show the world your creative side," I added.

He smiled and nodded, then returned to painting. I watched him, filled with optimism.

Inspired, the next day I went right out and bought a snappy new car, a red and gray Oldsmobile, ready to drive toward all that life had to offer.

These unexpected endeavors, as well as television appearances in *Adventures in Paradise*, *Wyatt Earp*, and *Mike Hammer*, kept me fully occupied. I also received news that I would have a star placed on the newly proposed Hollywood Walk of Fame, to begin construction in early 1960. I was one of more than fifteen hundred film, music, and stage celebrities whose names would be embedded on individual stars in the sidewalks next year. And once again, I was the first and only Chinese-American actress to be included among those big-name Caucasian movie actors and actresses, which reignited many emotions and memories in me. How quickly life had changed. I was receiving a Hollywood Star and being seen regularly by American television audiences! Who would have thought?

I don't intend to take things so seriously anymore, I wrote to Fania. *Apparently, life has its own damn plans, and all you can do is hope for the best.*

At fifty-five, after my haphazard search for religion through the years, I finally found a home when I embraced the teachings of Dr. Sue Sikking at the Unity School of Christianity, where I attended workshops with Hollywood friends. With a positive outlook on life, everything was finally falling into place again as I kept blissfully busy.

"WHERE ARE WE GOING?" I asked.

"You'll see."

Richard smiled as he backed the Oldsmobile out of the driveway, and soon we were sailing down the avenues, past apartment buildings and houses that eventually faded away to busier streets with crowded intersections that I knew led to downtown. The Oldsmobile was a wise purchase, allowing us afternoon drives to the beach on sunny days or to see the latest movies. We drove to dinners at Lulu's house and visits in Chinatown with family and friends.

"Downtown?" I said, turning toward him.

"Close."

"Sunset Boulevard?"

"Nope."

"Chinatown?"

"We can go to any of those places, but we aren't."

I stopped asking questions for a moment and paid attention to where Richard was driving us. Traffic became heavier as we approached Hollywood Boulevard. I saw construction along all the sidewalks, and then it dawned on me.

"The Hollywood Walk of Fame," I said. As I rolled down the window, the noise of a jackhammer blew in like an unexpected guest.

"Bingo!" Richard said.

He slowed as we approached Vine Street, where I'd been told my star would be located. A cement truck blocked the view, and I wondered what *ma ma* would say about the position of my star, and if it would bring good *feng shui*. I couldn't imagine it being better placed than on the corner of Hollywood and Vine. If nothing else, there would be a lot of foot traffic.

"You're a real Hollywood movie star now!" Richard said.

I laughed. "By the looks of things, not quite yet," I answered.

"You'll be there soon," Richard said, proudly.

"Yes, soon," I said, thinking, Finally.

"Do you want me to park?" he asked.

"No," I said. "There's nothing to see right now. Let's drive out to the beach."

Richard nodded and turned at the corner.

I wanted to escape the traffic and commotion, to go where there was only ocean and sky, where all I could hear was the crashing of waves as I walked along the sand at the water's edge, where everything was constantly renewed again by the ebb and flow of the tides.

"Santa Monica?" Richard asked.

I smiled and nodded, then rolled up my window, leaving the noise and heat behind.

NEW YORK
1960

I close the notebook where it ends with me rolling up the car window and shutting out the noise. Five days later, I left on this trip. Now I flip through the last thirty or forty blank pages. The rest of my life, I think to myself. It has all come down to these last empty pages. Does my life warrant a book? Let's see how the story continues.

I forage through my bag for a pen, turn back to the next blank page, and begin to write.

IN JUNE OF 1960, I formally announced my comeback with a small part in a much publicized movie, *Portrait in Black*. I was also in talks with Ross Hunter about a major role in his next big feature with an all-Chinese cast called *Flower Drum Song*. And there was talk of another movie, *The World of Suzy Wong*, starring a young up-and-coming Chinese actress named Nancy Kwan. At last, Hollywood was making small steps in the right direction, using real Chinese actresses, and hopefully wiping away all those monstrous yellowfaces.

When I was told that I would be doing a press tour for *Portrait in Black*, I was surprised and pleased that they were taking my small role seriously. I'd like to believe it's a bit of payback for passing me over for so many films in the past, or maybe it's a glimpse of what lies ahead, but I'm not that naive. To get here, I have endured years of quiet but aggressive prejudice, of lesser roles due to anti-miscegenation and lower salaries. I did the best I could with what little was given to me. From silent films to the talkies to the small television screens in everyone's living rooms, my life reflects a kaleidoscope of time and place. I never married and never had children, but I have an enduring family of siblings and friends. To have lived through this, to have paved the way, and most importantly, to have reached the other side reasonably intact is significant. I've always been as much Chinese as I am American, though I wasn't always accepted as either. It's taken me this long to realize that I've remained the best of both, Chinese American. Isn't that what *baba* wanted us to be?

I STOP WRITING WHEN there's a knock on my compartment door, and Joseph lets me know the train will be arriving at Penn Station in an hour's time. Do I need anything, he also asks me.

A good stiff drink is what I want to say but instead answer, "No, thank you, Joseph. You've been wonderful."

"I feel mighty lucky to have met you, Miz Wong. Gonna tell my family I met a real movie star when I get home," he says, and smiles.

"I'm going to tell my family I met you too," I say, and we both laugh.

"I'm looking forward to seeing your next movie."

"Thank you," I say.

Joseph tips his hat and closes the door behind him. I hear his voice as he moves from door to door down the car until it fades.

And so it begins.

AS SOON AS I step down from the train, I hear the trembling and sigh of it settling, crowds of people moving to and fro on the platform, announcements coming over the loudspeaker. For just a moment, it's all discombobulating and I'm ready to run back to my small, safe train compartment. I clutch my bag tighter. My schedule is crowded and begins first thing early tomorrow morning. There's a twinge in my gut. I have to be in top form, knowing that this may be my one chance to find my way back.

Take your time, take a step, no one's chasing you anymore, I think to myself.

"Anna May!"

"Anna May!"

I hear my name called, just loudly enough to rise above the steady commotion. I look up to see Carl and Fania, waving and waving, their faces flushed with happiness to see me. Smiling, I wave back. They're still here after all these years. I'm suddenly filled with such gratitude for them, for this film that has brought me back to New York, for all the struggles near and far that I've somehow managed to overcome.

I feel the tears push against the back of my eyes as I step through the crowd to walk toward them.

LOS ANGELES
Autumn & Winter—1960–1961

I returned from the press tour for *Portrait in Black* exhilarated but tired, followed by commitments in Alaska in the autumn of 1960. During the holidays, I wrote Carl and Fania that I'd come down with a virus, keeping me under the weather and in bed. Dr. Bloom wasn't happy with me. Come January, I rallied enough to do two episodes of *The Barbara Stanwyck Show*, but the illness returned full force, and Dr. Bloom began calling to check on me daily and dropping by weekly to give me injections of a diuretic to ease my swollen belly and ankles.

"It's a good thing I like you," I told him, coaxing a smile from him. "I see you more than I see my family."

He'd cut his hair shorter and looked more settled.

"The feeling's mutual," he said.

"Then patch me up and send me back out into the world."

He looked at me. "You don't make it easy."

I heard the whisper of sadness in his voice. I wanted to tell him that I'd met him halfway. I had quit smoking, but yes, I did cheat on the alcohol.

Instead, I said, "Nothing is ever easy in life."

He glanced up knowingly, wiped alcohol on a cotton ball cool across my arm, and stuck the needle in and out so quickly I barely felt the pinprick. Now that his hair was shorter, I found other things I liked about Dr. Bloom: his light touch and warm hands.

IT WASN'T JUST THE dull ache in my abdomen but the constant fatigue, and an occasional debilitating pain that struck like a bolt of lightning and claimed a bit more of my spirit each time it raced through my body. I was more than sad when I had to relinquish the role of Auntie Liang in *Flower Drum Song*, a role I'd waited forty years for. Ross Hunter, dear man, who had been championing me from the beginning, was just as disappointed as I was.

There would be other opportunities, I told myself, but in the same breath I was already thinking, Would there be?

EPILOGUE
SANTA MONICA, CALIFORNIA

February 3, 1961

I'm up early this morning, feeling well enough to putter around the house, talking to my plants and to my cat, Smoky. The sky is clear and bright, and it looks to be a very good day. I spend most of the morning feeling almost well again. Perhaps I should call Ross and have him reconsider my return to *Flower Drum Song*. Richard hovers over me like Lulu would. After we've had lunch, I tell him, "I'm going to take a nap, but afterwards be ready to drive me out to the beach before dinner. It'll be nice to get some fresh air." When he smiles, I see my carefree little brother once again.

I SLEEP AND WAKE and sleep again, those boys in the schoolyard, those dark-suited men from the studios, flitting in and out of my consciousness like evil spirits. When I wake again, I will them to fade away like the end credits on a movie screen. They're my past now, captured in the pages of my notebooks where they'll remain. It feels good to know I no longer have to please anyone but myself. The thought brings calm as the sunlight seeps through the curtains and falls warmly across my bed.

My well-being is short lived when a strange numbing sensation spreads through the left side of my body. I begin to perspire profusely, struggle to catch my breath. I try to call out for Richard but I don't have the energy. What I'm feeling is different from the stomach pains; this is something else. The numbness spreads, followed by an explosive pain like another bolt of lightning, this time striking right in the middle of my chest. The weight of the pain is crushing, and I can barely swallow. Like a child, I find myself counting to "thirty Mississippi," waiting for the thunder to come next . . . One Mississippi, two Mississippi, three Mississippi, four . . .

I CLOSE MY EYES and see my sister Mary. I'm sitting in front of the mirror in our old childhood bedroom in our house behind the laundry. Ten-year-old Mary is standing behind me, her hands on my shoulders, and a smile on her face. I'm so happy to see her, young and filled with spirit and curiosity again. We stare wide eyed at each other in the mirror before she blinks first and laughs.

Mary watches our reflections with a thoughtful gaze before asking:

Who did those boys see?

Chink, Chink, Chinabug.

Who did you see?

Wong Liu-Tsong.

Who did those men see?

A damsel in distress.

A dragon lady.

Who do you see?

I lean forward, look into the mirror, and smile.

I see Anna May Wong.

ACKNOWLEDGMENTS

I'm deeply grateful to my agent, Joy Harris, and to my editor, Tara Parsons, who supported and championed this story from the first page, and to Judith Curr and everyone at HarperVia who helped to bring this book to fruition.

I'm indebted to my longtime writers' group: Abby Pollak, Blair Moser, Cynthia Dorfman, and Catherine de Cuir. And to Karen Joy Fowler, Nancy Horan, Elizabeth George, and Jane Hamilton, who listen, encourage, and inspire. Thank you also to my brother, Tom, and to my family and friends for their unfailing support.

Lastly, my gratitude to Anna May Wong, who dared to step out of the box. Her courage and perseverance inspired this story, allowing me to reimagine her life, letters, and friendships. While this is solely a work of fiction, I hoped to capture the chronology of her life as accurately as possible. The sources available to me online, in articles, and through libraries and bookstores were invaluable, particularly: *Anna May Wong: From Laundryman's Daughter to Hollywood Legend*, by Graham Russell Gao Hodges; *Anna May Wong: Performing the Modern*, by Shirley Jennifer Lim; *Perpetually Cool: The Many Lives of Anna May Wong (1905–1961)*, by Anthony B. Chan; "Anna May Wong" in *Notable Asian Americans*, by Helen Zia and edited by Susan B. Gall; *Anna May Wong: A Complete Guide to*

ACKNOWLEDGMENTS

Her Film, Stage, Radio and Television Work, by Philip Leibfried
and Chei Mi Lane; the Carl Van Vechten Papers, Yale Collection
of American Literature, the Beinecke Rare Book and Manuscript
Library; the New-York Historical Society; and the UCLA Film &
Television Archive.

Here ends Gail Tsukiyama's
The Brightest Star.

The first edition of this book was printed and
bound at Lakeside Book Company in
Harrisonburg, Virginia, June 2023.

A NOTE ON THE TYPE

The text of this novel was set in Horley Old Style, released by Monotype in 1925. It was designed as an answer
to Frederic W. Goudy's highly successful Kennerley
typeface. It's proven to be a reliable, appealing font for
a variety of text work, and at larger sizes can be effective
for display work.

HARPERVIA

An imprint dedicated to publishing international voices,
offering readers a chance to encounter other lives and other
points of view via the language of the imagination.